10/1/15

D1016990

DISCARD

INFINITE
in
between

Also by Carolyn Mackler

TEEN

The Future of Us
(coauthored with Jay Asher)

Tangled

Guyaholic

Vegan Virgin Valentine

The Earth, My Butt, and Other Big Round Things

Love and Other Four-Letter Words

MIDDLE GRADE

Best Friend Next Door

INFINITE
in
between

CAROLYN MACKLER

HARPER TEEN

An Imprint of HarperCollinsPublishers

HarperTeen is an imprint of HarperCollins Publishers.

Infinite in Between
Copyright © 2015 by Carolyn Mackler
All rights reserved. Printed in the United States of America.
No part of this book may be used or reproduced in any manner whatsoever without written permission except in the case of brief quotations embodied in critical articles and reviews. For information address HarperCollins Children's Books, a division of HarperCollins Publishers, 195 Broadway, New York, NY 10007.
www.epicreads.com

Library of Congress Control Number: 2015940714
ISBN 978-0-06-173107-5 (trade bdg.)

Typography by Michelle Taormina
15 16 17 18 19   CG / RRDH   10 9 8 7 6 5 4 3 2 1

First Edition

To Stephanie Rath,
my lifelong friend

IN THE BEGINNING the five of them made a promise. It was the day before the first day of high school. They wrote those letters to their future selves, hid them in a secret place, and vowed to unearth them at graduation.

From the noisy, crowded gym at freshman orientation (day 1) to the noisy, crowded gym at graduation (day 1,387), four years of high school seemed infinite.

On that first day they had no clue that one of them would experience the worst of losses (day 691) and another would watch her family break apart (day 38) and another would fall deeply and dangerously in love without buckling up for the ride (day 1,045). There would be a fatal car accident (day 123), a supreme betrayal (day 489), a kiss with the most unlikely person at a waterfall in the woods (day 943), and a walk along the Seine in Paris (day 352), where a long-held secret is definitely not discussed.

And then there would be that night (day 1,386) when it all unraveled.

But back to day one. The beginning.

FRESHMAN YEAR

SEPTEMBER

GREGOR

"DO YOU REALIZE this is going to be life-changing?" Dinky asked Gregor.

Gregor opened his eyes wide like *shut up*, but Dinky didn't seem to notice. Sometimes his friend missed social cues. Or maybe he just didn't care.

They were in the backseat, speeding toward the high school. The air smelled like fruity skin cream, and on the floor at Gregor's feet, there was a pair of turquoise sneakers and a pink sports bra. Gregor tried not to look at the bra, but his eyes kept wandering back to it.

"By life-changing," Dinky said, "I mean, this year is going to *change our lives*."

Gregor's sister, Erica, groaned from the front.

That was exactly what Gregor didn't want, to give his sister any ammunition. She was only a year older, but she acted like she was twenty.

"Seriously," Erica said as she smeared moisturizer onto her calves. She smirked at her friend Callie, who was driving. Erica didn't have her license yet. She didn't even turn sixteen until next

June. "It's your *freshman year* of high school, guys. It's not like you're going to law school."

"Newbies," Callie murmured, flicking on her blinker and turning into the nearly empty parking lot.

"Exactly," Erica said. "Newbies."

Gregor stared out the window, his cheeks burning as hot as his bright red hair. It was bad enough that his dad had insisted Erica take him along when she and Callie went to cross-country practice. He thought it would be good for Gregor to see the high school before anyone was there, to find his locker and homeroom and the orchestra room. Gregor was relieved when Dinky agreed to join, but now he wasn't so sure that was a good idea.

As they got out of the car, Erica said to Callie, "Russell might be picking me up after cross-country. If he does, can you take my brother and his friend home?"

"Sure." Callie stretched her arm into the back and grabbed the turquoise sneakers but not the pink sports bra. "I guess that's fine."

"If you talk to Mom or Dad, don't tell them I went with Russell," Erica said to Gregor as she shut her door. "Get out at Dinky's house and walk from there. Tell them I went for a run."

Without even saying good-bye, the girls jogged toward the track, leaving Gregor and Dinky alone in the parking lot, staring at the massive brick building that was going to be their school in, *oh man*, three days.

"Your sister is hot," Dinky said, grinning. They started toward the side door. It was propped open with a brick. "Forget that Russell dude."

Gregor punched Dinky's arm. Dinky and his sister? No way.

"That's what high school will be like," Dinky said, popping his shoulders as he walked. This was Dinky's version of a strut. "Cute girls. Big dudes with facial hair. You have to think about being cool. I want to be drum major, maybe even next year. You should go out for band with me. Do drums too."

"I've got cello," Gregor said. He'd been playing since he was five. That was who he was, what he did.

"You're a prodigy on cello. We all know that. But you can play drums, too. Girls like drummers."

Dinky pulled the side door open, and they peered down the long corridor. It was quiet and dark in there, and the floors were so shiny, they seemed wet. Gregor had been to Hankinson High School before, for Erica's holiday concert and a few school plays, but now it felt huge and intimidating. He unwrapped a piece of gum for himself and handed another one to Dinky.

"Should we go in?" he asked.

"I guess," Dinky said quietly.

Neither of them moved. Gregor squished the gum between his molars. With his braces he wasn't supposed to chew gum, but he could do it as long as he was careful.

Just then they heard the tinny jingle of "Pop! Goes the Weasel." It was getting closer and closer. The ice cream man.

"Do you have any money?" Dinky asked.

Gregor reached into his pocket. "Yeah . . . some."

"Should we?"

"Sure. We can look around the school at orientation instead."

They sprinted across the closely cropped emerald lawn and

waved down the ice cream man. Dinky ordered a Chipwich. Gregor got a Creamsicle.

"Awesome," Dinky said, spitting his gum into the napkin. "Thanks."

The ice cream truck blared its music and steered up the hill toward the football stadium.

"Anytime," Gregor said as they sat on the curb.

Gregor licked his Creamsicle, sucking the sweet flavor out of his braces. The cheerleaders were shrieking in the stadium, and the runners were doing stretches over at the track. The whole thing made his stomach flip like crazy.

"High school is big, you know," Dinky said, gnawing at his frozen cookie. "You start out one person and finish as someone completely different."

Gregor wiped his chin with a napkin. He wasn't sure how he felt about that. So far in his life, nothing major had happened. It was mostly cello, school, video games, his family, his friends. He'd made out with a girl from orchestra last year. It was awkward, about as sexy as kissing a Pez dispenser. Maybe his life was a little boring, but he wasn't so sure he wanted it to be changed.

ZOE

THE DRIVER STEPPED out of the black SUV and nodded at Zoe. "Are these your bags?"

"Yeah," she said quietly. Her hair was pulled into a messy ponytail, and she was hot even though it was only sixty. Zoe glanced down. She was wearing ripped jeans and a yellow tank top. Her mom, who was Sierra Laybourne, always said yellow wasn't her color. There were toothpaste droppings on Zoe's left boob that looked like bird poop. She hoped no one would recognize her in the airport and take a picture. If they did, she'd smile and act like everything was fantastic. That's what she'd been doing her entire life.

The driver slammed the back shut and walked around to open her door. His square jaw was frozen into a frown. He reminded Zoe of her mom's bodyguard from last spring.

Behind the driver, their house loomed majestic with massive stone columns. She and her mom had been in Coldwater Canyon for a year, and this place was huge even by LA standards. It freaked Zoe out—all the long hallways and empty rooms. It didn't help that kids back in eighth grade told her that a producer drowned in their pool twenty years ago. That was a creepy image whenever Zoe went swimming.

Zoe buckled her seat belt. It hadn't started out as a terrible day. Just this morning she and Sierra had gotten pedicures by the pool. Her mom let her pick the color for both of them, and she'd gone with purple. It had seemed like a typical day, a flurry of texts for her mom, a rug being delivered, a cook who specialized in raw foods. The one strange thing was that her mom's manager, Max, had locked himself in the office, hissing into his phone.

But then, an hour ago, their housekeeper had walked into Zoe's room. "I'm so sorry to be the one telling you this," Rosa said, "but you need to pack."

"For what?" Zoe asked. She'd been texting with a few girls, planning what to wear for the first day of ninth grade. "Are my mom and I going somewhere?"

Rosa pinched the bridge of her nose. They no longer had a nanny on weekends, so the housekeeper was Zoe's main point of contact.

"No, it's you," Rosa said, her eyes crinkling sympathetically. "I'm sorry, Zoe. Max just told me too. Your mom's already left for Arizona. She's going to be getting help again. Longer this time."

Back when Zoe was in seventh grade, her mom had gone to rehab to "rest and focus on her goals," as she'd described. It was only for two weeks, so Zoe had stayed in LA with her nanny.

"So where am I going?" Zoe asked after a second.

"Max said you're flying to Hankinson this afternoon," Rosa told her. "He set it all up."

Zoe bit at her thumbnail. She knew things were getting worse with her mom, but it wasn't like anyone was talking about it. It wasn't like anyone ever talked about *anything*.

"*What?*" she asked, her voice rising.

Rosa touched her arm. Their housekeeper was on the older side and had a granddaughter around Zoe's age who she sometimes brought over.

"I know it's not fair," Rosa said, "but you can try to make the best of it."

"Where *is* Hankinson, anyway?"

"It's in New York State. Your aunt lives there. That's nice, right? You're going to stay with her for a while."

Her *aunt*? She'd never even *met* her mom's sister. The only evidence she existed were pictures of her in old albums, and the fact that she always sent birthday presents for Zoe—a sweater or a necklace. She signed the cards *Aunt Jane.* That was more than what Zoe knew about her father, which was nothing. No evidence at all. She'd asked about him, but her mom had always said it wasn't important.

Rosa disappeared into the hallway. She came back a few minutes later wheeling two pink suitcases.

"The car will be here in an hour," she said. "I'll go get your ski coat, and then I can help you pack."

"But it's September," Zoe said. "Why do I need my ski coat?"

Rosa wiped at her eyes like she was tearing up. "It gets cold in New York."

As the SUV meandered down the long driveway and waited for the gate to open, Zoe realized that packing her ski coat meant that Rosa knew she'd be in Hankinson until winter. She cried the whole way to the airport while the driver adjusted the volume on the music.

• • •

Two days later Zoe was twenty-seven hundred miles across the country at her aunt's house in central New York State. Her feet were tangled in the sheets, her belly cramping like she was getting her period.

She clutched her phone, quiet in her hand. A zit was erupting on her chin. Great . . . her period, a zit, and a new school all in the same day.

"Zoe?" Jane shouted upstairs. "Ready for breakfast?"

Jane was her mom's older sister. She'd told Zoe to call her Aunt Jane, but that felt too weird. From what Zoe had pieced together, her mom and aunt had had a fight before Zoe was born and had barely talked since.

"Orientation starts in forty minutes," Jane added.

Zoe pressed her face into the pillow. She *so* didn't want to go to freshman orientation at some school she'd never heard of until two days ago. She checked her phone. Still nothing.

"Zoe?" Jane was walking up the stairs. "Are you awake?"

"Yeah, I'm up," Zoe said. She was wearing only underwear and a tank top that stretched tight over her stomach. She never let anyone see her this naked—not even her mom. That's what her mom's outburst in London had been about. Zoe wouldn't let her into the dressing room to see how flabby she looked in that stupid bikini. Her mom's body was so perfect, straw-thin thighs and her famous Pilates-flat stomach. How could Zoe have known that someone would record her mom screaming outside her dressing room door and that it would go viral? The thing was, her mom wasn't even a shouter. Usually, when she was mad, she'd go in her room and give Zoe the silent treatment. Zoe guessed that the meltdown meant her mom was drinking again, which she hadn't done since she went to rehab two years ago.

"I'm just checking that you didn't fall back asleep," Jane said through the closed door. "The waffles are almost ready. Do you want yogurt, too?"

So far Jane seemed nice enough, though Zoe was less than thrilled that she was forcing her to go to orientation today and to start at the local high school tomorrow.

"I don't get why I have to go," Zoe had told her over dinner the night before. It was make-your-own tacos, something she'd never done before. Just like she'd never had ice cream at a roadside stand or done her own laundry or been inside a Walmart. "As soon as Sierra gets home, I'll be going back to *my* school." Zoe went to a private school in Santa Monica called Topanga Day. She'd gone there since fourth grade.

Jane had shaken her head. "You're here, so you'll go to school. It's what your mom would want."

How could Jane even *know* what her mom would want? They hadn't talked in fifteen years.

That was last night. Now Zoe sat up in bed and touched her volcanic zit. She'd give it a good squeeze later, after orientation. Jane sneezed. She was right outside the door.

"Just waffles, please," Zoe said. She slid her phone into the small orange bag that her mom bought her in London before everything had fallen apart.

"See you downstairs," Jane said. "I don't want to harass you, but we need to leave in twenty minutes."

As Zoe wriggled on a bra under her tank top, she paused to

examine her toenails. On the airplane ride east, she'd decided to leave her purple polish on until she saw her mom again. She texted her mom to tell her that, but Max had written back instead. *Sierra doesn't have her phone with her in Arizona.* That was all he said.

JAKE

JAKE HOPPED ON his mountain bike and hung a left. It was hot out, almost ninety. It didn't feel like it should be high school orientation today. It was more like a day to be cooking out at the lake. By the time Jake went over the train tracks, his calves were burning and sweat was slipping down his back.

As he rode, he kept an eye out for people he knew. It was stupid because as soon as he saw someone, he'd duck and try to disappear. Hankinson was a decent-sized city, but it still felt like there was nowhere to hide.

Jake locked his bike to the rack and crossed the road to the high school. The varsity football team was practicing on the south field. They were grunting and slamming into cushions. Jake clenched his fists. He was supposed to go out for junior varsity football, but then he'd bailed.

He shouldn't even be *looking* at the football players. Jake kicked at the grass under his sneakers. People wouldn't say anything to his face, but he could feel them watching, waiting for him to make his next move. Well, he was done with moves.

Some girls disappeared through a side door, their elbows linked.

He recognized Kyra, short and curvy with a helmet of black hair. Her mom had hired Jake to mow their lawn over the summer. Kyra was always lying out on the deck in a bikini, her pink phone in her hand. She giggled whenever Jake pushed the mower by her. He'd never said anything. Maybe it was a jerk move to ignore her, but what was he supposed to do? He didn't want to lead her on.

Jake pushed his hair off his face. His best summer friend, Mona Lisa, had convinced him to grow it out, and it was finally getting long. Hopefully high school would be different. He took a shallow breath and walked into the building.

Up on the bleachers, Jake was wedged between a skinny dude picking at his fingers and this small girl everyone was staring at. She had long brown hair and bright purple toenails.

As he jiggled his knee up and down, he scanned for Teddy, hoping to see him. Or maybe not. Maybe hoping Teddy had moved over the summer. That would suck. Or not.

"Welcome, students!" A man wearing a striped tie tapped a microphone.

Jake glanced at the girl with the purple toenails. He noticed two kids holding up their phones to take pictures of her while she stared straight ahead like it wasn't happening.

"My name is Mr. Bauersmith," the man said. He had a bushy mustache that looked like a caterpillar. "I'm the principal at Hankinson High School. In four years you're going to be sitting in this same gym for graduation. But first things first . . . welcome to the beginning."

A few girls clapped. Jake knew one of them from eighth grade.

Marin Banerjee. They'd gone to the winter semiformal together. They'd kissed on the dance floor and he'd said that her breath smelled like candy corn. Marin had spent the rest of the night crying, encircled by a pack of angry girls. Jake couldn't figure that out. It wasn't like candy corn was a *bad* thing. He'd told his friend Mona Lisa about it this summer. She was from Atlanta, but her grandparents had a cottage down the road from his family's cabin on Cayuga Lake. Mona Lisa said girls didn't want to be told that their breath was anything less than perfect.

The principal talked for a few more minutes and went over some school rules. He paused to stroke his mustache with his thumb, which gave Jake the chills. Jake didn't have much facial hair yet, but whatever peach fuzz he had, he shaved off.

"As we do every year," Mr. Bauersmith said, "I'm going to have all the incoming ninth graders break into small groups. Every group will have a peer advisor who is a junior or senior and has been assigned to guide you through your ice-breaker activity."

A few people groaned. Jake actually didn't mind these kinds of activities. It was like student council. Another thing he hadn't gone out for this year. In eighth grade he'd been the vice president of his class.

"It's your choice what you do," the principal said. "Your group can do a time capsule or a make a collage or help change the letters in the marquee outside the school. I'm going to pass out sheets with suggestions. But before I do, I'll leave you with the words of Ralph Waldo Emerson. 'Life is a journey, not a destination.'"

As the principal began calling names and numbers, Jake pushed his hair out of his eyes. He saw a few guys from middle school across the gym. They were probably talking about football. He turned away.

"Jake Rodriguez!" the principal called out. "Group eighteen. Alicia Montaine is your peer advisor."

Just as Jake stepped off the bleachers, he noticed Teddy by the victory banners. His hair was bleached golden and he'd gotten taller. The last time he'd seen Teddy was at junior high graduation. The last time they'd talked was on the bus home from the eighth-grade trip to Washington, DC.

Jake felt like he was being pulled under a wave, churned out of control, not knowing which part of his body was going to smash the sand. He was about to look away, like they'd done last spring, but then Teddy smiled at him. It was light and easy, as if nothing had ever happened.

WHITNEY

WHITNEY COULDN'T BELIEVE that Zoe Laybourne, daughter of Sierra Laybourne, was in her orientation group. Five people in each group, and she got Zoe!

This *more* than made up for the fact that her *sister* was her peer advisor. Who thought of that messed-up idea? She and Alicia had the same mocha skin and hazel eyes, but other than that, they were nothing alike. Mostly, they hated each other.

Whitney had recognized Zoe Laybourne as soon as she walked into the gym. It was surreal, seeing the long brown hair and wide-set eyes that she'd always seen in pictures. Zoe was shorter in real life, but it was *definitely* her. Whitney pointed her out to her new friend Laurel and some other girls. Within seconds everyone was whispering and sneaking pictures of Zoe.

As her group settled under the basketball hoop, Whitney kept her cool. She said her own name, Whitney Montaine. The two guys and that girl Mia introduced themselves. But then, when it was Zoe's turn to talk, Whitney lost it.

"I can't believe you're here!" she gushed to Zoe. "It's just so—"

"Whit," Alicia said to her. "Chill."

Whitney felt like a moron, but then she let it slide. Maybe it sounded stuck-up, but she was used to people liking her. Alicia said someday Whitney would crash, that her life couldn't always be so charmed. Well, Whitney wasn't going to let Alicia get her depressed with that kind of talk. Her mom's friend Glenda did her braids yesterday, and she was feeling great in her skirt and gold sandals. Even her best friend, Kyra, said she looked cute, and Kyra never complimented her. Mostly, she just whined about wanting Whitney's clothes.

Kyra's dad, Mr. Bauersmith, was the principal. Maybe Kyra knew why Zoe Laybourne, daughter of a *movie star*, was in Hankinson. Maybe it had to do with that clip of Sierra Laybourne that went viral a few weeks ago. Oh my god! She'd been yelling at *Zoe* in the clip, saying things like "Let me the hell in now, Z!" and "You're being a spoiled brat!" Whitney reached for her phone but then set it down. Alicia would murder her if she texted Kyra to ask what she knew. Her sister didn't understand how close she and Kyra were. Back in middle school people called them *Whitra*. Either that or *Kyrney*.

Whitney checked out the freckles across Zoe's nose. She didn't look like a spoiled brat. She also didn't look anything like her famous mom. Maybe Zoe resembled her dad? Whitney had read how Sierra Laybourne had never told anyone the identity of Zoe's dad, but Zoe probably knew. It was probably just a publicity stunt.

"I'm Zoe Laybourne," Zoe said. "I know it's random that I'm here. I'm staying with my aunt."

"Who's your aunt?" Whitney asked.

"Jane Morrison. She lives on Breakneck Hill."

"That's so cool!" Whitney smiled at Zoe. Her mom was a real

estate agent, so she'd have to ask her to look up all the info on Jane Morrison's house. "I used to take a drama class on the hill. We live ten minutes from there."

"Whitney," Alicia said. "Let Zoe talk."

"It's okay," Zoe said. "There's not much to say. I got here a few days ago." She fiddled with the buckle on her adorable orange bag. It probably cost a thousand dollars.

"Is your mom here with you?" that guy Jake asked.

Whitney was glad he said it because she was *dying* to know. Jake was cute with longish blond hair. When he'd introduced himself, he said he went to Loch Middle. Laurel, her new friend from summer soccer, also went to Loch. She was planning to drill Laurel about Jake, see if he had a girlfriend.

"No . . . my mom's in Arizona," Zoe said, smiling. She had perfect teeth and didn't even wear braces. Whitney was counting the seconds until her braces came off.

Mr. Bauersmith clapped his hands into the microphone. "Students! Now that you've all introduced yourselves, you should begin talking about your ice-breaker activity."

"Any ideas?" Alicia asked.

"What about a time capsule?" Jake suggested. "I'm into art. I could draw a picture or a cartoon for it."

This small red-haired guy raised his hand. What was his name again? Gregor?

"We could put on a recital for senior citizens," he said, his cheeks flushing. "I play cello."

Whitney wrinkled her nose. She couldn't stand being around old people. They smelled icky, like mothballs and pee.

"That's an interesting idea, Gregor," Alicia cooed. Whitney glared at her sister. Alicia was faking nice and would no doubt make fun of Gregor and his recital later. Alicia could be brutal that way.

"I play piano," Zoe said.

"The thing is," Alicia said, "it's not community service. We're supposed to do the activity *today*."

"I play piano too," Mia said quietly. Mia had gone to Weston Middle with Whitney. She was tall and supersmart but also bizarre, like she could stare at nothing for a whole period. People said she was always stoned, but Whitney seriously doubted that.

"That's nice to hear," Alicia said in her fake-friendly voice.

Whitney rolled her eyes. Kyra's dad had made that speech about how they were all going to be here in four years wearing caps and gowns, collecting their diplomas. Maybe they could do something that tied into that. . . .

"I've got it!" she said. "Let's meet up again at graduation, the five of us. Right here under this basketball hoop. It's kind of like, *See you on the other side.*"

"And . . . what?" Alicia asked. "That's your whole idea?"

Whitney ignored her sister. Zoe was smiling at her, and that was all she needed. "No, what I was going to say is that we could write notes today. Letters to our future selves. We'll seal them all together. When we meet at graduation, we can open them."

"That sounds cool," Jake said.

Alicia rotated her nose ring. Whitney's dad was furious when their mom had taken Alicia to get her nose pierced. Her parents had gotten into one of their epic fights over that one.

"I don't think I'll be here in four years," Zoe said. "But I can write a note."

"Okay." Whitney grinned. "That's what we'll do."

Alicia shook her head. She was two years older than Whitney, but they'd never hung out. She hadn't seen Whitney in action, had never seen how much people followed her.

"You," Whitney said, pointing to Alicia, "need to find a place in school to hide our letters."

"How am I supposed to do that?" Alicia asked.

"Ask around," Whitney said. She reached into Alicia's lap for paper and pens. "We need a big envelope for the letters. Can you find that, too?"

Alicia sighed as she stood up. She'd gained a lot of weight over the summer. It was like she hated Whitney for staying thin.

"Now let's write our letters," Whitney said.

Which was exactly what everyone did.

GREGOR

GREGOR'S PALMS WERE moist, and his braces were chafing his dry lips. He'd never met a girl like Whitney Montaine. She was gorgeous and funny and also really nice.

Gregor eyed the lined paper that Whitney had just handed him. He wasn't going to write her name, but he knew exactly what his hope and dream for high school was. *Girl. Gorgeous. Funny. Really nice.*

"There's a hole inside a fire extinguisher cabinet near the stairwell in the basement," Whitney's sister Alicia said, looking up from her phone. "If you reach behind the fire extinguisher, you can find it. People used to stash . . . *ahem* . . . illegal substances there last year. But they graduated."

Gregor glanced nervously at the others. The tall girl Mia was staring straight ahead like she hadn't even heard *illegal substances*. The famous girl was smiling serenely. The only person Gregor knew from middle school was Jake Rodriguez, but he was in the popular crowd. Drugs were probably no big deal to him. *Wow.* Welcome to high school.

"Who told you about that space?" Whitney asked.

"Like I'd say," Alicia said.

It was cute the way Whitney and her sister bickered, but you could see they were close. That was the opposite of how things were with Gregor's sister. All Erica cared about was running and her sleazy boyfriend. A few times this summer Russell had slipped his hand up Erica's shirt while Gregor was watching TV *in the same room*. Gregor fantasized about beating the crap out of Russell, punching his face and giving him a bloody nose. Of course, Russell was double his size and solid muscle. But a guy could dream.

When Whitney leaned over to continue writing, Gregor looked at the tan skin on her back where her shirt was sliding up. He felt pulsing deep in his gut as he imagined touching her there.

Stop!

Gregor was wearing loose shorts, but still. The last thing he needed was to be the guy with a boner at freshman orientation.

MIA

MIA WATCHED EVERYONE texting and talking as they left the gym. She crouched over, tugged open the laces on both her sneakers, and then slowly tied them again. She was trying not to make it look obvious that she was stalling for time. Not like it mattered. Everyone probably already thought she was weird. She knew that in middle school people said she did drugs, which was nuts. She'd never even *seen* drugs before.

When the gym was empty, Mia slipped out to the hallway and walked toward the basement stairs. The thought of starting school tomorrow in this huge building filled with twelve hundred people made Mia want to throw up.

Mia was tall, almost five-eight, and she hated the way she looked. Nothing was happening in the boob department, her eyes bulged, and her short hair was greenish from swimming in Sophie's pool. It didn't help that Mia's mom kept saying she should *do something* about her appearance. Like she had any clue what to *do*.

When she finally reached the basement, she checked her watch. Her dad wasn't coming for another half hour. Maybe it was dorky to wear a watch, but it was something to fixate on when she was nervous, like when Whitney's sister made her introduce herself. She'd practically regurgitated the strawberry Pop-Tart she'd eaten for breakfast.

Mia paused at the bottom of the stairs. There it was, the fire extinguisher cabinet. Just looking at it made her heart race. She opened the glass door, angled her hand behind the shiny red fire extinguisher, and then pinched her fingers into the hole, pulling out the curled-up envelope.

On the front, Alicia had written *Group Eighteen Freshman Orientation Project. Do not open until graduation!*

The first letter Mia pulled out was her own.

> *Dear Mia,*
> *To future you: I want to do well and get good grades and travel. Maybe leave the country? But most of all I want to get out of Hankinson for college. In four years I'd better have a clear escape plan.*
> *Mia*

It wasn't like Mia was going to write something profound. Not if she thought people were going to see it. She set her letter on the floor and pulled out the next one.

> *Dear Gregor,*
> *My hope and dream for high school involves a girl. I don't even need to write her name. In four years I'll remember who she is. I hope I make first chair cello, and I think maybe I'll start drums. I hope I like high school. I can't believe I'll be eighteen the next time I read this. I'll be driving. I'd better be going to college. If I'm not,*

then get your (our) act together, okay? Like, now!

   Gregor

He probably liked someone with sun-streaked blond hair and a real bra size. Guys always fall for the obvious girls. Mia reached for the next letter.

   Jake,

   I want to buy a new phone with the money I made mowing lawns this summer, but that's short-term. Hopes and dreams for high school: student council? Get back into sports? In four years . . . maybe I'll go to art school like my dad. Honestly, I can't picture what life will be like in four years. Will people still have iPads? Will all cars drive themselves? Well, this was kind of dumb. I can't think of anything else to say.

   Take care,

   Jake

Jake was cute in an all-American way. Definitely out of Mia's reach. Like she even *had* a reach.

The next letter was from Sierra Laybourne's daughter. Mia couldn't wait to tell Sophie about Zoe. Sophie went to Immaculate Conception, an all-girls Catholic school where despite the reference to egg meeting sperm, *nothing* exciting ever happened.

   Dear Zoe,

   I don't know what to say. If you're reading this someday, Whitney and Jake and the others, thanks for not making me feel like a freak today. I doubt I'll be at graduation when you open these letters. I'll probably be back in LA. Look me up if you come out there!

    Z

Mia folded up Zoe's letter. A few weeks ago she'd seen that clip of Sierra Laybourne screaming like a crazy woman and calling her daughter a brat. Even when she saw the video, before she *ever* imagined she would meet her, she felt so bad for Zoe. Mia would die if her mom were famous and did something like that. Mia would also die if people stared at her the way they did at Zoe today.

The last letter was from Whitney.

> *Dear Whit,*
>
>   *Hey, future me! I want to do well and be in school plays and travel and have fun. But most of all I want to get out of Hankinson. When I'm reading this in four years, I'd better have an escape plan.*
>
>   *Love,*
>
>   *Whit*

Mia spread her letter out next to Whitney's. Mia had gone to middle school with Whitney. She was gorgeous and talented and the only popular kid who'd never made fun of her, never asked if she was on drugs.

But then *this*! Back at Weston Middle, no one would have believed that Whitney Montaine and Mia Flint had the same goals, that they both wanted an "escape plan." And yet here it was. In writing.

Mia fitted the envelope back into the hole. If she had a girl crush, it would totally be on Whitney. Not that she'd ever tell *that* to Sophie.

JAKE

Jake: Truth or dare?

Mona Lisa: Hey, summer friend! Haven't heard from you since July. And . . . truth.

Jake: Hey to you, too. Okay, truth. How many boys have you kissed?

Mona Lisa: Eight. Yes, that's three more since I got back home to Atlanta after I saw you this summer. Do you think I'm a slut?

Jake: Ask me the same question.

Mona Lisa: How many girls have you kissed? I know that girl Marin with the candy-corn breath and someone from your Dominican heritage camp.

Jake: The SAME question.

Mona Lisa: Oh, you mean how many BOYS you've kissed?

Jake: One. A guy from my new art class. His name is Owen.

Mona Lisa: Does this mean you're over Teddy? I don't think I can spend another summer vacation at the lake with you moping about him.

Jake: It means I finally kissed a guy.

Mona Lisa: Please tell me you're over Teddy.

ZOE

ZOE DEFINITELY SHOULDN'T have come to the cafeteria. At least it was just ninth-grade lunch and not the upperclassmen, too. The older kids were nymphos. Every time the bell rang this morning, she'd had to push through packs of them grinding all over each other.

To top it off, people were staring at her in the halls. It was the same at orientation yesterday. They'd known right away who she was. She could hear them whispering about that video of her mom from London. People were saying how Sierra Laybourne had a mental breakdown and that was why Zoe was here. Whenever Zoe heard her mom's name, her throat tightened and she felt like she couldn't breathe.

"Zoe?" shouted a girl from her orientation group. It was Whitney, the bubbly one. She was waving at her. "Hey . . . Zoe!"

Whitney was sitting at a round table with two other girls. One was blond and Barbie-doll pretty. The other had black hair, blue eyeliner, and was in her math class this morning. Kyra, maybe? Zoe could tell right away that these were the popular girls.

Zoe started across the cafeteria. Most kids were wandering

aimlessly with their trays, but Whitney and her friends were totally chill. Zoe sat in the empty chair and set her pizza and fruit cup in front of her. *Of course* she landed at the popular table on day one. That's how it was when your mom was a celebrity. It didn't have anything to do with you.

"I'm Laurel," said the blond girl.

"You were in math with me," the girl with the blue eyeliner told Zoe.

"Yeah," Zoe said. "You're Kyra, right?"

Kyra squealed. "She knows my name! I can't believe she knows my name!" She screamed like she was trying to get people to look over.

A bunch of kids turned and stared at Zoe, checking out the greasy pizza on her tray. She should have gone with the salad bar.

"Shut up!" Whitney hissed. "Talk about her like she's *here*!" Then she turned to Zoe. "How's it going so far?"

"Fine, I guess." Zoe peeled back the foil on her fruit cup.

"Is everyone being stupid because of your mom?" Whitney asked. "Not like I'm the exception."

It was cool the way Whitney put it out there. Most people never mentioned Zoe's mom, and yet the entire conversation revolved around her in an unspoken way.

"A little," Zoe said. "A teacher asked if I could get him my mom's autograph."

"Damn!" Whitney shook her head. "They're not supposed to do that. Who was it?"

"No big deal," Zoe said, trying hard to breathe. *Oh god.* Watch one of them post *that* online. Then Max would call and give her the lecture: *be discreet, you're in the public eye, we have an image to preserve.* She'd gotten that lecture her whole life. She could probably sing it to the tune of the "Star-Spangled Banner." Max was her mom's manager, and he called the shots about everything in their lives.

"If that teacher keeps bothering you," Kyra said, "tell me, and I'll tell my dad."

"Kyra's dad is the principal," Whitney said, sipping her water. "Mr. Bauersmith. She's going to work the favors in high school."

"Lucky!" Laurel said. "My dad never gets me anything."

"Not too lucky," Kyra said. "He's cheesy. Did you see his mustache?" Kyra glanced at her phone and then at Zoe. "Besides, I'm not lucky like Zoe. You must get everything. Do designers send you free clothes? Do you have a chauffeur?"

The canned pear tasted sour on Zoe's tongue. She dropped the plastic spoon onto her tray.

"Stop it," Whitney said to Kyra.

"Whatever." Kyra craned her head around the cafeteria. "Did you see Brock? Wasn't he going to join us at lunch?"

"Kyra and Brock are together," Whitney explained to Zoe.

"We just celebrated three months," Kyra said.

Zoe pressed the heel of her hand to her forehead. Was she really going to have to puzzle together the friendships and couples here at Hankinson High School? None of it would matter once she went back to LA.

"Was that clip of your mom calling you a spoiled brat for real?" Kyra asked all of a sudden. "Or was it a publicity thing? I've heard that—"

"Kyr!" Whitney slapped her palm over Kyra's mouth. "Shut up. *Shut up.*"

"Whatever," Kyra said, pushing Whitney away. "God, high school is so boring."

To stop the tears from coming, Zoe studied the clock on the wall. She'd only been in lunch for eleven minutes.

MIA

THE DOORBELL RANG, several insistent buzzes. *Sophie.*

"Come on in!" Mia shouted, but she didn't get off the couch. She was indulging in her latest obsession: looking up pictures of Zoe. It was wild to type *Zoe Laybourne* and see images from Zoe's toddlerhood when she clutched a panda bear, her zitty period—probably seventh grade?—all the way until the paparazzi had gotten pictures of her and her mom in the airport leaving London after that horrific video went viral. In those pictures Zoe was wearing a black tank top and huge sunglasses and seemed grown-up and glamorous. That was what fascinated Mia. Like, how could that girl be the same Zoe she saw in the halls? At school Zoe seemed small and lost, definitely not a celebrity. Too bad they didn't end up in any classes together, because Mia would *really* like to bond with Zoe and help her adjust to life in Hankinson. Of course, Mia hadn't worked up the nerve even to smile at her yet.

Sophie was knocking hard on the door and turning at the knob. Mia's parents must have locked it when they went to the gym. Mia closed the screen with Zoe's pictures and hopped up to let Sophie in. She'd come over early for their standing Saturday night movie date.

"Finally!" Sophie said, kicking off her sandals and glancing at the tablet in Mia's hands. "What took so long? Were you getting your Zoe Laybourne fix again?"

Mia wished she hadn't told Sophie about her little hobby. Even though Sophie was her closest—or maybe only—friend, Mia sometimes felt like she couldn't trust her, like Sophie wouldn't think twice about slinging dirt if she needed to.

"No," Mia said. "Just doing homework."

"They're giving you homework already?" Sophie twisted her long sandy hair into a pile on her head. Classes at Immaculate Conception didn't start until Monday.

Mia nodded. She'd actually done all her homework this morning. It had taken only twenty minutes. So far high school seemed like a cakewalk.

"Did you do it?" Sophie asked. She smoothed her short blue sundress around her thighs. Sophie was much curvier than Mia and already had real hips and woman boobs. Whenever she wasn't in her Catholic school uniform, she wore minidresses. She liked to brag that guys checked out her legs. Personally, Mia thought Sophie's thighs looked like two honey-baked hams. Not that Mia would say that to Sophie, even though Sophie didn't think twice about telling Mia that she was a skeleton.

"Do what?" Mia asked.

Sophie rolled her eyes. "Shave your legs. When we texted two hours ago, you said you were finally going to do it."

"Oh yeah," Mia said. She was probably the last girl in the world to shave. Sophie said it was time she stopped having hairy Neanderthal legs. "Yeah, I sort of did it."

Sophie leaned down and swiped her hand across Mia's bare calf. "Nice. Does it itch?"

"A little."

"Hang on," Sophie said, touching Mia's other leg. "Why did you only shave one leg?"

"Oh." Mia adjusted her shorts on her hips. They were size zero and still loose. Size-zero hips and a double-A bra. Puberty was definitely taking its sweet time. "That's what I meant by *sort of*."

Sophie wrinkled her nose. "Why on earth would you shave one leg?"

Mia shrugged. Back when she was in the shower it had seemed like a good idea. "I wanted to make sure I liked it."

"*Liked it?* What's that supposed to mean?"

"I don't know. I guess like how you wear new shoes around inside before you go outside with them."

"You're weird," Sophie said. She grabbed a glass from Mia's cupboard and poured herself some milk. Mia hated plain milk—it actually made her gag. Another way that she and Sophie were different. Sometimes Mia wondered if they'd even be friends if they didn't live on the same street.

"Where're your parents?" Sophie asked, setting her empty glass in the sink and wiping off her milk mustache.

"Where do you think? The gym."

Mia's mom and dad worked out seven days a week. That was *their* obsession, along with their jobs. When they left for the gym every morning or evening, Mia wondered how they could possibly tone another part of their bodies, but in general they were more robot than human.

"I'm bored." Sophie nodded toward Mia's parents' room. "Want to try on your mom's clothes?"

"Okay . . . I just have to pee."

When Mia got back from the bathroom, Sophie was standing in front of her mom's closet, tugging her sundress over her head. Since Sophie's face was obscured by blue fabric, Mia stared at her boobs. They swelled out of her beige bra and formed a thin slit where they met in the center. Mia wished she could touch right there, the cleavage, to see if it felt sweaty or squishy or *what*.

"Should I try on your mom's green emerald wraparound or her cocktail dress with the satin?" Sophie asked, dropping her sundress onto the floor.

Mia quickly looked away. The last thing she wanted was for Sophie to know she'd been checking out her boobs. She didn't even know *why* she did that. Did it mean she was gay? Her uncle was, so maybe it ran in the family. But whenever Mia watched a movie, she thought the *guys* were cute, not the girls. And at school there was Brock Sawyer. Mia would give anything to kiss Brock. She couldn't see what he liked about horrible Kyra. Kyra did *not* deserve someone as amazing as Brock.

Maybe it was that Mia wanted to check out other boobs until she got her own.

Or maybe boobs were interesting even if you were straight.

Or maybe Sophie was right. Maybe Mia was just plain weird.

OCTOBER

WHITNEY

————

"YOU COULD HAVE knocked," Whitney said as Alicia opened her door and walked right into her room. *God.* At least she was just trying on lip gloss and not changing into pajamas.

"Dad is taking us camping this weekend." Alicia plopped onto the edge of Whitney's bed. "I thought you'd like to know. He just left to buy hot dogs. And that color's not right for you. Too pale. You look dead."

"Camping?" Whitney studied her reflection and then wiped her lips with a tissue. Whitney's family used to go camping when she was younger, but they hadn't been in forever. "All of us?"

"Mom's got open houses," Alicia said. "Plus, it's not like we want them together and arguing all weekend. I can't stand them sometimes. Anyway, Dad told me we're going to the campground with those boulders by the lake."

"Mosquito heaven?"

"Yep."

"Can we get out of it? I have plans tomorrow night."

Alicia checked out her nose ring in the mirror. She loved sharing the bad news. "Dad says he needs to talk to us, and he wants somewhere away from it all."

"He should have had two boys," Whitney said.

An hour later Whitney found her dad in his office cleaning his tropical fish tank. Their dog was sleeping in a knot on the sofa. Whitney's dad was a chemistry professor at the college. People called him *brilliant*. Sometimes Whitney wondered if people made a big deal because her dad was black, and there weren't a lot of black chemists around here.

"Dad?" Whitney asked.

Whitney's dad pushed his reading glasses up onto his head. He wore his hair short, and it was graying around the temples.

"I'm just wondering . . . do I have to go camping tomorrow night? I'm supposed to go to the mall with Kyra and this other girl, Laurel. She's a new friend."

Her dad examined the thin strip where he was testing the pH of the tank water. "This is the time to do it," he said. "Before you and Alicia get busy with your activities and the weather turns cold."

Whitney stood in the doorway, rising on her tippy-toes and slowly lowering again. Alicia took a psychology class last spring and got really into analyzing everyone. She told Whitney that their dad was a self-centered narcissist. She also said their mom compulsively shopped to fill the unhappy voids in her life. Whitney wasn't sure if any of it was true.

"Laurel's mom is driving us," Whitney said. "I know Laurel from summer soccer, and now she goes to Hankinson."

Whitney's dad jotted something in his notebook. Whitney had been hoping Zoe Laybourne would come shopping too, but when

Zoe didn't show up at lunch all week, Whitney assumed Kyra had scared her off. Sometimes she wished she could dump Kyra, but that would make her life hell.

"What did you say again?" Whitney's dad asked. He squirted a few droplets into the tank. It sent ripples into the water, making the fish flutter their iridescent tails.

"I'm supposed to go to the mall tomorrow night."

"Sorry, Whit," her dad said. "I need to talk to you girls. The mall will always be there. The campground closes for the season in a few weeks."

Whitney bit her lip. She decided not to tell him how she and her friends were planning to search for leopard-print unitards to wear on the homecoming float. The freshman homecoming theme was "Back to the Jungle." Her dad would say it was trivial. That was what he thought about most things that were important to Whitney.

GREGOR

GREGOR'S MOM MADE spaghetti the evening of the homecoming parade. Spicy red sauce and extra Parmesan, exactly the way he liked it. It was just Gregor and his parents because Erica was getting Chinese food with Russell, her sleazy boyfriend who drove a blue pickup truck with oversized tires.

"I've got something for you," Gregor's dad said. His eyes were teary as he reached toward the counter for a wrapped present.

"Smile, sweetie," Gregor's mom said. She had her phone up, recording the scene.

Gregor set down his fork. Thank god Erica wasn't here. She was always making fun of the way their parents babied Gregor. "Why did you get me something?"

Gregor's dad smiled. "Just open it."

Gregor carefully peeled off the tape. Inside was a brown leather journal with his name engraved in gold letters on the front.

"It's the same kind of journal I had when I was your age," his dad said. "My dad gave it to me on my first day of high school. I had to backorder yours. That's why it's a little late."

"Thank you. I love it." Gregor flipped through the blank pages, wondering about all the things that hadn't happened yet but would feel important to record in one, two, even three years.

It was exciting to think about that. It made Gregor wonder about Whitney.

After dinner his dad dropped him off downtown and then headed over to Nana Margaret's. His parents took turns bringing meals to his dad's mom, who was eighty-two and lived alone. Gregor waved good-bye and then walked toward the small crowd gathered along the street for the homecoming parade. He rubbed his hands together, wishing he'd brought gloves.

"Hey, Gregor!" Dinky called, waving him over.

Dinky was standing with some other ninth-grade guys from band. The first week of school, Gregor had started drums with Dinky. It was a lot, running from drums to orchestra and practicing two instruments, but it was also fun to do something different. With drums, Gregor could let loose. Cello was much more precise.

"It's crazy cold, right?" Dinky asked. The marching band was passing so he had to shout.

Gregor watched the band closely. Freshman percussion practiced with the marching band, but they didn't perform with them until spring.

"They're playing that song from *The Jungle Book*," Gregor said, blowing warm air on his fingers. "How come?"

"Because of our float," Dinky said, pointing down the street. "The freshman theme is 'Back to the Jungle.' Didn't you hear all those announcements about decorating it?"

An old-fashioned fire truck rolled past them. It had a banner tied to the side that said GO, HANKINSON WILDCATS. Behind that, an SUV was pulling a flatbed with a plastic palm tree and a bunch of people shrieking.

Gregor laughed. Even his braces felt cold. "What does 'back to the jungle' *mean*? Like, how can we get *back* to the jungle? Hankinson never was a jungle—"

The freshman float rolled in front of them. And there, dancing and waving, was Whitney Montaine. She was wearing a low-cut black shirt, a beaded necklace, and a swath of leopard-print fabric tied around her waist.

Whitney was in two of Gregor's honors classes. He tried not to be obvious, but he watched her all the time. She was left-handed and wore gold earrings with the letter *W* on them and made a squeaky sound when she sneezed.

As the float passed, Gregor raised one hand to wave at Whitney. For an amazing second it looked like Whitney was waving back at him. But then he saw her eyes moving over the whole crowd, smiling at everyone and no one.

JAKE

JAKE PULLED HIS shirt over his head. The locker room smelled like chlorine and cleaning fluid, but at least it was quiet. At least he was the only one in here. Jake had made a deal with the PE teacher to go to the art room instead of freshman gym if he swam laps in the pool during his first-period study hall. He just didn't want to face the other guys in the locker room. For the last few weeks of eighth grade, after people found out what he'd said to Teddy, guys turned away from him when they changed, like they didn't want him to see them in boxers. That made Jake feel like crap almost more than anything else. *Almost.* Losing Teddy's friendship was worse.

Just then the door to the locker room opened.

Teddy.

Jake quickly crossed his arms over his bare chest.

"Oh . . . hey," Teddy said.

"Hey," Jake managed.

"What's up?"

"Not much. Just swimming."

Teddy wasn't in any of his classes, but they said hi in the halls.

Once, in the lunch line, Jake handed him a bag of SunChips and Teddy said thanks.

"I lost my sweatshirt after football yesterday," Teddy said.

Teddy had gone out for JV football. Jake saw him wearing his jersey on the first game day. He'd painted his numbers in blue on his cheek. They were supposed to have done JV football together. Jake should have had numbers on his cheeks too.

"Maybe check the lost and found bin?"

"Yeah." Teddy stayed in the doorway, his bag slung over his shoulder.

Jake glanced at his T-shirt crumpled on the bench. He wished he could put it back on without seeming obvious.

"How's football going?" Jake asked.

"It's cool. We've lost most of our games, but whatever. We suck. I'm sure that's my fault."

Jake laughed hoarsely. They'd done a football clinic together in junior high, and Teddy always said how much he sucked. Jake and Teddy had known each other since elementary school, but they'd gotten to be best friends through football. After practice they'd go to Teddy's basement and share a beer. They hated the taste but wanted to build up tolerance for high school.

"What's up with you?" Teddy asked.

"Not much." Jake wished he had some great story to tell Teddy, but nothing was coming to mind. "I'm taking an art class downtown."

"Are you going out for Halloween?"

"Probably not."

That sucked to admit. Jake's middle-school friends had

regrouped, and he hadn't made any real friends in high school yet other than casual acquaintances from the art room. More than anything, he missed Teddy. Whenever he thought back to the bus ride home from Washington, DC, he wished he could take it back. He'd been sleep-deprived from the trip. He hadn't been thinking clearly.

"People are talking about this freshman slaughter thing that happens on Halloween," Teddy said, "but they're probably full of shit."

"Oh," Jake said. "Good to know."

"Listen." Teddy snapped his fingers a few times. He wasn't looking Jake in the eye. "There's something I want to tell you."

Jake's heart started racing. Was Teddy going to apologize? It wasn't like Teddy did anything wrong, though. Jake found out later that some girls had overheard him on the bus, and they'd told everyone. *Jeez.* All he wanted was to put his stupid T-shirt back on.

Teddy hoisted his bag farther up on his shoulder. "I'm with Marin. We're going out. Whatever."

"Marin *Banerjee*?" Marin was the girl who Jake had taken to the semiformal last year and kissed during a slow dance. Teddy knew this! Teddy also knew that Jake wasn't into her.

It wasn't like he and Teddy had ever talked about how maybe they liked guys instead of girls. But they *did* things. A few times, when they were playing video games, Teddy had held Jake's hand around the remote. And once, they were wrestling in the basement, and Teddy had stretched his body on top of Jake's. They'd stayed like that for a long time, inhaling each other's exhales.

"Marin's cool," Jake said. "That's cool."

"Yeah, she's awesome. You're really not going out for Halloween?"

"I guess not. I don't know."

"Well, see you around."

Once Teddy was gone, Jake realized that he never did come in and look for his football sweatshirt.

NOVEMBER

MIA

MIA RUSHED TO her locker after last period, hugging her folders tight to her chest. It was Mr. Maguire's fault that she was so late. Her earth science teacher was one of those cliquey teachers who buddied around with the popular kids. That morning he'd matched up everyone except Mia for the soil lab. By the time she worked up the nerve to tell him, all the dirt had been taken. She had to go back after school and sample the fungus levels, or Mr. Maguire said he'd dock it off her grade.

Honestly, it wouldn't have been a big deal, except Mia missed the bus and it was drizzling out, too wet to walk. That meant she'd have to take the late bus with the JV jocks who did afterschool sports. They weren't teasing her this year or saying she was stoned, but she didn't want to be alone with them on the bus either.

Thinking about all this, Mia was in a lousy mood when she stood at her locker. She was just loading her notebooks into her backpack when she noticed that Kyra Bauersmith's locker was slightly open. Kyra's locker was two down, which gave Mia a front-row seat to Kyra and Brock's daily makeout sessions. Kyra didn't deserve someone like Brock Sawyer. But there he was, pressing himself against her melon boobs every morning.

The hallway was empty. All Mia could hear was the distant clanking of the vending machine in the teachers' lounge. She eased Kyra's locker all the way open. Inside were lip glosses, a pack of gum, tags from expensive clothing, selfies of her with Whitney and other girls, and pictures of her and Brock together. Mia had been lusting after Brock Sawyer since middle school. Brock, with his amber-brown eyes and a playful dimple in one cheek. In eighth grade, she'd filled pages of notebooks with signatures like *Mia Sawyer* and *Mia Flint Sawyer* and *Mrs. Brock Sawyer*.

Quick as lightning, Mia peeled a small photo of Brock from Kyra's locker and slipped it into her backpack.

In this universe, Brock was Kyra's boyfriend.

In an alternate universe, he belonged entirely to Mia.

That evening the house was empty. Mia's mom was on a business trip and her dad was at the gym. Mia did her homework and practiced piano for thirty minutes. Then she microwaved a pizza bagel, cut up an apple, and carried the plate to her room. She sat cross-legged on her carpet and found the photo of Brock in her backpack. It was a rectangular picture, like from one of those photo booths at the mall. It must have been taken over the summer, because Brock's skin was as tan as a new penny.

Mia had never stolen anything before. But she'd been doing some crazy stuff recently, like googling *penis* to see what would come back. And the other day, when Sophie wasn't even around, she tried on her mom's lacy nightie and posed in front of the mirror. She envisioned explaining all that to the principal if she got busted for stealing the photo, and it made her cheeks so hot she ran into the bathroom and splashed cold water on her face.

The next morning Mia jolted awake in bed. She had stolen a photo of Brock Sawyer!

She showered, tugged on jeans and a T-shirt, and got out the pink Chucks from her uncle George. When he'd given them to her over the summer, they seemed too cool, like they were for someone who wanted to call attention to herself. But today she was ready for them.

She was just approaching her locker when she heard Kyra's voice.

"Where's my picture of Brock?" Kyra asked Whitney and this other popular girl, Laurel. "Who stole it?"

Mia froze. Just before the bus had arrived, she'd put Brock's picture deep into her jeans pocket. Maybe it was risky, but she liked having it near her.

As Mia opened her locker, Whitney sidestepped out of the way.

"How do you *know* someone stole it?" Laurel asked. "It could have fallen out."

"Yeah," Whitney said. "Tape has a tendency to unstick."

Being so close to them was making Mia's heart go wild. They were having this conversation about the photo *because of her.*

"You realize that you two are the only people who know my locker combination," Kyra said.

"Are you accusing us of *stealing*?" Whitney snapped. "Why would I want a picture of Brock?"

"Because you always get everything you want," Kyra shot back. "And if you don't get it, then you take it."

Whitney lurched back like she'd been slapped. "This is about homecoming queen, isn't it? You're still mad that I got it and you didn't."

"Guys, chill," Laurel said. "I'm sure you can find the picture."

"That's exactly what I'm going to do." Kyra slammed her locker. "I'm going to my dad's office. Come on, Laurel. We'll see what he says."

"You're seriously going to involve the *principal* in this?" Whitney called after them.

Once Kyra and Laurel were gone, Whitney pressed her thumbs to her temples. Mia stared into her locker.

"You probably think we're dumb," Whitney said.

Mia shook her head quickly.

"We *are* dumb," Whitney said. She flipped her long braids over her shoulder and started to walk away, but then she turned back. "I like your Chucks, by the way. Cool color."

Mia skipped homeroom. She hurried through the hallways and down the stairs to the basement. She checked that no one was coming and then opened the door to the fire extinguisher cabinet and reached for the hidden envelope. Mia pulled the photo of Brock out of her pocket and tucked it inside with the letters from freshman orientation.

ZOE

A WEEK BEFORE Thanksgiving, Zoe finally got the text she'd been waiting for. She had a window seat on the school bus and was listening to music, watching the sunrise, trying to block out the world. That was Zoe's mission these days. She'd wear her noise-canceling headphones the whole way to school, eat lunch in an empty study hall room, and take a nap as soon as she got home.

The text was from Max, her mom's manager. Okay, it was *almost* the text she'd been waiting for.

Can you talk to Sierra at four p.m. today? Eastern time. I will arrange the call.

Zoe peeked at the guy next to her to make sure he didn't see that and start gossiping about her. He'd introduced himself as James on the first day of school. He was a junior with lots of zits and a knobby Adam's apple. He'd told Zoe that he failed his road test, which was why he was on the bus.

Yeah, Zoe wrote back to Max. *Four is good.*

Zoe clutched her phone in her lap. She hadn't talked to her mom in three months. Jane had told her that the rule at Sierra's "place" was no outside contact. Zoe knew what *place* meant. It meant rehab, but no one was saying it.

Zoe could see that the guy next to her was talking to her. She pushed her headphones down onto her neck.

"I was saying that I like your phone," James said to her.

"Thanks." She hoped he wasn't trying to start a conversation. She didn't think she could do that right now.

"Is that the new one?"

"Not really," Zoe said. She stared out the window. It was going to be hard to make it until four o'clock.

Zoe slid an English muffin into the toaster and was just opening the fridge for jam when Jane walked through the door, home early from work. For a second Zoe was embarrassed to be helping herself to food. She still felt like a guest here.

"I wanted to get a jump on Thanksgiving cooking," Jane said. Her eyes darted to Zoe's phone on the counter, which made Zoe suspect she was there to make sure things went smoothly with today's call. Even though Max had texted Zoe to set up the call, Jane seemed to be talking to him quite a lot. It was Jane who told her that Max said her mom was returning from Arizona in two days. Also, Jane and Max had decided that Zoe would fly to LA for Thanksgiving then come back to Hankinson to finish up the fall semester. Over Christmas break she was moving back to California for good.

The toaster popped, which made Zoe jump. She reached for a butter knife but accidentally dropped it onto the floor.

"You can help me cook if you want," Jane said, bending over for the knife. "After your call."

"Okay . . . thanks," Zoe said.

At four on the dot Zoe's phone rang. She was sitting on her bed, examining her toenails. On both big toes she still had a smudge of purple from the pedicure she got on the last day she and her mom were together.

"Mom?" she asked hoarsely.

"Zoe? This is Lani," a woman's voice said. "I'm your mom's counselor. I've heard a lot about you."

Lani spoke slowly, like Zoe was a preschooler.

"I'm about to put your mom on," Lani said. "I'll be on the call too. Your mom is excited to talk to you, but she's still vulnerable. I'm sure you understand. Let's be strong for her."

Before Zoe had a chance to ask what that even *meant*, Sierra said, "Hey, Z. How's it going?"

Zoe's eyes welled up. She tried to say hi back, to sound strong, but she felt like crying.

Lani jumped in. "I know this is hard for both of you. It will be wonderful to see each other at Thanksgiving next week."

Zoe wiped her eyes. "Will Lani be there?" she asked her mom.

"No," Lani said. "I won't."

"Are things—" Zoe paused. "Are they better?"

In a million years she could never say *alcoholic* out loud. Back in October, Jane had driven Zoe to an Al-Anon support group at a church in downtown Hankinson, but Zoe couldn't get out of the car. Her legs literally wouldn't move.

"Can you explain for me?" Sierra asked Lani.

"Recovery is a process," Lani said. "Your mom will need everyone's support on her journey."

Zoe picked at her toenail. When they hung up a few minutes later, Zoe realized she'd never actually talked directly with her mom. Lani was the go-between for the entire call.

A few days later Zoe was helping Jane bake a pecan pie. Paul Simon was playing. Jane was explaining how her son, David, was coming for Thanksgiving and he was bringing a few buddies from Downing College.

Jane worked as an administrator at Downing, the small college forty-five minutes away. David went there and lived in the dorms. He came home every few weeks to do laundry. Zoe hid in her bedroom whenever he was here. She'd never had a sibling or even a cousin before. She didn't know how to do the family thing.

"Rich is coming with his wife, Glenda, and their daughter," Jane said. Rich was Jane's ex-husband, David's father.

"Isn't it awkward to have your ex-husband over with his new family?"

"It's been a lot of years." Jane cut open a bag of pecans. "A lot of water under the bridge. We go with it."

Zoe nodded. It was cool how Jane talked to her like an equal. She'd even told Zoe a little about her grandparents, Sierra and Jane's mom and dad, who had died in a car accident more than twenty years ago. Sierra rarely talked about them because it upset her too much, but Jane told her stories about them, and even explained carefully how Sierra had been in bad shape after they died. The one thing they never discussed, though, was why Sierra and Jane had had a falling out.

"You should know," Jane said as she handed Zoe a measuring cup, "that the best recipe for pecan pie is on the corn syrup bottle."

"Really?" Zoe studied the label on the glass bottle.

Jane's phone rang. She glanced at the counter. "Max."

Zoe wrinkled her nose. "Why's he calling again?"

"Not sure." Jane wiped her hands on a dishrag. "Hello?"

Zoe reached into the pecan bag for a few nuts.

"Oh. Oh no." Jane walked into the living room and sat down on the piano stool.

Zoe tried to drum her fingers to "Graceland," but all she could hear in her head was pounding, like her brain was on the spin cycle of a washing machine.

A few minutes later Jane came back into the kitchen.

"Okay, so . . ." Jane said, turning her phone around in her hands. "Max talked to Lani. . . . Sierra didn't come home today. She's still at . . . the place. She needs a few more weeks."

"What's wrong?" Zoe asked, her throat tight. "Did I say something wrong on that phone call?"

"Oh no, honey. No, no." Jane reached over and touched Zoe's arm. "He didn't say what was wrong exactly. I'm sure she's just working things through. But you'll stay here and have Thanksgiving with us."

Lani had promised that her mom would pick her up at the airport in Los Angeles. Zoe was going to bake her a pecan pie and somehow carry it cross-country.

"I'm sorry." Jane set her hand on Zoe's shoulder, but Zoe wriggled away.

She ran upstairs to the bathroom and grabbed the nail polish remover from the cabinet. With a few swipes she erased all the remaining purple from her toes.

DECEMBER

WHITNEY

OF COURSE KYRA had to go all drama queen at the mall. She and Whitney were shopping for their lucky audition shirts, but Whitney was also planning to tell Kyra that her parents had separated. Her dad had told her and Alicia that awful weekend that he forced them to go camping. Her mom had moved into a rental house *six weeks ago*.

Kyra's mom had dropped them off at the mall. Christmas music was blasting, and holiday shoppers were shoving around with their armfuls of bags. Whitney wanted to find their shirts for the *Grease* auditions and then get to Auntie Anne's so they could share a cinnamon-sugar pretzel and she could tell Kyra about her parents. She'd already told Laurel, but then made her promise not to say anything. It was stressful keeping her stories straight. Whitney was so stressed, she'd gotten a migraine a few days ago and stayed home from school, puking in pain.

"It's not fair!" Kyra shouted, pushing her bottom lip out.

They'd just left the cashier at Bloomingdale's. Several people looked over at them.

"We'll find you a good shirt," Whitney said, dropping her wallet into her purse.

They'd been shopping for an hour and still couldn't find anything that fit Kyra's chest. She kept saying everything made her look fat. And then the *only* shirt she liked happened to be the gauzy gold one that Whitney just bought. Whitney found it first, on the sale rack.

"Let's check the sale rack again," Kyra said. "Just to be sure they don't have another."

Whitney shrugged. "I really think it was the only medium."

"But it's not fair," Kyra said. "You'll get a good part in *Grease*, and I'll just stand around looking fat."

"You're not fat," Whitney said, taking Kyra's hand and pulling her out of the store. "Plus, we can't audition in matching shirts."

"You're just saying that because *you* have the shirt," Kyra said. "You'll probably get a lead. You're so lucky you're black. No one wants to cast another white girl."

"Biracial," Whitney said. "My mom's white."

"You know what I mean. My dad says diversity is a big advantage."

Whitney pressed her lips together. Kyra had been in a terrible mood since Brock dumped her in November. Also, Kyra was jealous that Whitney and Laurel did soccer together and had gotten closer this fall.

That was why today was supposed to be a *good* thing. Laurel was home with strep, so Whitney and Kyra were going to shop together and bond. If only they could find Kyra a shirt. Then everything would be okay.

• • •

"Look, there's Jake," Whitney said, leaning in close to Kyra. She pointed at the guy with the longish blond hair and blue North Face jacket. He'd been in her freshman orientation group. "He went to Loch Middle. Don't you think he's really cute?"

Jake saw them looking at him and nodded with his chin. It was such a dude gesture that Whitney and Kyra collapsed into giggles. Whitney had to squeeze her legs tight not to pee her pants. Jake veered into the bookstore.

"Jake Rodriguez," Kyra said, panting. "He's your type. Pretty boy. Supposedly, he's a really good artist. His dad is an artist, like, for real."

Whitney wiped at her eyes. "Do you know him?"

"He mowed my mom's lawn last summer, but it's not like we talked. He thinks he's better than us. Which he's not." Kyra clapped her hands. "Hang on! Laurel went to Loch Middle too. Let's ask her about him."

They both whipped out their phones and raced to see who could text Laurel first.

"Yes!" Kyra said, pumping her phone in the air. "I got Laurel! She just texted me."

"What'd she say?"

"Whoa." Kyra opened her mouth wide. "Whoa."

"*What?*" Whitney tried to peek, but Kyra was clutching her phone to her chest.

Kyra wrote Laurel back and then turned to Whitney. Her mouth was puckered like she was sucking a lemon lollipop. "It sounds like your pretty boy likes . . . pretty boys."

"No way! How does she know?"

Kyra's phone pinged again. "Hang on," she said, staring at the screen.

"What?" Whitney asked. This was getting annoying.

"Girls, too, possibly. He went to a dance with that Indian girl, Marin, last year. They kissed."

"So he's bi." Whitney swung her bag in her arms. "I can live with that."

"Right." Kyra linked arms with Whitney as they walked past Book Nook. "Like you, with your commitment issues, need to have a guy who can't decide whether he likes you or a dude."

"I don't have commitment issues. I'm just waiting for—"

"I figured it out!" Kyra pulled Whitney toward Victoria's Secret. "I'll get a gold camisole and wear something see-through over it. I've got ta-tas. Why not show them off?"

Whitney followed Kyra into the store. Maybe she'd wait to tell her the news about her parents.

MIA

MIA COULDN'T PUT this book down, even though she was reading it on the floor of Book Nook. Her parents were in the Nordic outlet buying yet more beige furniture. Her mom had handed her a credit card in the hopes that Mia would splurge at the mall and transform herself into a preppy rah-rah girl. Mia went to the bookstore instead.

The novel was called *Impossible*, and it was about a family curse and a girl discovering a letter from her long-lost mom behind a bookshelf. It reminded her of the envelope her orientation group had hidden at the start of the year.

Mia looked up from her book and saw Jake Rodriguez—from her orientation group!—sitting in the children's section. He was leaning against a shelf, his long legs stretched in front of him, flipping through . . . *Captain Underpants*? In his faded jeans and blue jacket, he looked like a model. It seemed unfair that a guy had better hair than she did. She'd been growing hers out since September, but it still wasn't past her earlobes.

Mia wondered if Jake even remembered her from orientation.

He was really cute and had that popular attitude going on. He probably had more important things in his life than to think about her.

Jake set Captain Underpants on a kiddie table and stretched his arms over his head. His shirt lifted up, revealing his stomach with a slight tickle of hair and the black band of his boxers. Mia's stomach flipped. She wondered if he'd had sex yet. According to statistics, 30 percent of American ninth graders had had sex. Thoroughly shocking, but facts were facts.

Mia watched Jake head out of the store. As soon as he was gone, she hurried across the children's section and scooped up *Captain Underpants and the Perilous Plot of Professor Poopypants*. She tucked it under *Impossible*, carried both books to the register, and bought them with her mom's credit card. Her mom hated real books. She complained that they got too dusty, and she was always trying to get Mia to read on a tablet. Oh well. It wasn't the first time her mom would be disappointed in her.

JAKE

JAKE JIGGLED ONE leg over the other. Christmas Eve mass was taking a million years. His family wasn't even really Catholic. His mom had grown up Jewish. His dad was Dominican and called himself a Christmas-and-Easter Catholic because those were the only times he dragged them to church.

Finally, *finally*, it was over and they got into the car. As his mom pulled out of the parking lot, Violet moaned that her tights were itchy. His little sister was always freaking out about tags and seams and elastic that was too tight.

"I want to take them off," she cried.

"Just wait until we're home," his dad called from the front.

"No!" Violet wriggled onto her side and began stripping in her seat.

Jake shifted around the backseat. He couldn't sit still either. Deciding to tell his parents had taken a year. Now he just wanted it over with.

Christmas Eve took another million years. His family had all these quirky holiday traditions like making homemade waffles and saying what they were grateful for and dancing to the Chipmunks as they hung their stockings on the mantel.

Jake used to be embarrassed by his parents, but not anymore. The way he saw it, his family was weird in a cool way. His mom wrote books about mythological creatures, and his dad illustrated them. People couldn't believe that was what they did for their actual jobs. Jake's little sister was eight. She was a chess genius and probably a regular genius too. Jake had always been the normal one in the family, with his friends and his football and his all-American blond hair.

But then things changed last spring, and Jake didn't feel so normal anymore. That was what he was sick of keeping inside.

"I don't get it," Jake said to his mom when his dad finally brought Violet up to bed. They were sitting at the kitchen table, wrapping stocking stuffers. "Everyone says she's brilliant, but she still believes in Santa Claus?"

Jake's mom rolled green tissue paper around a tube of peppermint ChapStick. "You believed in Santa for a long time too."

"No, I didn't." Jake began wrapping a purple pencil sharpener. "You and Santa had the same handwriting."

She laughed. "Guilty as charged."

"Who's guilty?" Jake's dad pulled a beer out of the fridge and joined them at the table.

Jake's mind went blank. After hours of waiting, there was nothing stopping him now.

"What would you think—?" he said really fast. He couldn't figure out how to finish that sentence.

Jake's dad tilted the beer into his mouth. His mom ran her finger along a strip of tape. They had no clue what he was about to say.

"What would you think if I told you something about me?" Jake asked.

His mom shot a look at his dad, who set his beer on the table. Then, after a second, he passed the beer to Jake. Jake shook his head. He was too nervous to swallow.

"The thing is . . ." Jake rapped his knuckles on the wooden table. "I might like boys instead of girls."

There it was. Jake's heart was pounding. His underarms were moist.

"We'd say"—Jake's mom took his hands—"that we're glad you feel comfortable telling us."

"Enough bullshit!" Jake's dad pounded his fist on the table so hard, the bottle rattled. "We'd say it's about time you figured that out. Now maybe you can look happy again."

He wrapped Jake in a hug, squeezing him tight. Jake's mom put her arms around both of them.

The next morning, after Jake had opened his sketchpad and oil paints and a navy blue hoodie, and Violet was building her new Lego set, Jake's mom handed him a large gift that had been sitting in his dad's lap. It was wrapped in green tissue paper.

Jake ripped it open. Inside was a stash of YA novels. He skimmed the titles, pausing to read the inside flaps. *Boy Meets Boy. Geography Club. Aristotle and Dante Discover the Secrets of the Universe.*

"You've given me gay lit," he said quietly.

Jake's parents were smiling and wiping back tears.

Jake was confused. "But I just told you last night."

"We've had the books since last year," Jake's mom said. "We've read them all."

"We were waiting to give them to you until you told us," his dad said.

"Modeh ani," Jake said to his parents. That was a Hebrew expression of gratitude. *"Gracias."*

"De nada," Jake's dad said.

"You're welcome," Jake's mom said.

GREGOR

ON NEW YEAR'S Eve, Gregor and his parents and sister were at Nana Margaret's house. They went every year and ate pound cake and put on a cello-violin duet. Tonight they were also planning to watch *One Precious* because it had the most classic New Year's scene ever.

Just as they were getting ready to start the movie, the doorbell rang. It was Erica's lame boyfriend. According to Erica, Russell was taking her out for pancakes. Gregor's dad went to the door. Her mom was in the kitchen with Nana Margaret.

Gregor curled his fingers into quote signs. "I wonder what 'pancakes' actually means."

"What do you know?" Erica huffed, shoving her violin into its case. She looked into the oak-framed mirror in the living room, adjusting her reddish-brown hair behind her ear. In Gregor's opinion, she had way too much makeup on.

The front door opened. They could hear Gregor's dad say, "I hear you're taking Erica for pancakes."

Gregor snorted. He couldn't help it. Russell was a dick. Someone had to give Erica a hard time about it.

"Screw you," Erica said. She slid on even more lipstick and skipped out to the foyer.

Gregor meandered after her.

"Yes, sir," Russell was saying. He was wearing dark jeans and a black leather jacket, his hair slicked back with gel. "I'll have Erica home right after midnight."

"Be home at twelve fifteen," Gregor's dad said. "The clock strikes, and you get into the car. I hope you're not planning to drink because—"

"God," Erica said, wriggling into her coat and slipping past their dad. "We're not stupid."

"And you'll remember to drive safely, Russ? You know that this is the worst night to be on the road."

"Russ*ell*," Erica said.

"Yes, sir," Russell said again. When he smiled, his teeth were clenched and a muscle in his jaw was twitching.

This was awesome. Gregor was loving it.

"When's the last time you had your truck serviced?" Gregor's dad asked Russell.

"Dad!" Erica cried. The tip of her nose was getting red, which was what happened before she lost her temper.

"Charlie?" Gregor's mom said, coming into the foyer and touching his arm. "Don't you think we should let them go?"

With that, Erica and Russell took off down the driveway.

"Doesn't Julia Roberts' daughter go to your school now?" Nana Margaret asked, steadying herself on the edge of the couch. They'd just paused *One Precious* so she could use the bathroom.

"That's not Julia Roberts in this movie, Mom," his dad said. "It's Sierra Laybourne."

"And yeah," Gregor said. He felt around in his pocket for the tiny scrap of paper he'd tucked in there, touching it with his fingers. "Her daughter goes to my school. Her name is Zoe."

"Have you asked her out yet?" Nana Margaret walked slowly toward the bathroom, holding the wall to support herself. "I'm sure Julia Roberts has a beautiful daughter."

Gregor saw his dad glance at his mom. Recently they'd all been noticing that Nana Margaret was forgetting things and mixing up words.

Gregor slipped into Nana Margaret's room. It smelled like baby powder, and she had faded floral sheets with ruffles on the pillow-cases. When Gregor and Erica were younger, they would sleep over here. The three of them would pile into her bed and watch romantic comedies until midnight. As always, there was a landline on Nana Margaret's nightstand. Gregor pulled the paper out of his pocket. It was Whitney Montaine's home phone number, listed under *Clark Montaine*. He'd found it in an old phone book in Nana Margaret's pantry, when she'd sent him searching for canned cherries for the pound cake.

He sat on the edge of the bed and dialed the number.

After several rings, a girl asked, "Hello?"

Gregor's mouth went dry as he thought of all the things he'd like to say to Whitney.

Instead he hung up.

Maybe next year.

WHITNEY

"HELLO?" WHITNEY SAID into the phone for a second time.

She'd been stepping into the car when they heard the phone ring. Her dad was driving her and Kyra and Laurel over to her mom's house. That was where they were sleeping for New Year's Eve. Her dad had sent her inside to answer the phone because he said no one called the landline anymore, so maybe it was an emergency.

It sounded like the person on the other line had hung up. Whitney set the phone down and walked out to the car.

"Wrong number," she told her dad as she opened the passenger door.

Just at that second there was a loud crash at the end of the driveway, metal on metal, glass shattering. Whitney and her friends screamed.

"Stay here," Whitney's dad said. He grabbed his phone from the drink console and ran out into the dark.

"Do you think he's calling 911?" Laurel asked.

"I guess," Whitney said, hugging her knees in the front seat. She hadn't even closed her door yet. It was freezing out, but she was too scared to move.

"Do you realize," Kyra whispered, "that if you hadn't gone inside to get that phone call *we* could have been hit?"

Whitney gasped. "Oh my god. That wrong number person saved our lives."

"That's so true," Laurel said.

"We could have died," Kyra said.

There was shouting down in the street. Whitney could hear her dad's voice, but she couldn't tell what he was saying. She was trembling all over.

A minute later sirens wailed in the distance. Whitney pulled her door shut and then turned and took her friends' hands. They sat in the dark holding hands as the sirens got closer and closer.

ZOE

ZOE STARTED TO dial 911 but then hung up. Even though Max hadn't specifically mentioned it, she guessed that calling 911 on her mom was off-limits. She tried Max again. He hadn't picked up the other four times she'd called tonight.

"Please answer," she whispered into the phone. "Please, please, please."

The call went straight to voice mail. Zoe's lungs felt icy. It was almost midnight on New Year's Eve, and her mom might be dying. Or maybe she wasn't, but how was Zoe supposed to figure that out?

Her mom had been in her room since eight. At first Zoe thought she was resting, but when she didn't come downstairs for the movie they were supposed to watch, Zoe went to wake her up. She found her mom passed out on her bed with drool trickling out of her mouth. Her blond hair was tangled, and it looked like she was barely breathing.

This had happened once before, back when Zoe was in seventh grade. Actually, Zoe wasn't sure exactly *what* had happened that time because when she'd gotten home from school, her mom was already at Cedars-Sinai. Later she'd overheard a doctor say it had been a combination of alcohol and sleeping pills. Her mom went into rehab a few days after getting out of the hospital.

Ever since Zoe returned to California last week, her mom seemed a little sad. She'd been talking a lot about how they didn't have family to share the holidays with. This afternoon, Zoe found her crying by the pool. Sierra said she'd been thinking about her parents and missing them.

Zoe scrolled through her phone. These were the moments when she wished she had a father, someone she could always turn to and count on. She saw *Jane Morrison* in her contacts. It was three in the morning on the East Coast, but she called anyway.

"Zoe?" Jane's voice was groggy. "What's wrong, honey? Is everything okay?"

"I think my mom's been drinking," Zoe said quietly. "I'm not sure if she's even conscious. She may have taken pills, too. I don't know. Maybe I'm wrong. I shouldn't even be telling anyone this."

"I'm not anyone," her aunt said. "Do you know what she took? Or how much? Has this happened before?"

Zoe's hands were shaking as she told her about seventh grade and the private room at the hospital and then rehab.

"I need you to call 911. Tell them exactly what you told me." Jane was speaking slowly, but her voice was high.

Zoe felt like there was a noose around her neck pulling tighter and tighter.

"Zoe . . . can you do that right now?"

"*Can* I?" Zoe asked.

"What do you mean?"

"Isn't it too public? Wouldn't Max—"

"Call 911," Jane said. "In the meantime, I'll be on the next plane to LA."

JANUARY

MIA

AFTER WEEKS OF pleading, Mia finally got her mom to book her an appointment with a dermatologist. Her mom totally didn't believe she had skin cancer on her elbow, but it's not like *she* was the one touching the blackish mole on a daily basis. It had appeared suddenly over Christmas break, and Mia was convinced it was melanoma.

Mia's mom picked her up from school early on the big day. Her beige Volvo still had a brand-new smell that made Mia queasy. As her mom drove, she chewed four pieces of green-tea gum in fifteen minutes, spitting them into a tissue one by one. Mia's mom was a sales director at a pharmaceutical company, and she lived to work. On the drive to the Kirkland Medical Complex, she checked her phone at every light. Mia bit down on the insides of her cheeks, wondering how long it would take to die from skin cancer.

The dermatologist's name was Dean Kimball. It said so in gold letters on the glass door. Mia imagined that he'd look like a Ken doll, muscular and tan with a Trident white smile. His office was full of fliers about laser hair removal. Mia's mom slipped a few pamphlets into her bag just as her phone rang.

"I have to take this call," she said. "It'll be a while."

"Aren't you coming in with me?" Mia asked.

Her mom handed her the health insurance card and hurried back out the glass doors.

The woman at the front desk gave Mia a clipboard. There was a form about her skin history that had two outlines of a body, one labeled *front* and the other *back*. The instructions said to put an *X* over areas of concern. Mia considered *X*-ing out the entire picture of the body, front and back. That was how she felt most days, like her body was full of uncertainty. Her boobs had finally started growing, except that the left was coming in bigger than the right. She had some hair under her arms but none down *there* yet.

Mia handed the paperwork to the receptionist and picked up *People*. The cover story was "Sierra Laybourne in Distress." There was a grainy image of Sierra Laybourne being rushed into the emergency room on New Year's Eve. The article was about how the official cause was dehydration, but anonymous sources said it was an overdose, that she may have spent last fall in a secluded rehab.

Mia had read this online already. People at school were saying that was why Zoe had returned to Hankinson after Christmas break when she'd told people she was moving back to California. Mia wished she could tell Zoe that she hoped everything was okay with her mom, but she was still too intimidated to talk to her.

"Mia Flint?" a woman in pink scrubs asked.

Mia's heart was beating fast as she followed the woman into an examination room.

"Change into this gown, open to the back," she said to Mia. "Panties on and bra off."

No one had said anything about stripping down. The mole was on her *elbow*. She wished her mom were here to tell this woman she could stay dressed.

"Any questions?"

"I really have to take my clothes off?" Mia asked quietly.

"How else is the doctor going to examine your skin?"

When the woman walked out, Mia slowly pulled off her jeans and shirt and wrapped herself in the thin green robe. Her boobs looked lopsided, and her legs were dry and stubbly. She wanted to curl into a knot on the paper-covered table and disappear.

A moment later the door opened. The woman was back and this time the doctor was with her.

"I'm Doctor Kimball," he said, extending his hand. He was short and potbellied with nest of gray hair. At least he wasn't a Ken doll.

Even so, Mia stared at her hands, lacing them tightly in her lap.

"So . . . Mia," he said, glancing at the computer on his desk. "What brings you here?"

"A mole on my elbow," Mia whispered. "I want to make sure it's not cancer."

"Have you been reading books about kids with cancer?"

Mia shrugged. She actually *had*, but what did that have to do with anything?

The doctor laughed. "I'm just playing with you. Have you ever had a dermatological exam before?"

Mia flushed as she shook her head. The woman was reading a chart and didn't even look up.

"Do you have a parent here with you?"

"My mom's on a call," she said.

"Well, let's have a look."

Dr. Kimball's hands were cold and smooth as they raced over Mia's back and front, legs and arms. He paused for an extra second at Mia's elbow, shining a bright light on the mole. Mia squeezed her eyes shut. Her stomach felt as sour as curdled milk.

"So," he said, switching off the light, "everything looks good. That mole isn't going to kill you. You won't end up like a character in a book. You'll get your happily-ever-after, or whatever it is you kids want."

As he turned to his computer he and the woman laughed like it was a big joke. Like Mia's entire *life* was a big joke.

MARCH

WHITNEY

MOM JUST TOLD me that she and Dad saw a custody mediator today, Alicia texted.

Whitney adjusted the band on her yoga pants and looked around to make sure no one else had seen that. She and some other people from the chorus were in the back of the auditorium at a rehearsal for *Grease*. They were chatting and swapping shoulder rubs. Whitney *so* didn't want to think about her parents' divorce right now. These days, rehearsal was the one place she felt good. She didn't even care that she didn't get a big part. The chorus had become really close. Plus, the choreographer was putting her in front for all the dances.

Okay . . . whatever, Whitney texted her sister. Hopefully, that would shut her up.

The custody stuff was probably Alicia's fault. After they split up, their parents had agreed that Whitney and Alicia would divide their weeks between their mom and dad. Except then Alicia decided she hated their dad and was refusing to go there. That left Whitney alone to haul her stuff back and forth every three days and eat take-out Chinese alone with her dad and hear all about his tropical fish.

No, it's worse than that, Alicia texted back.

Worse than what? Whitney wrote, but instead of keeping up this conversation with Alicia, she tucked her phone under her leg. Alicia needed to get a life. It was like she enjoyed making Whitney upset.

"Did you know that today is the Ides of March?" Gus asked. He was a sophomore and a three-season jock. A hamstring injury had kept him out of basketball this winter, so he'd tried out for the play and had gotten into the chorus. He also happened to be Whitney's boyfriend.

"What's that?" Laurel asked.

"March fifteenth," Gus said. "The day that Brutus killed Caesar."

Whitney positioned herself behind Gus and squeezed her fingers into his wide shoulders. He stretched his neck from side to side. She and Gus had been together for two weeks. He was cute with short curly hair and he'd just gotten his license. They made out in his car after they dropped Laurel off every night.

Laurel was definitely Whitney's best friend now. When Kyra didn't get cast in *Grease*, not even in the chorus, she stopped talking to Whitney. A total freeze-out. Kyra sat at a different lunch table and turned her head when she passed Whitney in the hall. Whitra was dead and so was Kyrney.

Whitney's phone pinged under her leg. She ignored it. It pinged again and then again.

"I think someone's trying to text you," Laurel said.

Whitney leaned in and kissed Gus's neck. He moaned a little and squeezed her thigh. Maybe she'd let him go to second base after rehearsal tonight.

"Want me to see who's texting you?" Laurel asked, reaching for Whitney's phone.

"No!" Whitney said, pulling away from Gus. The last thing she wanted was to have anyone see those texts from her sister. She slipped her phone out.

You wanna hear how bad it is? Alicia had written. *They went in to fight over custody of our DOG. I hate them.*

Whitney was aware of her friends, chatting happily around her, totally oblivious.

Custody of Vic? she wrote to Alicia. That was their white Jack Russell terrier. Since her dad had stayed in the house after the separation, he'd gotten the dog.

Are there other dogs in the picture? Alicia texted back. *Of course Vic.*

Why can't they just figure it out on their own? Whitney asked.

Because they're immature infants, Alicia wrote. *I hate them both.*

"Do you ever wonder what Caesar thought?" Laurel asked, taking a sip of water from Whitney's bottle.

Whitney set down her phone. Her head felt woozy. "What he thought when?" she asked. She wanted to pretend things were normal, that her parents weren't going through a divorce and fighting over a dog and her sister didn't hate everyone. She wished she could live in this world of *Grease* and never leave.

"When Brutus was coming at him with a knife," Laurel said.

"It wasn't just Brutus coming at him," Gus said. "It was the entire Senate."

"Brutal," Whitney said.

Everyone laughed. When her phone pinged again, she turned it off.

APRIL

GREGOR

GREGOR DID *NOT* see this coming. At least they were doing dishes so he didn't have to look his dad in the eye.

"As I imagine you know," his dad said, "there are several brands. When you do need a condom, I recommend starting with a conventional maker like Trojan or Lifestyle."

At least his mom and Erica weren't home. They were searching for prom dresses at the mall. He and his dad had made burgers and eaten in front of the TV. Things had seemed normal until . . . this. Gregor's cheeks felt feverish, and his ears were ringing.

"Do you know about lubrication?" his dad asked, handing him a sudsy plate.

Gregor stooped over the dishwasher, taking extra time to fit the plate in.

"I guess," he finally managed. "It's moisture, right?"

"Exactly." His dad handed him two forks. "A condom with lubrication will be more comfortable for your partner . . . and for you. Spermicide is important too. I'll buy you some condoms to try on when you're ready. It's good to have practice."

Now his dad was going too far. *Way* too far.

"Dad." Gregor's voice was barely a squeak. "I'm kind of dying here. Can we change the subject?"

"Too much?"

"Maybe a little," Gregor said. "Maybe a thousand times more than a little."

"Got it." Gregor's dad tossed him a sponge to clean the counters. "Here's a good story for you. This is an embarrassing one from when I was in high school."

"It's not about condoms, is it?"

His dad shook his head and then squeezed dishsoap into the frying pan. "One morning my mom was dropping me off outside the band room."

Gregor tried to picture his grandmother as a mom, driving her son to school. Nana Margaret had gotten her license taken away a few years ago when she'd knocked over three mailboxes in a five-day period.

Gregor's dad continued. "She was driving a green Oldsmobile station wagon with a bumper sticker that said *My Child Is An Honor Student*."

"Sounds bad," Gregor said, grinning. He was still recovering from the condom talk, but he liked stories from when his dad went to Hankinson.

"I opened the passenger door, got my oboe case, and stepped out. Just at that moment, Nana Margaret backed up, rolling over my foot. But instead of continuing to reverse, she braked to remind me I had an orthodontist appointment that afternoon."

"She drove over your foot? Were you okay?"

"No!" Gregor's dad laughed. "But just as I was about to scream, I saw three cute girls on the path going into school, watching me."

Gregor groaned. He tried to imagine that happening to him. It was too horrible to think about. "What did you say?"

"I said 'Back it up, Mom.'"

Gregor winced. "You said it like *that*? What did the girls do?"

"They were laughing like crazy."

"How was your foot?"

Gregor's dad smiled as he turned off the faucet. "Two broken toes. I couldn't run cross-country for the rest of the season. But the girls seeing it was probably worse."

Later that night Gregor sat on his bed with his journal open in his lap. No denying it, his dad had been a dork in high school. The "Back it up, Mom" story was total proof.

He chewed on his pen cap. He could hear his parents *oohing* and *aahing* in the other room as Erica modeled her prom dress. Russell was a junior, which was why Erica was going to the prom even though she was only a sophomore.

The thing was, Gregor's dad *had been* a dork, but he'd eventually grown taller and gotten his braces off. He went to Reed College out in Oregon and then Cornell Law School. That was where he met Gregor's mom. They got married and moved back to Hankinson and bought a house and had kids and this really nice life.

Gregor imagined a similar situation playing out for him. That was what he was planning to describe in his journal, except when he started writing, this was what came out instead:

April 11
Condoms

He scribbled that out so that no one could ever see it. Even the word *condom* freaked him out. Sure, he got boners, but to imagine needing a condom was insane. That would mean a girl was in the picture. And whenever Gregor thought of a girl, he thought of Whitney. Which was even more insane.

ZOE

"YOU NEED A thing," Aunt Jane said to Zoe.

They were hanging out in the kitchen, waiting for the mac and cheese to finish baking. Zoe had made the béchamel sauce by herself.

"What do you mean?" Zoe picked a chunk of Gouda off the cutting board and popped it into her mouth.

"Interests," Aunt Jane said. "Sports, music, a cooking class. You need to do something, start hanging out with other kids. Your grandmother loved cooking, you know. She passed it on to me. I can look into some classes. . . ."

Zoe shook her head. *No,* she wanted to say. *I'm not ready. I can barely make it through seven hours of school without wanting to fall asleep.* That was how it had been since she'd gotten back from California. She was even supposed to return to Hankinson, but then New Year's happened and everyone decided it was better for Zoe to be here while Sierra figured her life out.

Her phone rang. It was Whitney Montaine.

"A girl from school," she said to her aunt.

"Go ahead and answer," Aunt Jane said. "We're not eating for a few minutes."

"No, it's okay. I can—"

"This is what I was just saying. You need *things* in your life. Answer your phone."

Zoe hurried into the living room so Aunt Jane couldn't listen in. "Hello?"

"Hey, Zoe? How's it going?"

Of all the girls at Hankinson, Whitney was definitely the nicest. Whenever Zoe braved the cafeteria, which was maybe once a week, Whitney waved her over. Whitney picked her in gym, and she was always inviting her out with her and her friends. But Zoe never said yes. Whitney was too gorgeous and perfect. Being around her made Zoe feel blurry.

"A few of us are going to the mall tomorrow night," Whitney said. "They're having a sale on prom dresses. But it's not like we're only looking at dresses."

Zoe knew from the lunch table that Whitney was going to the prom with a popular senior, Tripp, who was Brock Sawyer's older brother. She'd broken up with Gus when Brock's brother asked her to the prom. Brock was the cute guy who used to go out with Kyra. Kyra used to be Whitney's best friend, but they didn't talk anymore. Or maybe they were talking again. It was exhausting to keep it all straight.

"That sounds cool," Zoe said, sitting on the piano bench. She definitely didn't want to be stuck at the mall with Whitney and her friends.

"My mom is driving us. It'll be me and Laurel and maybe Kyra if she's talking to me tomorrow." Whitney giggled. "We can also hang out, try on bikinis. Can you believe it's almost summer?"

Zoe scratched at a pimple on her arm. She'd been trying on a bikini in London when Sierra flipped out and screamed at her. That was what had started all of this. Or maybe not. Maybe things were going to fall apart no matter what.

"I'm sorry," Zoe said. "I'm busy tomorrow night. Thanks for asking."

"That's okay," Whitney said. "I just thought I'd ask. Wish me luck with the dress search."

After they hung up, Zoe played a little Chopin on the piano. She didn't want to face Aunt Jane. She didn't want a *thing*.

"What's wrong with helping her shop for dresses?" Aunt Jane asked over dinner. "It'll be fun. If you want, I can drive you separately and wait at that bookstore."

"It's just . . ." Zoe served herself more mac and cheese. "I don't feel like it."

"The girl who called you . . . Whitney? Did you say her last name is Montaine?"

"Yeah . . . why?"

Aunt Jane nodded. "Her dad is a chemistry professor at the college. People say he's brilliant."

"Of course he's brilliant," Zoe said. "Whitney's perfect."

"I doubt that. Besides, look at your mom. People probably think that about you, too."

Zoe shook her head.

"What? You don't think so?"

Ever since Christmas break, Zoe's face was disgusting with zits. It was almost as bad as that guy James, the one who used to sit next to her on the bus last fall. She never saw him anymore. He probably got his license and was driving to school now.

"People look at me and think *what happened*? I don't look anything like my mom."

Aunt Jane shook her head. "You're so pretty, Zoe. You don't see that? You've got a Laybourne chin and those adorable freckles."

Zoe rolled her eyes. "All everyone cares about is asking how my mom is and whether she was in rehab. I never know what to tell them."

"What about the truth?"

"Yeah, right."

Aunt Jane wiped her lips with a napkin. "Here's the deal. You go with those girls to the mall tomorrow or you go to Al-Anon. There's a meeting downtown at seven. I'll drive you."

Zoe's stomach started churning. She wished she hadn't eaten so much mac and cheese.

"I know it's tough love, but you're free-floating," Aunt Jane said. "We need to start grounding you."

The next evening Zoe zipped up her raincoat and texted Aunt Jane that she was going with option two.

By the time she got downtown, the rain had stopped. She sidestepped a puddle and wandered into a café called Bean. She sipped hot chocolate and leaned against the brick wall. A few people looked over at her. Most people in Hankinson knew who she was by this point. Now and then people posted photos of her around town. Zoe put on some music and pulled on her headphones.

A little before seven she made her way to the church. But as soon as she got to the gray metal door, she froze. No way could she do this. Maybe it was anonymous for *most* people, but if word got out that Sierra Laybourne's daughter was at a support group for families of alcoholics, the media would flip out. Max would murder her.

"Hey . . . Zoe, right?"

Zoe spun around, her heart racing. *Oh no, no, no.* It was a girl from her global studies class. She had springy black hair and flushed cheeks. Last week she'd done her oral report on sweatshops in China.

"I'm Anna Kimball," she said. Her neck was turning purplish and blotchy. "I didn't think I'd see anyone from school. No one can know about my dad, is the thing. He's a doctor and could lose his license. Even my mom doesn't know I'm here. I told her I was going to Bean to do homework."

"I was just at Bean," Zoe said.

They both stood there for a moment. If Anna told people that *she* was here, it would be New Year's Eve all over again. Back in the hospital, Max had pulled her aside and yelled at her for calling 911. He'd squeezed her upper arm, his fingernails digging into her skin. And then those photos hit the tabloids. For all of January, Zoe jumped whenever her phone rang.

"I won't tell anyone you're here," Zoe said.

Anna smiled weakly. "Me neither. I mean, I know who you are. Of course I won't tell."

Zoe opened the gray door, and they headed down the stairs together.

MAY

JAKE

JAKE NOTICED SOMETHING wedged through the top vent in his locker. It looked like a gift wrapped in red reindeer paper. As he reached up for it, his arms ached. He mowed two lawns yesterday afternoon, and his upper body was feeling it.

It turned out to be a Captain Underpants book, *The Perilous Plot of Professor Poopypants*. Jake glanced down the hallway, but no one was around. There was no card, no inscription.

It was already a strange day. He'd just stopped by the guidance counselor's office to get a petition to run for member-at-large on the sophomore student council. Maybe it was crazy, but he was considering it. The thing was, he had to get fifty signatures to be on the ballot, which might be hard seeing as he hadn't exactly made fifty friends this year.

Anyway, what was up with this Secret Santa thing? Whoever gave him the book had to have known him for years. He and Teddy and the other guys were obsessed with Captain Underpants back in second grade. They even started their own comic strip. While most people had moved on from children's books, Jake still loved them. They felt cozy, like hot chocolate with mini-marshmallows or a new jumbo box of Crayola crayons. When Jake read Captain Underpants or Roald Dahl or the Diary of a Wimpy Kid books, he was transported back to being a kid again, pre-hormones, when life was so much less complicated. Last summer at the lake, Mona Lisa gave him her old copy of *The Lightning Thief,* and he read it in one afternoon.

Jake crumpled the wrapping paper into a wad and slid the book into his backpack. He was going to take it as a good sign, like maybe someone was watching out for him, like maybe he could win student council after all.

WHITNEY

OVER MEMORIAL DAY Weekend, Whitney and her mom hit the sales at Darien Shoppes. Her mom was obsessed with this new open-air mall because she said it raised the property value in that part of Hankinson. In the past month she'd sold two houses near Darien Shoppes. That was the reason for this shopping spree, to celebrate. Also, Whitney needed summer clothes. Her shorts from last summer were squeezing her hips.

"Want to stop for iced tea?" her mom asked, hooking arms with Whitney as they passed the art gallery. They'd been going strong for two hours and had gotten shorts, tops, new sunglasses, and even a skirt for the fall. "My feet are killing me. Plus, I have some news."

"What about?"

Her mom steered her toward the Darien Coffee Company. Whitney had an idea what this was about. Now that her parents' divorce was official, she was guessing her mom was buying a new house. They'd probably drive by it when they were done shopping.

"Save this for us?" Whitney's mom said, pointing to a round table under an umbrella. "Want a cookie?"

"Sure," Whitney said. As her mom went to order, she ripped the tag off her new silver sunglasses and then checked her phone. No word from Tripp. The prom had been last weekend. It was strange going to the junior-senior prom since she was only a freshman. Tripp and his guy friends were cool, but the girls ignored her. They'd all rented a suite at the Hilton afterward. Whitney had gotten a little drunk, and she and Tripp went further than she'd wanted. Like, inside-the-underwear far. She'd seen him in school this week and they'd hugged, but he hadn't texted since the prom.

"Hey, sweetie." Whitney's mom slid into a chair. She'd recently gotten her hair cut short and highlighted auburn. Alicia called it *divorce hair*. "I got us two iced teas and one jumbo chocolate-chip cookie."

"Thanks," Whitney said, picking at the corner of her cookie.

Whitney's mom shook Splenda into her iced tea. "I may as well get right to the news," she said. "I'm seeing someone. I have a boy-friend."

Whitney stopped chewing. The cookie felt dry in her mouth and way too sweet.

"I know," her mom said, smiling. "It was a shock to me, too. His name is Michael. He's a real estate lawyer. It's been a little over a month."

Whitney shook her head. Her mom couldn't have a *boyfriend*. That sounded so high school.

"Does Alicia know?" Whitney asked. Her right eye socket had started throbbing. She slid on her sunglasses and hunched close to the table.

"She does, but I asked her to let me tell you," her mom said, sipping her iced tea. "Michael came over to dinner when you were at

Dad's last week. But here's the problem. Michael is allergic to dogs."

Whitney was starting to feel nauseous. She saw a guy who looked like Tripp, carrying his tray to the garbage. Tripp was built like a football player with wide shoulders and huge arms. Oh, no—it wasn't Tripp. This guy was, like, thirty and had two kids tagging along after him. Whitney's head hurt, and she suddenly wished she hadn't gone so far with Tripp, or maybe hadn't broken up with Gus, or maybe could take away this past year and be back at the beginning of high school.

Her mom nodded. "The thing is, with your dad going away next year, and with Michael allergic to dogs, we're going to let Vic live with my friend Glenda. She has a house with a big yard and her daughter will love him."

Whitney touched her iced tea to her forehead. Even with her sunglasses on, the light was way too bright.

"Hang on," Whitney said, slumping forward onto her elbows. Her tongue was slick with saliva. "What did you just say about *Dad*?"

"He didn't tell you?" Whitney's mom inflated her cheeks and slowly let the air out. "That's just like him to forget something so important. He was supposed to tell you yesterday."

"Tell me what?"

"Whit, your dad got invited to lecture at the University of Chicago next year, and do research in their lab. Downing is letting him take a sabbatical year. He's leaving in early July, so I'll give up the rental house and move back home."

Whitney pressed her hands against her forehead. Everything felt so impossibly loud.

"You and Alicia will be full-time with me," her mom said, "but you'll go there for holidays. I know it's a lot to absorb. Dad was supposed to—"

Whitney puked. All over her sandals and the brick floor and the cluster of shopping bags.

Hours later, once it was dark, once Whitney had slept off the worst of the migraine, her mom spooned in bed with her, holding an ice pack to her eyes, rubbing her shoulders in small circles.

"Do you want to talk about it?" she asked softly.

Whitney moaned. She was too wrecked to think, too wrecked to care that she'd thrown up in public.

"No, it's okay," Whitney told her mom.

"I know it's a lot," her mom said. "Dad and I had a communication breakdown about Chicago. I'm sorry you had to find out that way. And about Michael. And the dog. I shouldn't have dumped it on you all at once."

"Really, it's okay. It'll be okay."

"That's my girl," Whitney's mom said, kissing her cheek.

JUNE

GREGOR

GREGOR FINISHED HIS global studies final and walked to the front to turn it in. Last final of freshman year! He glanced back at Dinky, scowling down at his test, his fingers tugging at his shaggy brown hair. He looked like he'd be a while.

To kill time before the ninth-grade party on the lawn, Gregor headed to the band room to grab his extra drumsticks. He was just opening his band locker when he heard crying in the hallway. He got a shiver down his spine. He recognized that cry.

He hurried out of the band room. His sister was sitting on the floor, hugging her knees and leaning against a locker. Her cheeks were streaked with tears, and there was mascara puddled under her eyes.

"Erica, what's wrong?" Gregor asked. "Are you okay?"

"He broke up with me," she sobbed.

"Russell broke up with *you*?" Gregor was shocked. Erica was so much better than Russell. Sure, she could be annoying, but she was pretty and smart and played violin and was a star cross-country runner. She placed fourth in the county last fall, and she was only a sophomore. And what did Russell have to show for himself? Greasy hair, no chin, and a pickup truck with stupid tires.

"He didn't just break up with me," Erica moaned. "He cheated on me. He was cheating on me when we went to the *prom*."

Erica was shaking so hard, her back was rattling the metal door of the locker. Gregor slid next to her and squeezed in close so they were side by side.

"Are you sure he cheated?" he asked. "How did you find out?"

"I saw a text from another girl on his phone. Her name is Holly. She doesn't go to Hankinson. I called him on it, and he admitted it. They even had sex."

Holy crap. Gregor's face flushed hot.

Erica wiped her nose with the collar of her T-shirt. "I feel like an idiot crying in school. I don't want him to see me like this."

"How are you getting home? Wasn't Russell supposed to—"

"Please don't say his name," Erica said. "I think I'll just walk. Or maybe run. I have my sneakers. Can you take my bag?"

"Are you sure? Want me to call Mom or—"

"No!" Erica shot Gregor an angry look. "You can't ever tell Mom and Dad about this. *God*."

Erica pushed her lavender tote bag toward Gregor. He held it between his knees, hoping Erica wasn't mad at him now too. He was just trying to help.

"Want to hear something crazy?" Erica asked. "I gave him *The Book Thief* for his birthday. I said it would change his life, but he never read it. Not even the first page."

"How do you know?" Gregor asked. He could picture the cover of *The Book Thief* on Erica's nightstand.

"Because it's in his locker. He never even took it home."

Gregor was still holding his spare drumsticks. He tapped a rhythm on Erica's bag. "Maybe Russell didn't want his life changed."

Erica sucked in her bottom lip. "But he changed my life."

"So you have that. He can't take that away."

"I guess." Erica smiled weakly. "Sorry about before. I didn't mean to be a bitch."

"It's okay."

He stood up and lifted his sister to her feet. He couldn't help feeling like a superhero.

ZOE

ZOE STOOD OUTSIDE the choir room. There was a sign on the door that said EXPECT TO BE ACCEPTED FOR WHO YOU ARE. Yeah, right. That was definitely not the story of *her* life.

For the past month Anna had been begging her to audition for next year's choir. The real tryouts already happened in April, but Anna said that Ms. Godfrey might make an exception in Zoe's case.

"Because of my mom?" Zoe asked.

"No, stupid." When Anna laughed, her cheeks got blotchy. "Because you've got a great voice."

Zoe and Anna had been hanging out constantly since they met at Al-Anon. Zoe had never had a best friend before. Now she always knew where she was eating lunch, and they sat next to each other in all their classes. They loved harmonizing together or accompanying each other on piano. Anna had taken piano lessons in middle school just like Zoe, and they'd both quit the summer after eighth grade.

"Door's open!" a woman's voice called from inside the choir room.

Zoe's heart started racing. Had Ms. Godfrey seen her loitering at the door? Now she had no choice but to go inside.

"Zoe Laybourne?" Ms. Godfrey pushed her glasses down so they were hanging on a gold chain around her neck. "I was hoping to see you."

Zoe nodded. She braced herself for Ms. Godfrey to say she was a fan of her mom's and to ask to take a selfie together.

"Anna told me about you," Ms. Godfrey said. "She said you're very talented. Do you still want to audition for choir?"

"If that's okay," Zoe said quietly. Maybe this was stupid. She wasn't even sure she'd be here in the fall. But it was true that she could sing any song she heard. The crazy thing was, her mom couldn't carry a tune at all. Maybe Zoe had inherited her voice from her dad. Sometimes she wondered about things like that.

"Can you do a scale for me?"

Zoe's mouth went dry. She hadn't really been paying attention. "A what?"

"A scale. *Do re mi*," Ms. Godfrey said. "Want some water?"

MIA

OUT ON THE archery field, Mia drank a Dixie cup of punch. The student council was hosting a gathering for all the freshmen. Actually, they were rising sophomores now. Mia touched the mole on her elbow, felt a flash of panic, and then reminded herself it wasn't cancer.

Mia couldn't believe that one fourth of high school was over. It hadn't been a terrible year. Better than middle school. Yesterday her guidance counselor called her in and told her she was ranked number one in her class.

"But don't think it'll be an easy ride for the next three years," she warned, clicking a pen open and closed.

"Okay," Mia said. She hated how adults always bubble-wrapped compliments with warnings. *You're smart, but don't let it go to your head. You have great skin, but watch it with the chocolate.*

Today was superhot, almost as hot as freshman orientation. Mia still thought about that day in the gym last September, sitting in a circle with Whitney, Jake, Zoe, and Gregor, writing those letters and promising to meet again at graduation. Maybe it was lame, but Mia actually cared about her group. She was always keeping an eye on them, hoping they were okay.

Right now she could see Gregor standing with Dinky and some other band kids. His backpack was on, and he was carrying a pale purple bag. Gregor was still as short as a sixth grader.

Zoe was talking to a girl named Anna, their faces leaning in close. Mia had seen them together a lot this spring. They'd even started dressing alike. Mia was jealous that Anna had landed Zoe as a BFF when Mia hadn't ever worked up the nerve to talk to her.

Whitney was laughing with a senior guy, Adam, from Mia's precalculus class. They'd moved Mia up two grades in math, which is how she knew Adam's name. Whitney was so gorgeous that guys from all grades flocked to her. Now that she'd gotten her braces off, she truly looked like a model. Whitney's friends, Kyra and Laurel, were fluttering nearby.

The only person from the orientation group who Mia couldn't find was Jake. She wondered if he'd ever gotten that Captain Underpants book she'd secretly given him last month. She'd held on to it since Christmas, waited until she spotted Jake at his locker, and then carefully taken note of his locker number. She'd returned the next afternoon and slid the book through the vents.

Mia chucked her cup in a trash bag and texted Sophie that she was ready to go. Sophie's dad was picking her up from school and bringing her back to their place. They were going to dye pink streaks in their hair. They'd already bought the Manic Panic. It was Sophie's idea. She said that girls like them had to find ways to stand out from the pack. Mia just hoped she wouldn't chicken out.

SUMMER AFTER
FRESHMAN YEAR

JULY

JAKE

Jake: When are you flying up from Atlanta? You're coming to visit your grandparents at the lake, right?

Mona Lisa: Of course! Just like every summer. I get there July 13. We can celebrate your birthday late.

Jake: Cool. Truth or dare?

Mona Lisa: I've got a truth . . . I almost went all the way this year.

Jake: Whoa!!!!

Mona Lisa: What about you? Truth or dare?

Jake: Truth . . . I ran for student council.

Mona Lisa: And?

Jake: I lost by a little.

Mona Lisa: Real truth. I actually went all the way.

Jake: Real truth. I actually got slaughtered. Hardly anyone voted for me.

WHITNEY

FOR A SECOND Whitney couldn't remember anything. Her brain felt like mush. There was sunlight streaming through her gauzy bedroom curtains. She could hear her dad puttering in the kitchen, listening to jazz.

But then Whitney saw the hearts on her hand, scribbled in pen, and it all came back to her.

Last night had been the end of drama camp. She'd done the camp with Laurel and a new friend, Autumn Cortez. They had their cast party after the show at this guy's house. Someone brought lime Jell-O shots. Whitney did a few shots and ended up making out with two different guys. One was this guy Adam who'd been flirting with her all spring. The other was Zach Ryder. The kiss was slurpy and he tasted like nachos. He rambled on about how he loved her and then drew those hearts on her hand.

Whitney yawned and checked her phone.

Whaddup? Zack had texted. *Wanna hang out today?*

There was also a text from Kyra. *I've been thinking about it, and I've decided we're over.*

Whitney read it again. It sounded like Kyra was breaking up

with her. The crazy part was, they'd been becoming best friends again! Just yesterday Kyra sent her a photo of Jake Rodriguez mowing her lawn, his blond hair damp with sweat. They'd agreed he was total eye candy.

Whitney could hear her dad in the other room, on the phone with the moving company. Kyra *knew* Whitney's dad was leaving for Chicago today. Kyra also knew that her mom's boyfriend, Michael, was helping her mom move back home later. Michael drank Red Bull and wore leather shoes with tassels. Whitney felt icky whenever she saw him touching her mom.

What do you mean OVER? Whitney wrote. But then, before she hit send, she backspaced and deleted the text. If Kyra wanted to dump her, let her do it. She'd be fine without Kyra. Better than fine. Instead she wrote to Zach.

Sure, let's chill this afternoon.

Maybe he wouldn't taste like nachos this time. At the very least, it would get her mind off everything else happening today.

AUGUST

GREGOR

GREGOR DIPPED THE net into the pool and fished out some pine needles. His parents were out for the morning, and his dad had made a deal with him to clean the pool in exchange for driving lessons. Not that Gregor had his permit yet, but they went to the parking lot behind the high school and worked on three-point turns.

Suddenly Gregor felt an intense pain on his ankle. He yelped and slapped at his leg. He'd just gotten stung by a bee! Seconds later his ankle, his foot, and his entire leg were throbbing. Then his lips started tingling, and his tongue was swelling in his mouth.

Gregor looked around for his phone. Nowhere. No one was home, either. He couldn't remember where his parents were—maybe grocery shopping? His leg was hurting worse, and his throat felt tight.

Somehow Gregor made it across the deck, through the glass door, and into the kitchen. As soon as he walked inside, he puked all over the floor. Then he slumped down, leaned his head against the fridge, and closed his eyes.

• • •

"Oh my god," Gregor's dad said.

Gregor blinked. The kitchen reeked of vomit. His leg was killing him, and his head felt fuzzy. Hang on . . . Where was his dad now?

A second later his dad was kneeling next to him. "Here goes," he said.

Gregor felt a pinch in his left thigh. His heart started pounding, and then his dad was lifting him, carrying him out of the house.

"Stay with me," his dad said as he lowered him into the front seat.

His dad didn't even buckle him in as he blew through every light in Hankinson on the way to the emergency room.

Life-threatening anaphylactic bee sting allergy, Gregor wrote in his journal that night. For the rest of his life he'd have to carry around an EpiPen and never truly relax when he was outside.

They kept him at the emergency room for nine hours to make sure things were okay. Now it was midnight, and he couldn't sleep. Gregor touched the bandage on his ankle. His leg was still swollen, but the pain was better. Mostly, he was freaked out about how something random could happen on a perfectly fine day and suddenly you were practically dying.

The doctor said it was a miracle that his dad had skipped the post office and come home and found that EpiPen they'd gotten after Erica had had an allergic reaction to cherries.

In Gregor's mind, there were now three miracles in his life. One was surviving today. Another was music. And the third was Whitney Montaine. Forget the fact that they'd never talked. She was still a miracle to him.

MIA

——————

"**I WAS IN** the ER yesterday observing sales reps," Mia's mom said. "I saw a boy from your school. Allergic reaction. Anaphylactic."

Mia looked up from her Honey Nut Cheerios. She'd been reading *The Catcher in the Rye*. She and her mom never talked during breakfast. Mostly, her mom was on her phone.

"Who was it?" Mia asked. "Did you find out his name? Is he okay?"

"He's okay. His dad gave him the EpiPen. Strange name. Gregor? Red hair."

"Gregor Lombard?" Mia asked, shocked. "I know him! He was in my freshman orientation group."

Her mom shook her head. "He could have died. His airways constricted. Lucky, they had an Epi at home. That's what we're working on."

Mia's mom's big account was selling epinephrine kits to schools and restaurants. Mia's mom said there was money in allergies. Mia thought that sounded cold, but also not atypical for her mom.

"By the way," Mia's mom said, "your new piano teacher is coming at four. Will you tell the cleaning lady to dust around the piano?"

The microwave beeped. Mia's mom picked up her coffee and disappeared into the bathroom. Mia got back to *The Catcher in the Rye*. She wondered what Holden Caulfield would say about her mom. He'd probably call her a phony.

ZOE

THE PARIS TRIP was very last minute. Aunt Jane had to rush order a passport so she could come. They hadn't made a decision yet about where Zoe was going to live sophomore year, even though school was starting next Wednesday. Sierra was on location in France, so Max arranged for Zoe and Aunt Jane to meet her there and figure it out.

"Paris!" Aunt Jane said on the ride to the airport. Max had sent an SUV with tinted windows to pick them up. "How many times have you been?"

"I'm not sure," Zoe said. She didn't want to sound like a spoiled brat, like going to Paris wasn't a big deal. "Three, I think. Maybe four."

Aunt Jane shook her head. "First-class seats to Paris. I can't get over this."

Zoe reached for a San Pellegrino water. Aunt Jane had no idea what Zoe's life had been like before she'd moved to Hankinson. Nobody did.

Max put them at the same hotel as Sierra. It was on Champs Elysee, a block from the Arc de Triomphe. The man at the front desk told them, *"Mille huit cent neuf."* And then, in a heavy French accent, he said, "That's 1809."

"What about my mom?" Zoe asked him. "Sierra Laybourne? Is she in 1809 too?"

The man stared at her with dull black eyes. He reminded Zoe of a weasel.

"I'm her daughter," Zoe said. "It's not like I'm coming to stalk her."

The man pressed his thin lips together.

"She's in 2010," Aunt Jane said, swiping her finger across her phone. "Max texted it to me."

The hotel guy frowned. As he handed them two room cards, Zoe blinked hard. She assumed she was staying in her mom's room. They spent all of July together, and Sierra told her she'd been sober for six months. Zoe only returned to Hankinson when her mom came to France to shoot this movie.

"I'm sure she's just tired," Aunt Jane said. "I wouldn't take it the wrong way."

An hour later Zoe met her mom in the lobby. They were going to take a walk along the Seine. Aunt Jane said she needed to catch up on sleep, but Zoe had a feeling she wanted to give them time alone.

"It's good to see you and Janie," Sierra said, sliding on her sunglasses and taking Zoe's hand as they ducked into the backseat of a waiting car.

Zoe had never heard *Janie* before. She hoped that meant her mom and Jane were patching things up. Zoe knew they'd been talking on the phone this summer.

As their car weaved in and out of traffic, Zoe studied her mom's new bodyguard. He was sitting in the front seat. His name was Kwame, and he was African. He and Sierra kept glancing at each other. Zoe wondered if they were sleeping together. It was gross to think about her mom having sex, but it wasn't like Zoe was an idiot. Celebs generally kept things in their inner circle, even if it meant doing it with people who worked for them.

"Where's Max?" she asked, suddenly surprised that he wasn't in the car with them, pushing Zoe to live wherever made the most strategic sense for Sierra.

"Two days off," Sierra said. "He went to the Loire Valley."

"Oh," she said, relieved. Then again, sometimes it was easier for Max to call the shots. If he didn't, then Zoe would have to think about what she actually wanted.

"Should we take a boat tour?" Sierra pointed to the riverboats docked along the Seine. "People say it's lovely."

Zoe shook her head. She was still queasy from the long flight. "I think walking is fine."

"Okay . . . sure. Walking is good." Sierra jiggled her knee. "I know I've told you that yellow isn't your color, but I like your shirt."

Zoe touched her yellow shirt from the Hankinson mall. It was nothing special, just a cotton scoop neck. Mostly, her mom seemed nervous, which was making her nervous too.

"You can get out of the car here," the driver said to them. He and Kwame made a security plan, something about Kwame walking behind to give them privacy.

The illusion of privacy, Zoe thought. She was never truly alone with her mom. Except, ironically, that night on New Year's Eve.

It was cooler down by the river. They passed a gaggle of Japanese tourists. Sierra adjusted her sunglasses and tucked her blond hair into a floppy hat. No one seemed to recognize her. Zoe glanced back at Kwame, but he was staring straight ahead.

"Want to go shopping after this?" her mom asked. "I'd love to get you some new clothes for school."

Zoe shivered. The last thing she wanted was to go shopping with her mom, especially after last summer in London. Also, she was stressed about the school thing. Aunt Jane said she could live in Hankinson for sophomore year. Her mom said she could go back to Topanga Day and have a live-in nanny until Sierra returned from France. Or staying here in Paris was an option, but then Zoe would need a tutor.

"I'm much better, you know," Sierra said. "Things will be different than before."

Zoe hugged her arms over her chest. She'd gotten into the choir in Hankinson. Also, she'd miss Anna if she left.

"Do you know what you want to do?" her mom asked.

She sort of did, but she couldn't bring herself to say it out loud.

SOPHOMORE YEAR

SEPTEMBER

JAKE

ON THE FIRST day of school, Jake saw Teddy and Marin in the cafeteria line. He hadn't seen either of them all summer. He cleared his throat and reached for a plate of chicken nuggets. He wasn't going to look. He wasn't going to care.

Okay, he looked.

They were holding hands and clutching their trays like they couldn't let go of each other for two minutes. Mona Lisa said that couples who were massively PDA were actually insecure about their relationship status, but from the looks of Teddy and Marin, they seemed massively in love.

Jake was behind them, waiting for his squirt of honey mustard sauce. If it were any other two people, he'd be like, *Hey, what's up? How was your summer?*

But with Teddy and Marin, no way.

Even *hello* got trapped in his throat.

Jake wanted sophomore year to be different. Not just with Teddy, but in general. He didn't want to hide in the art room all the time. He didn't want to run for student council but then be too scared to campaign. This year he wanted to be himself. He just didn't understand when that got so hard.

Screw the honey mustard. Jake paid for his lunch and carried his tray back to the art room.

WHITNEY

WHITNEY KISSED ZACH outside first-period English, and then skipped after Laurel down the hall. They hadn't seen each other yet this morning, but she spotted Laurel's long golden hair pulled into two loose pigtails.

"Do you have gym second period too?" Whitney asked as she tugged on Laurel's hair.

Laurel wrinkled her nose. "Unfortunately. Then we'll be gross and sweaty for the rest of the day."

"At least we'll be gross and sweaty together," Whitney said, smiling.

Laurel shrugged. She seemed sulky, but Whitney wasn't going to let it bring her down. She was wearing short linen shorts and these great wedges that she bought in Chicago when she and her sister flew out to see their dad. He wanted to take them camping at the Indiana Dunes, but Whitney and Alicia begged for a few days of shopping instead. Also, she and Zach had been together for seven weeks. It was her longest relationship yet. So much for everyone saying she couldn't make a commitment!

"At least it's the first day of school," Whitney said as she and

Laurel turned into the gym, "so we don't have to go to the locker room and—"

Kyra was standing right inside the double doors. As soon as she saw Laurel, she clapped her hands and jumped up and down.

"Laurel!" Kyra squealed. "I'm so glad you're in my gym! I asked my dad to make it happen, but you never know."

Whitney froze. She hadn't seen Kyra since that breakup text back in July. Whitney had never written her back. It was a total freeze-out.

"I love your shirt!" Kyra said, hugging Laurel.

Laurel smiled at Kyra. "Thanks! It's like the one you got last week at the Darien Shoppes."

"I'm so flattered," Kyra said, giggling.

Whitney tried to catch Laurel's eye. Laurel *knew* that Kyra had ditched her—they'd even talked about it at soccer yesterday. So why didn't Laurel tell Whitney that she and Kyra had gone shopping together and seemed to be becoming best friends?

"Hey, Whit," Kyra said coldly.

"Hey," Whitney said in an equally icy tone. Then she walked across the gym to Autumn Cortez. Autumn had done drama camp with her and Zach. She was totally cool the way she always wore tights and short dresses and dark lipstick.

"Hey, girl!" Autumn called out. "How's it going?"

Whitney gave her a hug. Forget Kyra. Maybe even forget Laurel, too. Autumn was going to become her new best friend this year.

OCTOBER

MIA

MIA DIALED *67 to block her dad's name from appearing on someone's phone. This was her standard routine. She made her prank calls from the landline, in the abyss of time between the end of school and bed. That's when she was always alone. Sophie's mom wouldn't let her come over on weeknights, and Mia's parents were usually working late or at the gym.

Tonight she was trying to reach Mott's applesauce. She dialed the toll-free number on the label and pressed about seven zeroes before she got a real person.

"Motts, I'm Justine," the woman answered. "How may I help you?"

Mia cleared her throat. "I have a question."

"That's what we're here for!"

"I'd like to feed your applesauce to my baby," Mia lied. "I'm wondering if she's ready."

"How old is she?"

"Six months." Mia twisted some hair around her finger. Her hair was down to her shoulders with faded pink streaks that her mom hated. In Mia's mom's opinion, hair should be only one color and that was sun-streaked blond.

"That's when I gave my kids solid food," the Mott's woman said. "You may want to talk with your pediatrician about it."

"Good idea," Mia said. "I'll call the pediatrician in the morning. Thanks!"

Mia hung up and rubbed her hands against her upper arms. Prank-calling left her with a dizzying rush of excitement and nervousness.

Mia's prank-call record was fifty-three minutes. That was with a travel agent. They'd debated whether Mia and her fiancé—Mia called him Brock, of course—should honeymoon in Hawaii or the Caribbean. Sometimes Mia called neighbors and invented random polls like who they were voting for in the upcoming election. She had to be especially careful to *67 these calls.

On Halloween night Mia passed out candy to princesses and superheroes. Her mom had left a bag of Snickers on the counter with a Post-it saying *Please distribute*. She and her dad were at dinner with customers.

Once the doorbell stopped ringing, Mia busted out the Manic Panic and touched up her pink streaks. She'd gotten compliments on her hair this fall. Some kids told her she looked Goth. Mia had started wearing all black and lots of eyeliner. This drove her mom crazy too. She'd already decided to ask her uncle George for Doc Martens for her fifteenth birthday in December.

By nine thirty, Mia was listening to Sonic Youth and eating mini Snickers. The house was pulsing with emptiness. Mia stared at the home phone. She pictured Whitney Montaine in English class this morning. She'd been wearing a headband with cat ears, and she had a charcoal smudge on her nose and whiskers across her cheeks. There was a white rose on her desk. Whitney had been telling Autumn Cortez that her boyfriend, Zach, put a rose in her locker every Friday.

Mia grabbed the iPad and typed *Montaine* and *Hankinson* into the search engine. There it was! Whitney lived at 236 Abbey Drive, and it even showed her parents' phone number. Abbey Drive was one of the nicest streets in Hankinson, with its Victorian houses and broad shady trees. On New Year's Eve last year there'd been a car accident on Abbey Drive, and a guy from school had died. He was a junior and his name was James. Mia didn't know him, but she went to his memorial anyway. When they played "Tears in Heaven," she'd started crying.

After a few rings Mia heard Whitney's voice. "Hello?"

Mia realized, way too late, that she'd forgotten to dial *67.

"Hello?" Whitney asked again. She sounded groggy, like she'd just woken up. "Is someone there?"

"Oh, hi," Mia finally said. "I'm calling . . . I'm taking a poll . . . about how people celebrate Halloween."

"Who's this again?" Whitney asked.

Mia slammed down the phone. She pressed her cheek against the granite counter, attempting to breathe. The home phone rang. Mia glanced at the caller ID.

Lydia Montaine.

It was Whitney. Mia frowned at the screen as the phone rang and rang and finally fell silent.

NOVEMBER

JAKE

"WE SHOULD PAINT a mural together," Allegra said in art class one morning.

Allegra Nichols was Jake's new best friend, at least according to her. Jake actually didn't like her, yet he couldn't get rid of her. She moved from Maine at the beginning of sophomore year and had latched on to Jake in the art room. She didn't care that Jake was gay. In fact, she considered it an accessory to have a gay BFF. That alone annoyed Jake.

"What kind of mural?" he asked. He'd been excited about taking advanced drawing until Allegra dropped out of her photography class to join him in his elective.

"You know that gray wall at the bottom of the stairwell in the basement?" she asked. "We should get permission to paint it."

Jake was working on his charcoal self-portrait. It counted for 20 percent of this quarter's grade. He glanced into the small mirror on the table and then added shading under his left eye.

"You know where I'm talking about?" Allegra asked.

Jake nodded. It was that stairwell where he and his freshman group had hidden the letters at orientation before ninth grade. Just yesterday he'd seen that quiet girl, Mia, walking into school. She'd gotten pretty in an exotic way, tall and skinny with large gray eyes and pink hair.

"We could design the mural and sketch it out," Allegra said, knotting her curly hair on top of her head. "I was thinking we could paint people holding hands and stars and inspirational quotes. Not cheesy, though. I did one at my school in Bangor. Want to see a picture?"

"Sure," Jake said. If he said no, she'd just show him anyway.

Here was another annoying thing about Allegra. She was hooking up with a guy who had a girlfriend. She wouldn't tell Jake his name, but other than that, she wouldn't shut up about him.

"Did you know we met at church?" Allegra asked on the phone. She called almost every night, which was also annoying. No one called. It was all text.

"The first *you know what* happened in the church bathroom," Allegra said. That was how she referred to blow jobs. "Is that gross? It didn't feel gross at the time."

"I guess it's more ironic," Jake said. He wasn't really paying attention. He was digging in his desk for his bank account number. With the money from mowing lawns, he might have enough for sailing camp next summer. He'd never sailed before, but he wanted to learn. His parents said if he came up with half the tuition, they'd pay the other half.

"Ironic, why?"

"I don't know . . . because of church?" Jake opened another drawer. He could hear his sister crying downstairs. She was nine and still had meltdowns.

"You totally want to know who he is, don't you?" Allegra asked.

"Whatever."

"I can't tell you. I wish I could, but I feel this moral obligation to, uh . . ."

Violet was shrieking, her feet pounding up the stairs.

"I want to protect his girlfriend," Allegra finally said. "He loves her, but she doesn't put out. Crude but true. Hey, did you think about that mural? I dropped off a proposal with the principal, and I wrote both of our names on it."

By the time Jake had hung up, his neck was tight. He turned off his light and lay on the carpet, his arms folded behind his head. What Jake didn't tell Allegra was that he knew the guy's name. It was Zach Ryder. He was the one who beat Jake for student council last year. He constantly saw Zach's texts on Allegra's phone.

As Jake lay in the dark, he thought about Zach's girlfriend, whoever she was, and how much it must be sucking for her right now.

After school on Thursday, Jake had an hour before his mom picked him up for his painting class. He zipped up his hoodie and was just heading past the track when Allegra caught up with him.

"Are you going to Bean?" she asked, fishing her sunglasses out of her messenger bag.

Jake shrugged. There were rusty leaves piled in heaps on both sides of the path. When he and Teddy were in seventh grade, they made a massive leaf pile in his backyard and cannonballed into it from his roof. It was nuts they didn't break any bones.

Jake and Allegra walked past the field where the JV football team was practicing.

"Idiots," Allegra said.

"Not all of them." He was thinking about Teddy, but also his other football friends from middle school who'd stopped talking to him. Actually, maybe they *were* idiots. Or maybe he was the idiot because he let it happen.

When they got to Bean, Allegra wouldn't shut up about the brick wall in the café and how they should paint bricks on their mural.

"If you look closely," Allegra said, "all the bricks aren't red. Every so often, there's a black brick. That's what we are, Jake."

Jake sipped his hot apple cider. It was too hot, and it scalded his tongue. "What's that supposed to mean?" he asked sharply.

"We're different." Allegra doodled a shooting star on the edge of Jake's math homework. "The wall wouldn't look right with *all* black bricks, but the red bricks wouldn't be as beautiful without an occasional black brick."

Jake had never considered himself a freak, and he wasn't about to start now. "I'm not a black brick," he said, erasing her star from his homework.

"Yes, you are. I was thinking, in the mural—"

"Forget the mural." Jake stuffed his notebook into his backpack. "Take my name off that. I don't want to do it."

"Will you chill out? I'm just saying—"

"Don't."

Jake reached for his cider, but Allegra snatched it first, holding the cup out of his reach.

"You know what sucks?" Allegra said. "I had something big to tell you."

Jake tried to get his drink, but Allegra stretched it over her head.

"Were you going to tell me it's Zach Ryder?" he said, his voice cracking. "The guy you're cheating with? Because I already know."

"Shut up!"

Screw the apple cider. Jake turned to leave, but then Allegra called after him.

"I was going to tell you that I'm moving back to Maine over Christmas break. I'm going to live with my dad again."

Jake froze. If only he'd put up with Allegra for another month, he could have avoided this dumb fight. He wished she'd told him she was moving *before* they'd gotten to Bean. He wished he'd never met her. He wished a lot of things, but so far nothing had come true.

GREGOR

GREGOR SWITCHED ON his bedside light. It was past midnight, and he couldn't sleep. He was thinking about Whitney again. It was so frustrating. He saw the guys she talked to in school. Guys like Zach Ryder and Brock Sawyer. Personally, Gregor thought Zach was a sleaze and that Brock's square teeth made him look like a horse.

He had to come up with a plan to get Whitney to notice him.

He uncapped a pen and started writing in his journal.

November 19, 12:33 a.m.

1. *I should start working out. Lift weights?*
2. *Become a drummer in a garage band. Talk to Dinky about this.*
3. *Switch from tighty-whities to boxer briefs.*
4. *Study for my learner's permit.*
5. *Read* The Book Thief. *Erica said girls love it when guys read this.*
6. *Talk to my orthodontist about hurrying things up.*
7. *Come up with a grand gesture.*

In the morning Gregor opened his journal and reread the list. He decided to start with boxer briefs and a grand gesture.

All day at school Gregor kept thinking about grand gestures. Guys in movies ran through New York City gridlock or decorated girls' rooms with rose petals, but neither of those seemed possible to pull off. Finally, at band practice after school, it came to him.

Gregor was playing cadence on the snare drum, keeping an eye on Dinky for time. Shockingly, Dinky had been voted drum major, the first time a sophomore landed that position in Hankinson history.

After practice Gregor wriggled out of the harness that affixed the drum over his shoulders. "Hey, Dink," he said. "Can I talk to you for a second?"

They were out at the stadium. Dinky set his clipboard on the bleachers. A few people were hovering around, waiting to ask him questions. "Sure, what's up?"

"Alone," Gregor said.

Dinky lifted his eyebrows and walked with Gregor a few paces across the playing field. The wind was picking up and the sky was gray. Hopefully, the game wouldn't be rained out tomorrow.

"Is there any chance . . ." Gregor glanced around to make sure no one was in earshot, and then he leaned in close. "Is there any way you can get the band to spell *I heart WM* at half time tomorrow night? Like, during the Notre Dame 'Victory March'?"

Dinky's lips spread into a slow smile. "Yo, Gregor, who's the girl?"

Gregor shook his head. Dinky was his closest friend, but he still couldn't tell him about Whitney.

Dinky twirled his long metal baton in his fingers. "Let me think about this. We'd need to schedule some extra time to practice that formation."

"It's really important."

Dinky nodded. "Got it. I'll see what I can do."

Best-case scenario: Whitney would be swept up by the grand gesture and come to the band room after the game, and Gregor would be there waiting for her.

Worst-case scenario: Things would remain exactly the way they were.

WHITNEY

"DUH, TWIT," ALICIA said to Whitney. They were eating Chex at the breakfast table. "Why else would the band say they love *WM*? Clue in. I thought you were smarter than the rest of the idiots here."

Whitney rubbed her eyes. She wished her mom were home, but she was sleeping over at Michael's. Whenever she thought about them having sex, it made her stomach clench tight.

"I just don't see why the marching band would spell my initials," Whitney said. She sipped some orange juice. "That's freaky. Some people said they were trying to spell 'Wildcats.'"

The Wildcats were the school mascot, after all. Either way, Whitney didn't want to be analyzing this. Last night's football game was awful. She'd gone with Zach, but he ditched early. Then, when the marching band did *I heart WM* in their formation, all these people whistled at Whitney. To make it worse, she hadn't been able to find Autumn after the game, so she had to ride home with Alicia and her senior friends. They were smoking weed in the car, which made Whitney feel like gagging. She was definitely not into weed. After some queasy hangovers in ninth grade, she didn't even drink anymore.

"You seriously think they were trying to spell *Wildcats* in their formation and they wrote *WM*?" Alicia clipped her hair in a barrette. Her sister was going natural these days, but it was brittle. Whitney wasn't about to suggest she go in for a deep condition. She'd jump down her throat about that, too. "You *know* someone in the marching band is in love with you."

"Whatever," Whitney said.

Alicia shook more Chex into her bowl. "What, you have a problem with that?"

"They're sort of . . ." Whitney scrunched her nose. She pictured those shabby Q-tip hats the marching band wore on their heads. "Band geeks. Not my type."

"You're so shallow," Alicia said. "Why not go out with a band geek? They're smarter than the average asshole, and they'll be grateful you're with them. Unlike Zach."

"Zach is fine."

As Alicia carried her bowl to the sink, she sang, *"Don't stop believin'. . . ."*

Whitney wanted to chuck a spoon at her. Instead she reached for her phone. Where *was* Zach anyway? For the past few weeks he'd been a flaky boyfriend. Sometimes he got frustrated that Whitney didn't want to go that far. The thing was, ever since prom night with Tripp freshman year, Whitney promised herself she wouldn't go inside the pants until it was love. Whitney guessed Zach was being flaky because he was on the varsity soccer team this fall, and practices were intense. Then again, she was on varsity soccer too, and she always found time for *him*.

Hey, sexy lady! Autumn wrote her a few minutes later. *Everyone's saying that WM was you. NOW is the time to dump Zach. You're gonna be the IT girl.*

Ha, Whitney texted her back. *I'll let Zach stick around.*

ZOE

ON THE AFTERNOON of Thanksgiving, the rain was beating so hard against the windows that Zoe could barely see out. She wasn't even sure what she was looking for as she watched the fuzzy outlines of cars with their headlights on. Aunt Jane's son, David, had driven up from college with his girlfriend, Tamara. They got so wet sprinting from the driveway that they threw their clothes in the dryer and changed into sweats and T-shirts. During a lull in the storm, David's dad, Rich, arrived with his wife, Glenda, and their five-year-old daughter, Mariah. Rich's father, Harris, came a minute later, propping his umbrella inside the door. Zoe pretended to watch the game with her cousin and Tamara. Not that she cared about football. But maybe no one did. Maybe they had a game on Thanksgiving for the sole purpose of people not having to talk.

Zoe's mom was still shooting in France. The movie was supposed to wrap by November, but now they were saying middle of December. That was why Zoe was doing Thanksgiving in Hankinson again this year.

After a while Aunt Jane shooed people away from the TV and into the dining room for appetizers. As Zoe watched everyone hovering around the veggies and dip, she thought about families. This family tree, with the stepmom and half-siblings and ex-spouses, would have branches crossing over branches and twigs like Zoe's— the estranged famous sister's daughter—sprouting completely out of nowhere.

Aunt Jane handed Zoe a lime seltzer to give to her cousin's grandfather. As she did, he extended a thick freckled hand to her.

"Call me Grandpa Harris," he said. His freckles were so round and orange, they looked like chewable vitamin Cs. "I met your mom a few times when Rich was married to Jane. I'm a big fan."

"Thanks," Zoe said. This was her first time meeting Harris. She looked from Harris to Rich, Jane's ex-husband. They were both bald with rosy cheeks and big bellies.

"Is Sierra working on something now?" Harris asked.

"A romantic comedy," Zoe said. "She's filming in France." She hoped he wouldn't ask her anything else. It made her uncomfortable talking about her mom's career. The whole room would get instantly quiet as people hung on to every word.

Thankfully, no one mentioned her mom again until dinner when David's girlfriend quoted *One Precious*, a movie Sierra starred in nearly twenty years ago.

"Oh my god," Tamara said, flushing. "I didn't even think about how she's your mom. That's so embarrassing."

David touched her arm. "No big deal."

"Happens all the time," Aunt Jane said, passing around the cranberry mold.

"Wasn't *One Precious* made around here?" Glenda asked. Rich's wife was African American and glamorous, with a long velvet skirt and dark red nails. She was a hair stylist in Hankinson. Zoe had met her one other time, at Thanksgiving last year. She'd said that Zoe had great natural highlights.

"It was filmed two hours away," Harris said. "Up by Lake Ontario."

Zoe saw Aunt Jane look quickly at Rich, and he cleared his throat. Something about seeing David's dad, Rich, and Rich's dad, Harris, made her wonder about her own father. More and more recently, she'd been thinking about him. When she was younger and asked her mom about her father, her mom always shut her down. After a while Zoe stopped asking. It was almost like he didn't exist. But he *did* exist. And if life had turned out differently, Zoe would have been sitting around some other table, another branch on another tree.

As Aunt Jane and David washed dishes, Zoe slipped up to her room to call her mom. She sprawled across her bed and unbuttoned her jeans, which were squeezing into her stomach. She was going to ask it short and simple: *Who's my father?* She was almost sixteen. She deserved to know.

Zoe had talked to her mom earlier that day. They'd made a plan to meet in Sun Valley for Christmas. Sierra was going to take her skiing.

It was late in Paris but not the middle of the night. For a second Zoe wondered if her mom would be drinking, if her words would be slurred. That had happened before, back when she used to drink.

Before she could chicken out, she hit *Mom*. The phone rang and rang that monotone European beep. When she got her mom's voice mail, she cleared her throat and then said, "Hey, Mom. It's me. I'm just calling because, well, I had some questions about who my father is. I know it's . . . I don't know . . . I'm ready to talk about it. Thanks."

DECEMBER

JAKE

"WANT TO THROW a football?" Jake asked his dad as he flopped next to him on the couch.

It was warm out, about sixty degrees. Jake had already taken a ten-mile bike ride, but he still had energy to burn.

"Now?" Jake's dad usually drank a few beers and watched soccer on Sunday afternoons.

"Yeah . . . sure. It's really nice out."

Jake's dad switched off the TV, dropped his empty bottle in the recycling bin, and went upstairs to change. When he came down, Jake was in the front yard, wearing shorts and a T-shirt, a football under his arm.

"Should we run to the park?" Jake asked. The weather was pumping him up.

"A run and football?" His dad laughed as he leaned over to tie his sneaker. "You want to kill me? Why don't you run and I'll meet you at the park?"

"That's okay. Walking is fine."

There were tons of people in Mount Olive Park. Women working out, kids scooting, guys shooting hoops. If it weren't for the bare trees and the Christmas decorations, it would feel like September.

Jake and his dad tossed the football, stepping farther apart with every pass. Jake still threw a tight spiral, and he was fast. When he received the ball, he charged past his dad, planting it firmly on a patch of brown grass.

"Touchdown!" a voice yelled.

Jake spun around. Teddy was watching them from the path.

"Theodore!" Jake's dad shouted. That was what he used to call him when they'd been younger. It was an inside joke.

"It's *Teddy*," Jake hissed to his dad, because they weren't younger, and he and Teddy weren't on inside-joke terms anymore.

"Teddy," Jake's dad said, waving him over. "Join us for a little football. It's been too long."

"Dad," Jake whispered. His face was hot, and he wanted to disappear. Or maybe not. Maybe he hoped Teddy would come over. Or maybe not. Maybe that would be too much.

"Hey, Mr. Rodriguez," Teddy said, tossing down his water bottle and jogging across the grass. "It's Ted now."

Ted? He scooped up the ball and spiraled it hard into Jake's arms. Jake caught it, stumbling slightly, and chucked it to his dad. His arms were wobbly, so it was a pathetic throw. He was trying not to look at Teddy's—*Ted's*—legs in his slippery blue shorts. He had hair on his legs now, and muscles that bulged out from his calves.

"Jake!" Ted received a ball from Jake's dad and then threw it to Jake. "What kind of throw *was* that?"

Jake caught it and spiraled it back to Ted. This one was a hard throw, and Ted had to run to get it. *Yes!* Jake was grinning so hard, his cheeks hurt.

"Not bad," Ted said. "Maybe you haven't lost it, after all."

They both cracked up and, just like that, everything changed. Jake and Ted and Jake's dad were laughing and shouting and working up a sweat. A few other dads came over and they started playing touch football, except it quickly descended into light tackle. Jake and Ted were good together, passing down the field, dodging the old guys.

The dads were getting their butts kicked, so they split Jake and Ted onto opposite teams. It was dusk, and the ball had become harder to see. On one long throw, Jake somehow caught it. He was weaving through the pack when Ted tackled him. They tumbled onto the ground, their bodies mashed together.

The earth was hard and moist and smelled like rotting leaves. Jake and Ted lay there, tangled around each other. Jake could feel Ted's bare arms and legs against his, and he could hear him panting. Ted pressed his hips into Jake, and Jake pressed back. When they did that, groin to groin, it felt like electricity zapping between their bodies. For a few seconds neither of them could move.

"All okay?" Jake's dad called from across the lawn.

Ted and Jake both leaped up. They brushed off their knees and shook out their arms.

"I better go," Ted said. "See you at school."

Jake nodded. He wasn't sure he could talk.

"Thanks, Mr. Rodriguez!" Ted called out to Jake's dad.

Ted walked across the field and grabbed his water bottle. Jake watched him go. The thing was, Jake knew that Ted wouldn't *see* him at school. He would look right through him like he didn't exist.

JANUARY

WHITNEY

"MOM? DAD?" WHITNEY called weakly. It was two in the morning. Her chest was hurting so badly, she could hardly talk.

"Mom? Dad?" she called again. "Can you come in here?"

Whitney felt achy and hot and trapped in this limbo between sleep and awake. She'd had a cough for the past week. She thought it was getting better, but then, last night, she and Zach had gotten into a fight on the phone and she'd crawled into bed feeling like crap.

"Whit?" Alicia asked, pushing her door open. "Did you just call for Mom *and* Dad? Do you realize Dad lives in Chicago now?"

"I don't feel so good." Whitney started to cough. It was a deep hacking cough that sent shocks of pain through her chest.

Alicia touched Whitney's forehead. "Oh my god."

"What?"

"I'm getting Mom," Alicia said, and then she left the room.

Whitney was trembling all over. She heard her mom and Alicia talking and then, seconds later, her mom burst in. She lay her hand on Whitney's cheek and called to Alicia, "Go heat up the car. And call the emergency room. Tell them we're on our way."

GREGOR

"SO WHAT'S THE deal for Saturday afternoon?" Dinky said as soon as Gregor answered his phone. "Want to get a bunch of people together?"

Gregor hit speaker and lay on his floor, looking out the window. It was only nine, but the sky was black. "What about bowling? They have great wings at the bowling alley."

"Or ice-skating," Dinky said. "Hey, did you see that thing about Whitney Montaine? Ice-skating would be cool. I'd probably fall all over my ass. Or bowling. I love wings."

"What thing?" Gregor asked, sitting up.

"Hang on, is Whitney the *WM* you had the marching band spell? I never thought about that until now, but—"

"What *thing* about Whitney?"

"The guidance counselor sent an email to all the sophomores. Didn't you see it? She's in the hospital with pneumonia. They didn't *say* she was going to die, but—"

Gregor meant to say good-bye, but his finger just hit end. Dinky called back, but Gregor didn't answer. With trembling hands, he opened his email and there it was, from two hours ago.

Dear Sophomore Class,

As some of you know, your fellow student, Whitney Montaine, is in University Hospital with acute pneumonia. It's a critical situation, and the doctors are . . .

Gregor wiped away the tears, but more kept coming. No one, not even his dad, could understand how he felt about Whitney. And now she was sick, and there was nothing he could do.

If he *could* do something, he knew exactly what it was. The other day, his mom had dragged him to Card 'n' Candle, and he'd seen a teddy bear that made him think of Whitney. It was small and red and said *Coup de Couer* on the belly. Gregor wasn't positive but he thought that meant "falling in love" in French.

What the hell. He was going to get it for her. If it wasn't snowing, he'd bike downtown after school tomorrow, buy the bear, and drop it off at the hospital. He didn't have to sign his name on the card. He just wanted her to have it.

FEBRUARY

ZOE

THERE WAS SOMETHING about being in Sun Valley with the altitude and the insanely blue skies that made Zoe feel like a different person. Back in Hankinson the skies had been soupy gray for months. No one there even knew she could snowboard.

Zoe's mom was finally back from France, and they were spending Presidents' Day weekend skiing with this boy Mac and his parents. Mac's parents were movie producers who were friends with Sierra, and they often rented ski chalets near each other. Mac was short and broad, built like a bulldog. Back in California, Zoe and Mac used to fool around when they were bored at their parents' parties. Not much, just groping. Mac was more into weed than anything. He was the kind of guy who smoked before school.

"I have something," Mac said to her.

They were on his bed. Zoe's long underwear was bunched around her ankles, but her panties were still on and she was fully clothed up top. They'd been snowboarding all morning and had gone to his place to heat up a pizza. After lunch Mac brought her to his room to roll a joint, but they ended up in bed.

"You mean you have a"—Zoe chewed at her thumbnail—"a condom?"

"Yeah," Mac said, kissing her. His breath smelled like pepperoni.

As he crossed the room to his dresser, she could see his boner poking out from his long underwear. Zoe looked away. She was still a virgin and hadn't thought she'd be having sex anytime soon. She hadn't even kissed anyone in Hankinson yet. Then again, it was another world here. She was a different Zoe.

"Here goes nothing." Mac sat on the end of the bed and tore the wrapper open.

Zoe tried to swallow, but her mouth was too dry. "I'm not sure I . . . uh . . ." She paused. *Oh god.* What was she even doing here?

"You don't want to?" Mac asked.

Zoe shook her head. She wriggled her long underwear back over her panties.

"That's cool," Mac said, chucking the condom into the trash. "Want to just smoke?"

Zoe shook her head. "But you can."

Mac reached for his joint. Zoe pulled the blanket around her chin. Maybe she wasn't a different Zoe here. Maybe there was just one Zoe. Sometimes it all felt so confusing.

Later that night, as Zoe and Sierra soaked in the hot tub, Zoe studied her mom, her blond curls matted against her face, her lids half closed. Did her mom have any idea she'd almost lost her virginity today?

"There's something I want to talk to you about," her mom said. "Remember what you asked me over the phone a few months ago?"

Zoe swirled her fingers in the steaming water. "Not really."

"Over Thanksgiving," Sierra said. "You left me a message."

Zoe suddenly felt woozy. "You mean about my father?"

"I've thought long and hard about this. You should understand that there are reasons I can't tell you much."

"Even a name is okay," Zoe said quietly. She was faint from the heat, but she didn't want to move in case it made her mom stop talking.

"Let's just say . . . it was while I was filming *One Precious*," her mom said. "Please keep this between you and me. It would be a PR nightmare if it got out."

Zoe rested her head on the edge of the tub. It was so surreal that one person's PR nightmare was another person's entire existence.

APRIL

MIA

_____

LAST PERIOD ALL the sophomores were herded to their home-rooms for a nationwide standardized math exam. Most everyone groaned, except Mia and a few others. Mia loved filling in those tidy bubbles with a number-two pencil. It was her version of Zen.

When the test was over, Mia was so energized that she ditched the school bus and walked home. It was over three miles, but the air was soft, and tulips were poking through the wet earth. As she walked she listened to music and thought about math. It sounded dorky, but when she was taking that standardized test or sitting in calculus, her brain was at peace instead of whirring in overdrive like it was most of the time.

Mia passed a shuttered pizza delivery store and eyed herself in the reflection. She'd finally stopped growing at almost six feet, and her hair was past her shoulders. It was streaked with green and purple. She was wearing her Doc Martens, short denim shorts, and fishnet tights. Her boobs—*both* her boobs—were now a satisfying size C. As she crossed onto a quiet street, she took off her sweater and tied it around her waist, the sun toasting her shoulders.

But then something caught her eye.

A scuffed van was idling at a stop sign. It was just sitting there, engine on. As she passed the van, she tugged off her headphones, clenching them in her fist.

A man with mirrored sunglasses was alone in the driver's seat. He grinned at Mia in this hungry way like he was going to eat her up. Mia hurried through the crosswalk, but then she heard the van behind her. Her legs went weak. She was too scared to take out her phone and call 911. Anyway, it wasn't like 911 could prevent her from being dragged into the van.

Panicked, she broke into a sprint, her heavy boots thudding against the concrete. She ran until she reached a house at the end of the block with a sprinkler arching across the lawn. As she rang the doorbell, her lungs burned and she could barely breathe. The van was at a stop sign thirty feet behind her.

Please be home, Mia thought as she jabbed the doorbell. *Please save me from this creepy abductor guy.*

Miraculously, the door opened, and there was Jake Rodriguez. Mia rarely saw him in school. All she knew about him was that he was gay and he mostly hung around the art room, oil paint splattered on his jeans.

"What's up, Mia?" Jake asked. He was wearing a white T-shirt and plaid shorts, and he was barefoot.

Mia's legs were trembling. She clutched the doorframe so she wouldn't collapse.

"Are you okay?" Jake asked.

Mia gestured to the van. Now it was driving slowly past them along the street. Jake raised his eyebrows like, *Yeah, that does look a little weird.*

Mia thought about blurting out, *I was the one who slipped the Captain Underpants book in your locker. Maybe it was a stupid gift, but please, please stay with me until the van is out of sight.* Instead she started crying.

Jake stepped onto the porch and wrapped his arms around her. Mia tried to relax, but it was hard. She'd never been hugged by a guy before.

"Want a ride home?" Jake asked, pulling back. "My mom is here. She can probably drive you."

Mia wiped her nose with her hand. "Yeah . . . if that's okay."

Jake disappeared for a minute and then came back with his mom. She was wearing a T-shirt and jeans, her hair in a loose ponytail.

"Are you okay?" she asked, touching Mia's arm. "Did something happen?"

Mia bit her lip. "No, I'm fine," she said quietly. The man in the van suddenly seemed far away, like maybe she'd imagined it, like maybe he wasn't even a real threat.

As they walked to the car, Jake asked for Mia's number. He pulled out his phone and added her to his contacts. No boy had ever asked for her number. Maybe this was the start of something new. Maybe something good could come from something bad.

MAY

WHITNEY

WHITNEY WAS GOING to be late for tennis, but she had something to deal with first. At least it was a home match. She could change into her outfit in two minutes and just miss warm-ups. The tennis coach was a laid-back Canadian guy who didn't even take attendance.

The thing was, Whitney had to find someone who could beat Zach for junior class treasurer. Stupid Zach, who cheated on her when she was in the hospital with pneumonia! Thank god Autumn told her so she could dump Zach before she looked like a total idiot.

But Whitney was not going to let him cruise through another student council election and feel all studly and popular when he was a cheating jerk. She had to get revenge.

She'd considered running against him. She could beat him easily, except then it would be too obvious. Everyone would think she was hurt. Which she was. But the important thing was not letting it show.

"Jake!" Whitney shouted. She'd just come out of the guidance counselor's office where she'd gotten a petition to run for treasurer.

And there was Jake Rodriguez walking down the hall toward her.

"Hey, Whitney," Jake said. "What's up?"

Whitney smiled at Jake. He was perfect. He was cute and friendly and people said he was a great artist. Also, he was gay, which would totally help. The girls all thought he was hot, and the guys weren't threatened that he was going to steal their girlfriends.

"Maybe this is crazy," Whitney said, "but do you want to run for treasurer for our class next year?"

"Uh." Jake shifted his sketchbook from one arm to the other. "Why?"

"Well . . ." Whitney paused. She and Jake had never really hung out. She should text him sometime. "I think you'd be good for it."

"I ran for student council last year and sort of . . . lost," Jake said.

"Really?" Whitney had no idea! If she'd known, she would have voted for him.

Jake looked down at his sneakers.

"Seriously, I'll make it happen for you," Whitney said. "I'll get all the signatures. Don't worry. You'll totally win."

Jake shrugged. He wasn't saying yes, but he wasn't saying no.

"Give me your number," Whitney said, pulling out her phone. "I'll text you when I have fifty signatures. That's all we need."

Jake paused for a second and then offered up his number.

Whitney gave Jake a quick hug and then sprinted to the locker room to change and grab her tennis racket.

By the time her first match started, she already had sixteen signatures on Jake's petition.

When she broke for water, she got ten more.

By the next day at lunch she had more than fifty.

This was awesome. Revenge was awesome.

She texted Jake at the end of the following day.

One hundred and eighty-two, was all she wrote.

They were going to murder Zach.

JUNE

GREGOR

"SUNSHINE?" GREGOR'S DAD asked him.

"That makes me think about swimming," Gregor said. He was brushing leaves and dead bugs and pine needles off the pool cover. "Or, I don't know . . . Maybe music?"

"With music, of course I think of cello," his dad said. "Bach. Tchaikovsky."

"Beethoven."

His dad repositioned the hose that was spilling water into the pool. "Vivaldi. I love hearing you play Vivaldi."

Gregor and his dad were opening the pool and playing a word-association game while they worked.

"What about chocolate?" Gregor's dad asked. "What do you think of when I say chocolate?"

"That yellow bag of Toll House chips. Also, I think of popcorn. I don't know why."

"Popcorn. I think of watching movies. Or maybe road trips. Remember how Mom always used to make popcorn for long drives?"

Gregor sprinkled baby powder on the pool cover to keep it from getting moldy over the summer. Speaking of driving, his dad had taken him parallel parking this morning. Gregor wanted to take his road test before he left for Michigan, where he was attending a music conservatory for three weeks in July.

"What about *happy*?" Gregor asked his dad. He slid his tongue over his smooth teeth. On Friday he'd finally gotten his braces off after two years of achy teeth and canker sores. "What do you think of?"

"Right now," his dad said.

Gregor smiled. That was exactly what he was thinking.

JAKE

Jake: Can you meet after school to give me the files?

Zach: Sure. Congrats on stealing treasurer from me.

Jake: Uh, thanks.

Zach: Hey, did you hear about Ted?

Jake: What about him?

Zach: Ask him yourself. Did you hear Allegra Nichols is moving back from Maine?

Jake: No! When?

Zach: August. You have to admit, she was cute. Did you hear a movie is being filmed in Hankinson? You should audition. I'm going to. You've got that Hollywood look.

Jake: Uh.

Zach: Don't take that the wrong way. You're hot and all, but I'm straight.

Jake: That's cool/fuck off.

Zach: You da man! Come to think of it, Allegra was annoying.

Jake: You guys were perfect for each other.

SUMMER AFTER
SOPHOMORE YEAR

JULY

ZOE

"WHAT?" ZOE ASKED. "Why are you staring?"

Lola grinned. "Something seems different about you. I'm trying to put my finger on it. Know what I mean?"

Lola was Rosa's granddaughter. Rosa had been Sierra's house-keeper for years, and Lola often tagged along. She was a year younger than Zoe and went to high school in LA. Of all the friends Zoe had left behind in California, Lola was honestly the only one she was happy to see again.

"Different how?" Zoe rolled up a fluffy white towel and slid it behind her head. They were sprawled on chairs next to the salt-water pool in the backyard. Sierra had spent a zillion dollars having it renovated this year. In honor of the brand-new pool, she kept offering to take Zoe for a brand-new bikini. *No, thanks.* Zoe was fine in her tankini top and paddleboard shorts.

"I don't know. . . . You seem more confident," Lola said. She giggled and twisted a strand of shiny black hair around her finger. "Did you do the deed? I've heard that changes people."

"Almost, but no." Zoe took a sip of water. "Why, did you?"

"I wish." Lola ducked in toward Zoe. "I did get drunk, though.

Don't tell my grandmother."

"I won't."

"Jack and Coke. I don't recommend it."

Zoe nodded. She'd never tried alcohol and didn't plan to. She'd learned in Al-Anon that addiction was hereditary.

"There is a guy, actually," Zoe said to Lola. Her stomach quivered with excitement. She hadn't told anyone what her mom had said about her dad. Not like she knew much, but Zoe was happy to have even a speck of information.

"I thought so!" Lola squealed. "Who is he? Is he hot?"

"No, it's not like that," Zoe said. She pushed aside her towel, stood up, and dove into the pool.

Lola splashed in after her. "What's his name?"

Zoe spit out a mouthful of saltwater.

"Not telling?" Lola asked.

Zoe swam underwater to the shallow end. She knew she wasn't making any sense, but it wasn't like she had anything else to share.

"No details whatsoever?" Lola squealed, paddling across the pool. "So unfair!"

"Tell me about it," Zoe said.

MIA

MIA WALKED TO the end of her driveway to check the mail. It was almost a hundred out, and she felt lightheaded as she opened the mailbox. Or maybe it was mental lethargy. Summer was stretching out, boring and endless, in front of her. She was doing some baby-sitting and taking extra piano lessons, but Sophie was at Catholic sleep-away camp, and her parents were always at work. Checking the mail had become a high point, even though it was just catalogs and bills.

Today a large yellow envelope sat on top of the usual offerings. It was addressed to the parents of Mia Flint from the Intensive Math Learning Institute. The sun scorched Mia's neck as she tore it open.

> *Dear Parents of Mia Flint:*
>
> *Congratulations on your daughter's stellar achievements! As you undoubtedly know, Mia is extremely talented in mathematics. This past spring a standardized math test was administered to every sophomore in the United States. In all areas of the test, Mia scored in the top percentile, gaining acceptance into the Intensive Math Learning Institute.*

For three weeks this August, IMLI will be hosting forty teenagers from around the country, all going into their junior year of high school, on the campus of Stanford University in Palo Alto, California. We will cover all expenses, both travel and program fees. The students will live with host families near campus and spend their days working with mathematics professors and graduate students...

Mia could hardly breathe. She skimmed to the last sentence.

... because of high demand for this program, please RSVP by July 10 to let us know whether Mia will be attending.

Mia closed the mailbox and ran back to the house for her phone. As she typed in the number at the bottom of the page, her heart was racing. She hadn't made a prank call since last fall. After the debacle with calling Whitney, she vowed she was done with them. But this wasn't really a prank. This was a *necessity*.

"Hello . . . IMLI," said a man on the other end.

"I'm calling on behalf of Mia Flint," Mia said. She kept her voice high and formal. "This is her mother, Susan. We're delighted to accept your invitation to IMLI."

When Mia hung up a few minutes later, she was beaming. Her escape plan was starting.

WHITNEY

"KYRA AND SCOTT did it on a *waterbed* last night," Autumn told Whitney as they waited with their pom-poms near the bleachers.

Whitney shaded her eyes with her hands. It felt strange to hear that Kyra, her former best friend, had lost her virginity. But so far *everything* about this summer was strange. For one, she and Autumn had been cast as cheerleading extras in a movie that was being filmed in Hankinson. It was called *This Is My Life*. It was low budget and sappy, and they weren't even being paid. But it wasn't like Whitney had anything better going on. She'd thought about lifeguarding this summer, but she was still recovering from pneumonia when they taught the Red Cross course in the high school pool.

"A waterbed is so cheesy," Autumn said. "Can you imagine them sloshing all over the place?"

"How do you know about this? Did Kyra call you?" Whitney stretched her legs in front of her and crossed one ankle over the other. The cheerleading skirts were seriously short. Every morning she woke up early to shave. When Lucas picked her up on the way to the stadium, he would run his hand up her calf for a stubble check.

That was another strange thing about this summer. Lucas

Bauersmith was eighteen and had just graduated from Fayette High, about twenty minutes from Hankinson. He also happened to be Kyra's cousin. He wasn't Whitney's boyfriend, but they'd been hooking up. The fact that Whitney was fooling around with Lucas had gotten her and Kyra talking again. They weren't best friends, but at least they were being civil.

"Kyra called me right after she did it," Autumn said. She buried her fingers into one of her pom-poms. "I mean, after Scott drove her home."

"Filming in two minutes . . . Quiet on the set!" a production assistant shouted into a megaphone. They weren't using the extras for this scene, so all the cheerleaders were hanging out on the grass.

"Why did Kyra call *you* after she did it?" Whitney whispered, leaning in to Autumn. When Kyra and Whitney had broken up, Kyra got custody of Laurel, and *Whitney* got Autumn. Whitney didn't even know Kyra and Autumn liked each other.

Autumn shrugged. "I guess Kyra needed someone to confide in, like, to process the whole thing."

A techie glared at them and held his finger to his lips. As they began filming, Whitney studied Autumn, with her white sunglasses and heart-shaped lips and reddish curls tied back in a ponytail. Why on earth would Kyra call *Autumn* to tell her she'd had sex? Something was up. Whitney could sense it.

"And . . . cut!" the director called out.

"Also," Autumn said, leaning in close. Her breath smelled like Altoids. "Kyra and I are going through the same thing right now."

Whitney stared at Autumn. Yet one more strange thing about this summer was that Autumn was together with Zach. Yes, *Whitney's* ex-boyfriend Zach. He was in the movie too, and he and Autumn couldn't keep their hands off each other. To Autumn's credit, she'd asked for Whitney's blessing before they got together. *God.* Sometimes Hankinson gave her a headache.

"*You and Zach* did it?" Whitney's throat was tight. She and Zach had been together for over four months. *Autumn* was the one who told her that Zach had been cheating on her with that girl Allegra and some other girls too.

Autumn pushed her sunglasses up on her head. "Uh-huh," she said, grinning. "Zach and I did it last week for the first time. And then . . . let's just say it's *happening*."

Whitney shook her head. It was one thing for Autumn to be fooling around with her ex-boyfriend, but another entirely for them to be having *sex*. Also, why didn't Autumn tell *her* last week? Why did she tell Kyra first?

"So what about you?" Autumn asked.

"Me what?"

"You and Lucas. He's eighteen. How long do you think he's going to wait? You've heard of blue balls, right?"

Among their friends, Whitney and Laurel were both holding off. Laurel was planning to have sex once she was in college. Whitney wasn't so definite. She figured she'd know when she got there.

"You're saying I should do it with Lucas because he's sexually frustrated?" Across the field, Lucas was guzzling water with the other football extras and then they were spitting it at each other. No way was he going to be her first.

"Don't you want to?" Autumn asked. "Aren't you ready to get it over with?"

"Filming in one!" the production assistant called into his megaphone.

Whitney whispered to Autumn, "Have you ever heard of *coup de coeur*?"

Autumn shrugged. "Is that French?"

"Yeah . . . it means 'falling in love.' But it's more than that. It's like falling in love instantly. A shock of love."

"And?"

"Maybe it's stupid . . . but that's what I'm waiting for."

Whitney lay on her stomach to watch the scene being filmed. Back when she was really sick with pneumonia, someone had anonymously delivered a small red teddy bear to the hospital. The bear had the words *Coup de Couer* across its belly. Her dad, who had flown in from Chicago, translated it for her.

Later that day Whitney's fever broke. Deep down she thought it was the bear that saved her life. She still slept with it every night.

GREGOR

AVA LOCKED THE door of her dorm room and then pulled off her striped sundress. Underneath, she was naked.

Gregor felt stirring between his legs and also an icy terror in his gut.

Ava was seventeen, played viola, and was a counselor-in-training at the summer music conservatory. On the first morning, Ava had flirted with him in the dining hall. That night they'd clandestinely held hands on the lawn during the outdoor movie, and they'd been fooling around ever since. They had to keep things on the down low, since Ava was a CIT and Gregor was a senior camper. Mostly, it was making out when Ava's roommate was away, but a few times they'd taken off their shirts and her bra and pressed their bare torsos together. Even when he was playing cello, all Gregor could think about was Ava's long brown hair, the way her skin smelled like sunblock and tasted like salt, her legs in those short shorts she always wore.

"Do you want to do it?" Ava asked. She set her glasses on her desk and pulled a box of condoms out of her dresser drawer.

Gregor glanced at the condoms and then at Ava again. Her head was tipped to one side, and she was smiling. Just looking at her made his stomach scramble.

He gestured to her roommate's side of the room. "She won't come back, will she?"

"She drove to Ann Arbor," Ava said. "She's not getting back until tonight."

The shade was pulled, but there was enough light for Gregor to see the hair between Ava's legs. It was in the shape of a rectangle. As he stepped closer to her, she wrapped her arms around him.

"Are you sure?" Gregor asked as Ava pulled his T-shirt over his head and led him to her twin bed.

"Sure, I'm sure."

They tumbled onto the sheets and started kissing. Ava had done it before. She'd told Gregor a few days ago. She also knew that Gregor was still a virgin.

Once he had his boxers off, she helped him roll a condom on. So this was really happening. He was really here.

Ava positioned him between her legs. "Now you just, sort of, move," she whispered.

Gregor thrust his hips forward. He was on top of Ava, and his cheek was pressed into her shoulder. He wasn't sure how much he was supposed to push, though. He didn't want to hurt her.

"You can do it harder," Ava said, clasping her hands on his lower back.

After a little shimmying back and forth, Gregor came. It was so intense that he saw swirls of colors behind his eyes.

"Was that okay?" he asked Ava. He was out of breath.

"Definitely. What about you?"

"It was good," Gregor said.

Who was he kidding? That was freaking awesome.

The next morning Ava rapped on the door to Gregor's practice room. Gregor was so immersed in Bach's Suite No. 6 that at first he didn't hear her. When she knocked again, he spotted her through the glass. He leaned his cello against the piano and waved her in.

"Hey," she said, pushing her glasses up on her nose. "There's a call for you in the main office. Roger says it's urgent."

Roger was the camp director. Gregor had only talked to him a few times. He picked up his phone from the piano stool. No missed calls.

"We should probably go right now," Ava said. "Let's leave your cello. We can lock the room and get it later."

Ava didn't say anything as they walked up the stairs to Roger's office, but Gregor could sense something was wrong. Probably Nana Margaret had another fall. She'd broken her hip last February, and the doctor warned them it could happen again.

Gregor watched Ava's legs, smooth and thin, and her flip-flops slapping against the stairs. He wondered if they were going to have sex again today. He hoped he wouldn't have to fly home early because of Nana Margaret.

AUGUST

JAKE

"I PICKED SOME blueberries for you," Mona Lisa said as she skipped onto Jake's front deck. She set a pint of blueberries onto the picnic table and flopped into a chair, kicking off her sandals.

Jake clapped his water shoes together over the ledge, trying to get the tiny pebbles out. He was leaving for sailing camp tomorrow and was getting everything organized.

"Thanks," he said. "Awesome."

"You should have seen me at the U-pick place," Mona Lisa said. "I must have eaten four hundred blueberries. I was cramming them in my mouth. I bet I'll crap an enormous blueberry tonight."

"Okay, that's disgusting."

Mona Lisa giggled and reached toward Jake, tugging him onto her lap. "I love grossing you out," she said, running her fingers through his hair. "And you love me for it, right?"

Jake rested his head on her shoulder. After nine years of being summer friends, he was used to how Mona Lisa acted all flirty and possessive with him.

"So you're going to sailing camp?" she asked, tugging at a thread on her cutoffs.

Jake got up off her lap and settled into the chair next to her. "Yeah, in the morning."

"How cool. I bet there'll be a lot of cute guys at sailing camp. Preppy guys."

"Here's hoping," Jake said. "Maybe I'll even meet someone."

Mona Lisa frowned and began picking at her toenails. They were painted bright orange.

"What?" he asked.

"Nothing."

"For real?"

Mona Lisa shrugged.

"Truth or dare," Jake said. They'd been playing an ongoing game of Truth or Dare since sixth grade, and it was their way of prying secrets out of each other. "And you have to pick truth."

"Okay, truth," Mona Lisa said. "If you get a boyfriend, I'll be jealous. I'll probably never talk to you again."

Jake raised his eyebrows. "You're joking, right?"

"Maybe. Sort of. But seriously, *I'm* the one with the boyfriends. You're my loyal sidekick. If you have a boyfriend, then you won't need me anymore."

"That's selfish," Jake said.

"Whoever said I wasn't selfish?" Mona Lisa laughed, scooping up a handful of blueberries.

Four days later and a quarter mile out on Cayuga Lake, Jake capsized the Sunfish. If that wasn't bad enough, there were menacing clouds taking over the sky.

He was twenty minutes up the lake from his family's cabin. He knew this lake well, knew how moody it could be. He shouldn't have been on the water, especially since he didn't sign out and didn't bring a buddy. If the counselors caught him, he was going to get hell for this. He'd probably be kicked out.

He wasn't even sure what had made the boat capsize. He'd been navigating the waves, but then the wake from a speedboat hit him, tipping the Sunfish to the right. Jake was chucked overboard, and the mast went upside down. The instructors had been hardcore about practicing how to right a boat. But it was one thing to flip a Sunfish in shallow water and another entirely to be two hundred feet deep.

Jake hoisted his chest up the side of the boat and reached for the dagger board, but then a wave splashed his face and he fell back down.

Damn Simon.

Simon was one of the reasons he ditched camp today. Simon came to sailing camp from a small town in North Carolina. Jake had no idea why he picked central New York. There were plenty of lakes down South.

Simon was cute in a Southern boy way with his polo shirts and short hair and *yes sirs* and *no ma'ams*. But as soon as he found out that Jake was gay, he wouldn't leave him alone. He kept signing up for chore shifts with him and asking him all these questions like *How did you come out?* and *What did your parents say?* and *Did people at school give you hell?* It was getting old. Especially since Simon was obviously queer but wasn't saying anything about *that*.

Also, it was bothering Jake the way everyone at sailing camp had bonded. It was like they were in a cult. They were always singing campfire songs and dressing alike and walking with their elbows hooked together. They weren't leaving him out, but he wasn't into it at all. That was stressing him out too, like, why didn't he want to make friends? Maybe Mona Lisa had jinxed him by saying she'd be mad if he got a boyfriend.

Jake rested his head on the side of the boat. His arms were tired, and his swimsuit was slipping off his waist. For some reason he thought of that girl Mia from school and how she rang his doorbell last spring, crying hysterically. He thought about how he'd hugged her. It wasn't like she asked him to or even told him why she was crying. He'd just known it was the right thing to do. Maybe it was twisted, but Jake liked being able to help her. Even now, he liked how that made him feel.

Jake grabbed at the dagger board and hauled the boat upright. This time it worked. He pulled himself onto the Sunfish and sailed back to camp.

MIA

TWO DAYS BEFORE Mia left for the Intensive Math Learning Institute, she was picking out the center of a croissant and nibbling the doughy innards pinch by pinch.

"Do you have to eat your croissant like that?" her mom asked, tossing Mia a paper towel.

"Can you take me to the mall today?" Mia asked.

Mia's mom looked up from her phone. Her thinly waxed eyebrows lifted like tiny umbrellas. "You want to go to the *mall*?"

Mia wiped the croissant flakes into the sink. Her mom hated her secondhand clothes. Just like how she hated the rainbow streaks in Mia's hair and her scuffed Docs. Her *dream* was to take Mia to the mall, to transform her into a blond, perky, gym bunny princess, but up until now that was Mia's nightmare.

"I want cute clothes for California," Mia explained. "And sneakers. I'm going to start running every day."

Her mom's mouth was open in shock. She was too surprised even to read the text coming in on her phone, which was tight in her hand.

"Can you also book me a hair appointment with Glenda?" Mia

asked. "I'm ready to go blond."

Mia's mom dropped her precious phone onto the floor. Mia scooped it up and handed it back to her. She was kicking her plan into high gear.

"You've always made fun of sun-streaked highlights," Sophie said when she pushed open the door to Mia's room the following evening. Sophie had come over to say good-bye. "And a pink manicure? A lavender tennis skirt? Where's my Mia? Did your mom clobber you unconscious and give you a makeover?"

"I bought new clothes for California," Mia said, brushing her newly blond hair. "My mom took me to the mall."

Sophie sank into Mia's desk chair. "I don't even know where to begin. Your *mom*? The *mall*?"

"I just wanted to . . ." Mia paused. Over the past year, just as she'd started feeling good about her body, Sophie had gained weight and broken out all over her face and back. "I'm trying out a new look for California."

Sophie reached into Mia's suitcase, which was open on her bed, and pulled out a seersucker tank top with the tags still on. She draped it across her chest and wrinkled her nose at her reflection.

"You can borrow whatever you want," Mia offered, but she didn't really mean it. She wanted to be the first to wear her new clothes.

"Like that tiny thing would ever fit me," Sophie said, tossing the shirt onto Mia's bed.

As Mia folded the tank top and set it back in her suitcase, Sophie said, "I guess it's cool. You'll see how the other half lives. I just hope you're not going to forget us little people."

"Of course I won't," Mia said, shaking her head.

What Mia didn't tell Sophie was that her plan for California wasn't about *seeing* how the other half lives. It was about *being* the other half.

The next day, Mia stepped into the orientation at IMLI. The sky was bright on the walk over, and there were palm trees lining the streets. She'd never been to California before. Whenever her parents went on exciting trips, they left Mia home with her uncle.

Mia pressed her name tag onto her pale pink sundress and tossed her blond hair over her shoulders. There were teachers greeting students at the door. Some pretty girls were sitting by the windows, laughing and chatting with a jocky Asian guy. On the other side of the room a bunch of pale kids were hunched over their phones. Right in the middle, a guy was studying the cheese platter. He was wearing a vintage gas station shirt and his name tag said *Jeremiah*. Not only was he cute, but her name was embedded in his name! As he grinned at Mia, her stomach flipped. His eyes were dark brown with long lashes. He had hair as blue as a blue-raspberry Slurpee, battered Vans, and an eyebrow ring. Total indie hunk.

No! This was not part of the plan. The plan was about fitting in, not hanging out with blue-haired guys.

As Jeremiah walked toward Mia, she pressed her glossy lips together and thought about Whitney Montaine. Whitney had this way of being friendly to everyone while only truly aligning with the popular people.

"I'm from Kansas," Jeremiah said, popping a cube of cheddar

into his mouth. "Maybe I'm a dork, but did you realize that *Mia* is in Jeremiah?"

His voice was sleepy. His eyes were chocolate. His breath was cinnamon.

But no. *No.*

"Oh," Mia said coolly. "I hadn't realized that."

Then she walked away from Jeremiah and toward the pretty girls and the jocky guy. This was her chance for a slice of American pie, and she wasn't going to throw it away.

JUNIOR YEAR

SEPTEMBER

JAKE

"YOU COULD WRITE notes to your future selves," Jake suggested to his group at freshman orientation. He was trying to help them come up with their ice-breaker project.

"That's dumb," said one girl. She frowned at Jake. "Like, what would we do with the notes?"

Jake looked around the gym at the other peer advisors sitting with their circles of ninth graders. His group sucked. He was two years older than they were *and* the junior class treasurer, and they weren't showing him any respect.

"You could hide the letters and get them out at graduation," Jake offered. He wasn't going them to tell where his group had hidden *their* letters, but he could always find another spot. "Or I could keep them and mail them to you in four years."

"Can't we just do a volunteer thing?" said a short guy. "Like, get it over with."

After a brief discussion, they agreed to paint a bench outside the school. Whatever. It wasn't like Jake was going to fight it.

As he headed over to get painting supplies, he thought about his own freshman orientation group. It wasn't like they were friends, but he still felt a connection to them. That was why he went out for peer advisor: to give that experience to a new group of freshmen.

Jake glanced across the gym. His group all had their phones out. None of them were even talking to each other.

Marin Banerjee was another peer advisor, but Jake hadn't talked to her yet. As his group went outside to start painting, he carried some forms over to the guidance counselor.

"Hey, Jake!" Marin said, tapping his shoulder. She was wearing blue shorts and a red tank top with visible bra straps. "Did you hear?"

"Hear what?"

Marin wrinkled her nose and smirked at Jake. He couldn't believe he'd kissed her at that dance. It felt like a million years ago.

"That I'm the last stop," Marin said, and then she laughed sharply.

"I have no idea what you're talking about."

"Ted dumped me on the last day of school. It was our twenty-one-month anniversary."

"He did?" Jake asked. Last spring that guy Zach mentioned there was news about Ted. That must have been what he was talking about.

"Which makes me the last stop on the gay highway," Marin said. "First you . . . and now Ted."

Jake stared at Marin.

"Yep," Marin said, nodding. "Ted came out. It's no big secret. I must have that effect on guys."

Marin spotted a friend, waved, and took off across the gym. Once she was gone, Jake dropped the papers he'd been holding.

WHITNEY

WHITNEY WAS WALKING to homeroom when she got a text from Autumn. They'd just driven to school together and said good-bye ten minutes ago.

Did you see Mia Flint? Autumn wrote to her. *Kyra and Laurel and I were like, HOLY MAKEOVER. You have to admit she looks good, but still . . . once a freak, always a freak.*

Whitney dodged a few freshmen scurrying into their home-room.

Mia's really smart, Whitney texted back. *You shouldn't give her a hard time for trying. I'm done with that.*

Autumn wrote her right away. *Duh, I was JOKING. You didn't have to go off on me.*

"Phones away," Whitney's homeroom teacher said as she walked in the door. "You should know that by now."

Whitney slid her phone into her bag and sat at her table, nod-ding at a few people. She closed her eyes and tried to focus on her breath. Life felt so topsy-turvy right now. Alicia left for college in Ohio last week. Two days later her dad got back from Chicago and rented a condo near Darien, so now she was dragging her stuff between parents every three days again. On top of everything, her mom and Michael were going to a bed-and-breakfast in Ithaca this weekend. Watch them come back engaged.

After homeroom Whitney pulled out her phone again. She'd gotten another text from Autumn.

I feel like you've changed since we were in the movie together, Autumn had written. *I heard what you said about me and Zach. Kyra told me.*

Whitney had no idea what she was talking about. *What did I say???* she wrote.

You told Kyra's cousin Lucas that I was being incestuous by hooking up with Zach!

Whitney scowled at her phone. People were pushing past her in the hall like she wasn't even there.

I didn't say that to Lucas, Whitney wrote, steering into a corner. *Besides, Lucas and I are over. You know that. He's a dick.*

A second later her phone vibrated. *Hey, it's Kyra writing from Autumn's phone. Thanks for saying shit about my cousin. Happy first day of school!*

Whitney barely made it to the bathroom before she started crying.

Yeah, right. Happy first day of school.

MIA

ON THE FIRST day of school, Mia passed Gregor in the science corridor. She'd always watched him, ever since her mom told her that he'd almost died from a bee sting. It was like she knew something about him that other people didn't know, and that was delicious.

But this time something was very wrong. Gregor's cheeks were hollow, his orange hair matted, his collarbones poking through his T-shirt. It was his eyes that killed Mia more than anything. She'd never seen such sad eyes in her life.

Mia wished she could run up to him and give him a hug, but he probably didn't even remember who she was.

GREGOR

ON THE DRIVE to the Kirkland Medical Complex, Gregor's mom tried to start a few conversations, but he wouldn't nibble. Finally she turned on NPR.

It had been two months since Gregor's dad died of a heart attack while he was running. He and Erica had been training for a father-daughter half marathon. He was forty-seven and jogged five miles every day. Gregor was at music camp when it happened, probably fantasizing about Ava at the moment his dad collapsed in Mount Olive Park. Erica had screamed for someone to call 911, but Gregor's dad was gone by the time the ambulance arrived.

The psychiatrist's name was Dr. Brunner, and his office had white walls, three chairs, and a low couch. Gregor sat in a chair and stared down at the trim carpet. It wasn't like he was here for being in a *good* mood.

"It's concerning me," Gregor's mom said after they'd all introduced themselves. The doctor's hair was thin, and he had a deep cleft in his chin. "He refuses to talk about his dad. He's quit cello and drums. He's not hanging out with his friends. I see their calls and texts coming in, but he's not answering them. I can barely get him to go to school every morning."

She looked guiltily at Gregor, but he kept staring at the ground.

"It's understandable," Dr. Brunner said. "You've been through a major trauma, Gregor. You've lost your father. I'm sure it feels like your entire world has been turned upside down in the worst possible way."

Gregor examined his fingertips. The calluses from his cello strings were almost gone. He stuffed his hands into his sweatshirt pockets.

"He barely leaves his room," Gregor's mom said. "I have no idea what he's doing in there."

Dr. Brunner nodded. "Do you want to talk about that?"

Gregor shook his head. For the past eight weeks he'd been flat on his bed, his hands laced behind his head, listening to Billie Holiday, picturing his dad's casket being lowered into the ground, wishing he himself were dead. He wasn't suicidal, but he couldn't imagine living in a world without his dad.

Gregor looked out the window of Dr. Brunner's office. The leaves were changing. It was the start of the first season that his dad wouldn't be alive to see. Gregor didn't want this season to happen, just like he wouldn't delete the voice mails from his dad on his phone or take down the Post-it that his dad stuck to his mirror the morning Gregor left for music camp. It said:

Gregor—
Stay true to yourself.
Love,
Dad

Dr. Brunner and his mom talked for a few more minutes, and then the doctor rotated his chair toward Gregor.

"I'm going to prescribe an antidepressant for you," he said. "It won't make you feel better immediately and it won't take away your terrible loss, but it will ease some of the pain. I also want you to start talking to a therapist. I'll give your mom some referrals. Does that sound like a plan?"

Gregor shrugged. He could see his mom wiping at her eyes.

"Did you want to talk about anything else?" Dr. Brunner asked Gregor. "Do you have any questions? I'll be seeing you next week to check in on how you're doing."

Gregor glanced out the window again. It was getting dark out, the end of day number sixty-one. Tomorrow would be day sixty-two.

OCTOBER

ZOE

DID YOU PASS?????!!

Two seconds later, another text.

DID YOU PASS?! TELL ME NOW!

Zoe had just taken her road test. Aunt Jane had gotten out of work early and driven her to the DMV.

Zoe wrote back to Anna, *Yes, I got my license.*

YAY!!!!!!!!!!!!!!!!!!

"Did you just tell Anna?" Aunt Jane asked. She'd offered her the wheel for the ride home, but Zoe said no. She needed a breather from driving right now.

"Do you think Anna would let me *not* tell her?"

Aunt Jane smiled. "What did you say?"

Zoe glanced at her phone. Another text from Anna had just come in.

"She said, 'Come pick me up now!'" Zoe read out loud. "Can I borrow your car?"

Aunt Jane turned sideways. "You didn't talk to your mom?"

"About what?"

Aunt Jane pulled onto their street. There, three driveways down, was a brand-new white BMW 5 Series.

Zoe's cheeks flushed. This car was LA all the way, a rich-girl car. Even though it had been more than two years since her mom's screaming fit in London, Zoe still didn't want people to think of her as a spoiled brat.

"Do you see it?" Aunt Jane asked. She was smiling hopefully.

Zoe didn't want to sound ungrateful. "I . . . uh . . ."

"I know," Aunt Jane said. "But it's the gesture that counts."

"Holy car!" Anna said when Zoe pulled into her driveway a half hour later.

As Anna slid into the passenger seat, Zoe said, "I know . . . it's kind of embarrassing."

"Your mom is a movie star!" Anna said. She wasn't usually this amped, but she'd bombed her road test twice and had all her freedom hopes pinned on Zoe. "Why not have a million-dollar car?"

"It's not exactly a million," Zoe said. She'd pictured asking her mom for a Honda or a used SUV.

"I could get used to this," Anna said as she slid her hands across the leather seat.

At Book Nook they celebrated with red velvet cupcakes, and piled a stack of books and magazines on the table between them. Zoe was reading *Cosmo* while Anna flipped through a book called *Women in Film*.

"Look!" Anna pointed to a chapter entitled "Women We Adore." "There's your mom when she was filming *One Precious*. I know it's cheesy, but that movie makes me bawl. I love the New Year's scene."

Zoe studied the page of candids from the set. *One Precious* was Sierra's most popular movie. It was from a long time ago. She played a baker who falls in love with a blind musician. It was the movie people watched when they wanted a good cry.

"She was so young," Anna said. "Look at her eyebrows. Did people not pluck back then? I wonder if I'll ever meet her."

"My mom? Maybe." Honestly, Zoe couldn't imagine her Hankinson life and her Los Angeles life colliding.

Anna rotated the book so Zoe could see better. In the pictures, Zoe's mom was in various stages of makeup and costume, on set with the director and costars and members of the crew. One man from the crew had his arm around Sierra in several shots. He had brown hair and he was on the short side. Zoe's stomach flipped as she remembered what her mom had said.

"Does it say what that man's name is?" Zoe asked. Her voice felt far away from her body.

"What man?"

Zoe touched the picture of the brown-haired man and her mom, laughing together on a pebbly beach. "Like, is there a caption?"

Anna leaned closer to the page. "Kevin," she said. "It says his name is Kevin G. Church."

NOVEMBER

JAKE

JAKE HAD FIFTY things on his mind when he pushed open the door to the locker room on Friday afternoon. *Swim laps in the pool, turn in art portfolio, drop off a budget at the student council office, make up the pre-calc . . .*

Oh, crap.

Ted was standing in the locker room in a green swimsuit. He didn't have a shirt on. Jake tried not to look at his chest. He tried not to look at how his wet swimsuit was clinging to him.

"Hey," Jake said, trying to breathe.

"Hey," Ted said, "what's up?"

"Not much."

"Me neither."

There was so much Jake wanted to say. Like, *Did you know you were gay when I told you on the bus back in eighth grade?* Jake still remembered exactly how Ted had responded when Jake said that he liked him. All he'd said back was, *Uh . . . that's kind of random.*

They'd been avoiding each other ever since Ted had come out. The way Jake saw it, he'd put things in Ted's court almost three years ago. Now it was Ted's turn to make the next move. Jake was surprised by how Ted's coming out had been a nonevent at school. He was still in football and he still had the same group of friends. Jake even heard from Marin that Ted had a boyfriend from another school.

"Are you going swimming?" Ted asked. He tossed a towel over his shoulders. "I just went and it's fucking freezing."

Jake glanced at a Band-Aid on the floor. "I think . . . I forgot something."

"Oh . . . okay. That's cool."

Jake hurried out of the locker room. Once he was down the hall, he hunched over his knees, trying to catch his breath.

"Guess who?" Allegra asked, coming up behind him and covering his eyes. She'd been back since September, but they hadn't hung out. From what Jake had observed, she was just as annoying as she had been sophomore year. "I heard you got your license. Do you feel like driving me around tonight? I want to get drunk."

"Sorry." Jake wriggled away from her. "I'm busy."

"Way to blow me off," Allegra called after him as he walked away.

At his locker, Jake loaded up his backpack and slipped his arms into his winter coat. Screw all the stuff he had to do. He was getting out of here. Student council members could leave school during free periods to run errands, which was basically how people got away with ditching if they didn't take advantage of it too much. What the hell. Jake was going to cash in on that privilege right now.

WHITNEY

———————

THE WEEK AFTER Thanksgiving, Whitney's mom hosted a "girls' night in" with her high school friends, Glenda and Nancy. Glenda lived here in Hankinson. She was the stylist who did Whitney's hair and also one of her mom's old friends. Nancy was visiting from North Carolina with her perfect husband and perfect son, Simon. At least that was what she kept bragging about in her loud Southern drawl. The moms were in the kitchen mixing blood-orange cocktails. Whitney was stretched on the couch, reading a script for the *Cat on a Hot Tin Roof* auditions.

From what she could hear, her mom and Glenda were in their angry-at-men mode. Michael had broken up with her mom a few months ago. And Glenda's husband, Rich, was out playing music at night and leaving her alone to care for their daughter and their dog, who actually used to be Whitney's family's dog before the divorce.

Whitney's phone pinged on her hip.

Hey, sexy, Brock Sawyer had written.

She and Brock had become friends in drivers ed over the summer. They flirted, but there was too much history with Brock and

Kyra, and also she'd gone to the prom with Brock's older brother, Tripp, freshman year.

Sorry, Whitney texted back. *Not gonna happen.*

Damn. Don't want to get blue balls.

TMI, Whitney wrote. What was it with people's obsession with blue balls?

"Whitney?" her mom called from the kitchen. "You've met Simon, right? Nancy wants to show you a picture of him and his girlfriend. They're gorgeous."

Whitney hiked up her yoga pants and headed into the kitchen. She'd met Nancy's son a long time ago, maybe when they were twelve. She remembered thinking he was stupid.

"Here's my boy," Nancy said, thrusting a phone in her face.

"Cute," Whitney said even though he wasn't. Simon was blond and doughy with a stubby upturned nose.

"If he wasn't with Lindsey, you two would be perfect together," Nancy said. "Like Halle Berry and that guy. Of course, if we didn't live in North Carolina . . ."

"That's the only interracial couple you can think of?" Glenda asked, examining her long nails. Glenda was much darker than Whitney. "Halle Berry's guy isn't blond. Plus, I think Whitney has a boyfriend."

"Not at the moment," Whitney said. She poured herself a glass of orange juice and slid into the kitchen nook. They had a bowl of sweet potato chips and a baguette next to some soft cheese on the table. Whitney spread a lump of cheese across a slice of bread.

"Remember sophomore year?" Nancy asked, toasting with her mom and Glenda. "Remember when we saw that guy get run over by a station wagon on his way in to school?"

Glenda sipped her drink. "It was just his foot."

"Charlie with the red hair," Whitney's mom said. "I always thought he was cute." She shook almonds into a bowl and held them out to Nancy. "Here . . . wasabi almonds."

"You thought *that guy* was cute?" Nancy clucked, scooping up a few almonds. "Yikes, spicy. What's in these?"

"Wasabi," Whitney's mom repeated. "From Trader Joe's."

Whitney took another baguette slice. It was funny to hear them talking about when they were in high school.

"I had a secret crush on Charlie," Whitney's mom said, swirling around her drink.

"Remember how he didn't even scream when his mom ran over his foot?" Glenda asked. "He just said, 'Back it up, Mom,' all low and deadpan."

The three of them collapsed into giggles. Whitney wondered if one day, in thirty years, she and Kyra and Autumn and Laurel would be in a kitchen laughing about high school.

"I should have married him," her mom said. She nodded at Whitney. "Of course *after* having you girls with your dad."

Whitney pressed her lips together. She hated when her parents talked about each other. Even though they tried to sound civil, she knew they hated each other's guts.

"Did you know he died?" Glenda said. "Last summer. I saw the obituary in the paper."

Nancy inhaled sharply.

"Charlie Lombard?" Whitney's mom's voice was tight. "He *died?"*

"He had a heart attack while he was running," Glenda said. "He had kids at the high school. You probably know them, Whit. Or maybe they graduated?"

Whitney gagged on the baguette and started coughing.

"Drink," Glenda said, passing her a glass of water.

"Are you okay?" her mom asked.

Whitney took the water. That was Gregor Lombard's *dad* who her mom had a secret crush on? It wasn't like she knew Gregor, except they'd been in the same freshman orientation group and he always said hi to her in the hall. She'd heard that Gregor's dad died over the summer. She kept meaning to tell him she was sorry, but then she always forgot to do it.

Whitney's mom crouched next to her. "Are you okay?" she asked again. "What is it? Do you know his kids?"

Whitney nodded. What she couldn't say was that she hated herself for being such a self-centered bitch that her own stupid world seemed so important while Gregor's tragedy was completely forgettable.

DECEMBER

ZOE

ON CHRISTMAS MORNING Zoe put on jeans and a powder-blue tank top and made her bed. She'd convinced her mom to let her cook breakfast. She was going to make a coffee cake, scrambled egg whites, and a mango salad. Nothing too complicated. She'd tried out the coffee cake recipe on Aunt Jane back in Hankinson. Zoe's mom wanted them to go to a restaurant, but Zoe had said no. She was going to cook.

Telling her mom what she wanted was a huge deal. But a lot was changing these days. For one, she had a crush. His name was Dinky. He was supertall with massive shoulders. They were always smiling at each other in American studies.

Zoe paused in front of her mom's door. Her mom was in her bed, rubbing moisturizer on her hands.

"Merry Christmas," her mom said.

"Yeah, Merry Christmas."

"Come on in." Sierra threw back the ivory comforter and patted the empty spot next to her.

Zoe's heart pounded as she stepped into the room. It had been two years since that horrible New Year's Eve, but it was still hard to be in here, to remember the paramedics barging in and flopping her unconscious mom onto a stretcher.

"Are you sure you want to do all that cooking?" her mom asked. "Let's just go to the Polo Lounge. They're open today."

"That's okay. I like being in the kitchen."

"You sound like Janie."

Zoe couldn't tell whether she was saying that in a bad way. The other day, she'd asked her mom why she and Aunt Jane weren't close, but all Sierra said was that some things were better left in the past. Zoe assumed their falling out happened around the time her grandparents had died. From what Aunt Jane had told her, her grandparents had been driving to Florida for Christmas when they'd been hit by a tractor-trailer and died instantly.

"Want some moisturizer?" Sierra asked. Her eyes were a little red, like maybe she'd been crying. Or maybe not. In so many ways, Sierra was a mystery to Zoe.

Zoe held out her hands, and her mom laced her slender fingers into hers. Her mom's hands were so tiny. Zoe's hands were thick, built for working a field. Maybe her father came from peasant stock. Last night, as they were driving home from Beverly Hills, Zoe had told her mom about the *Women in Film* book and asked if that man, Kevin G. Church, was her dad. Her mom had gripped the wheel and stared straight ahead.

"I've been thinking about what you told me," Sierra said now. She caressed one of her palms over the other hand. "About the pictures that you saw from the *One Precious* set."

Zoe held her breath. It was like her mom had read her mind!

"This is hard for me to talk about. It's true that that man . . .

Kevin . . . and I were briefly involved. But he's not the one." She dabbed at her eyes. "It was a hard time for me. I was very confused. Do you need a father figure? Is that the problem? Because Max can take you snowboarding, or even—"

"I should start the coffee cake," Zoe said. She stood up so quickly that she got a head rush.

"No butter, okay? Just a little canola."

"No butter," Zoe said, and she fled downstairs.

When Zoe got to the kitchen, she bumped into the edge of the marble counter and yelped in pain.

"Everything okay?" her mom called downstairs.

Zoe rubbed her hip. "Yeah. Fine."

She reached for the mixing bowl, but then dropped it onto the floor. Thank god it didn't break. She poured in two cups of Bisquick and way too much milk. What on earth did her mom just tell her? That she used to be a sex addict and didn't actually know who Zoe's father was? Because that was what it sounded like.

Zoe tore open the brown sugar and got to work on the crumble topping. She used canola instead of butter, but it looked wet and gross. *Screw it.* Zoe threw it into the trash and dumped the batter down the garbage disposal. Then she picked up her phone and called the Polo Lounge for a breakfast reservation. All she had to do was use her mom's name; they got a prime table within an hour.

MIA

***

MIA COULDN'T BELIEVE her parents were taking her to the Caribbean over Christmas break. It was *so* not like them to include her in anything. And they were even paying for Sophie to come along! If Mia was being cynical, she'd say her makeover was the reason. She finally looked like the preppy daughter they'd always wanted. Mia figured they invited Sophie along so they could still do their tennis lessons and have fancy dinners by themselves.

On the plane, Mia glanced over at Sophie listening to music in the seat next to her.

"I have a new goal," Mia said. She traced her finger across her tablet. She was reading *The Man of My Dreams* by Curtis Sittenfeld.

"A new *what*?" Sophie lowered the volume on her phone.

"A goal."

Sophie rolled her eyes. Over the past few months, Mia had become obsessed with goals. Growing her hair three more inches. Narrowing her list of college choices. Advancing in piano so it would stand out on college applications. Practicing driving. Taking her road test the instant she turned sixteen. That was two days ago, and she'd rocked it. Sophie said she needed to chill, but Mia didn't see the problem with self-betterment.

Mia's new goal was to kiss a boy. And not just any boy. Mia wanted to set the bar high. She wanted her first kiss to be with someone gorgeous.

"Do you think there'll be cute guys at the hotel?" she asked Sophie.

"What?"

Mia tugged out one of Sophie's earbuds. "Cute guys. Do you think we'll meet some at Royal Reef?"

"I hope so," Sophie said, shrugging. "Otherwise, why did I become anorexic for the past six weeks? Skinny doesn't come naturally to *some* people."

Mia watched Sophie fit her earbud back in and unwrap a piece of gum. She decided to keep her kissing goal to herself.

The Royal Reef Hotel overlooked the harbor. From their room, Mia and Sophie watched the cruise ships coming and going. The air was warm and moist and sweet with flowers. Mia woke up before Sophie every morning and went running on the mile-long beach. While Mia ran, she could see her parents playing tennis. They were always the first people on the court.

Every afternoon she and Sophie lay on towels near the pool. There were definitely cute guys at Royal Reef. The problem was, they were all older, and most of them had girlfriends.

"Skanks," Sophie called the girlfriends. "It's obvious they've had boob jobs because they're so skinny. At least mine are the real thing."

"Mine are real too," Mia said. She adjusted her new yellow bikini top. Her boobs weren't huge, but at least she wasn't flat anymore.

"Yeah . . . well," Sophie said, reaching for the sunblock. "You're you."

"What's that supposed to mean?"

"Nothing," Sophie said. "Can you do my back?"

"I found the cutest boy in the universe," Sophie hissed. She'd just returned from the bar where she'd gotten them glasses of tropical punch. "Man of my dreams. No skank in sight. Hubba, hubba, is he hot!"

Mia propped herself on her elbows. "Where?"

"He was getting a Sprite, but then he headed inside." Sophie plopped down next to Mia. "I should have followed him and offered him my sumptuous body."

Mia laughed. "And told him you have a friend. A threesome!"

"He's all mine," Sophie said, nibbling the maraschino cherry from her punch.

"If he's yours, then maybe you should give him that," Mia said.

They collapsed into giggles and sipped at their drinks.

That night, as they were having dinner with Mia's parents, Sophie dug her fingernails into Mia's thigh.

"Oww," Mia said, pushing Sophie's hand away.

Mia's parents were studying the wine menu and didn't notice anything.

"Hubba Hubba Boy," Sophie whispered. "He's at that table over there. I think he's with his parents."

Mia followed Sophie's gaze. The guy was their age, maybe a

little older. His hair was sandy brown. He had broad shoulders and a square jaw. He was a definite hunk.

Mine, Sophie mouthed.

"Let's say you were stranded on a desert island," Sophie said the next night as she was washing her face with her acne soap. "And you could pick one person to have with you. Who would it be?"

Mia sat on the edge of the tub. They'd seen Hubba Hubba Boy playing volleyball on the beach that morning. When he dove for the ball, they had to press their hands over their mouths to keep from cheering.

"Hubba Hubba Boy," Mia said. "You can rescue us in the lifeboat."

"First of all, finders keepers." Sophie flicked some water at Mia. "And no offense, but if I came to the island, I'd put you in the boat, stay with Hubba Hubba, and make little hubbie babies."

Mia dried her arm with a towel and then flopped into a chair by the window. As she stared at the lights over the harbor, she thought about Hubba Hubba Boy. Maybe they'd meet on the beach when Sophie was upstairs in the hotel room. Maybe they'd fall in love, and it would be happily-ever-after. Maybe someday they'd be honeymooning on one of those cruise ships, their naked bodies wrapped around each other on a private deck.

"What's wrong?" Sophie asked. She was on the bed tapping at her phone.

"Why?"

"You've been staring out the window for ten minutes."

"Nothing really." Mia tucked her legs under her. She'd just

shaved them and they felt silky smooth. "Don't laugh, but I'm think-ing about my new goal. I want to kiss a gorgeous guy. I mean, I'm *sixteen*." Mia snorted. "That's geriatric in the world of first kisses. I'm owed something amazing."

Sophie shook her head.

"What?" Mia asked.

"Do you remember back when you were so bony and just had, you know, bumps instead of boobs? I feel like you've changed since you got pretty, like it used to be *us* and now it's *you*."

"What's that supposed to mean?"

"Nothing," Sophie said, staring at her phone again. "Forget it."

On the last day of the trip, Mia and Sophie were walking on the beach. It was New Year's Eve day. Mia had her bikini on, yellow with white polka dots. She was swinging her hips, feeling sexy. Sophie was wearing a teal-green bathing suit with a blue sarong she'd bought from the gift shop.

"Hey!" Hubba Hubba Boy splashed out of the ocean and walked toward them. "You're staying at my hotel."

Mia's heart started racing. He was even more gorgeous up close. His eyes were speckled, and he had a tiny scar on one cheek.

"Yeah," says Sophie. "We're going home tomorrow."

"Where are you from?" he asked. He was looking at Mia.

Mia's throat tightened. Last summer, in California, she'd over-come her extreme shyness, but it still returned at the worst times.

"Hankinson. That's in central New York," Sophie said. "What about you?"

He glanced quickly at Sophie. "Colorado."

"I'm Sophie. This is Mia."

"I'm Marco." Hubba Hubba Boy grinned. "Does she talk?"

"Sorry." Sophie rolled her eyes. "Mia's a little weird."

Mia clenched her fists. She wanted to die right there on the sand.

"Mia," Marco said, nodding at Mia. "I've seen you around."

Mia could feel Sophie glaring at her. She still couldn't think of a single thing to say.

"Peace out." Marco started back down to the water but then turned and grinned at Mia. "Maybe I'll see you in the ballroom tonight. A lot of people are going for New Year's Eve."

Mia nodded and watched him splash into the water. She'd actually packed the perfect black dress. If she went down to the ballroom and she and Marco danced and the clock struck midnight, then—

"Peace out?" Sophie grumbled. "Who even says *peace out*? And what kind of cheesy name is Marco? I liked him more from a distance."

Mia didn't respond as she continued down the beach. She knew she wouldn't go to the ballroom tonight. Sophie would sulk in the hotel room and Mia would feel guilty and they'd watch movies and Sophie would complain about how *girls like us* never have fun. Mia didn't want to be a *girl like us* anymore. Plus, she was sick of Sophie calling her weird. She was over it.

FEBRUARY

WHITNEY

DURING THE INTERMISSION of *Cat on a Hot Tin Roof*, Autumn skipped into the dressing room and kissed Whitney on the lips. It wasn't a lesbian thing. It was just what Autumn was doing with all her friends this spring. Her boyfriend, Zach, said it was a turn-on.

"Hey, superstar!" Autumn said, pulling back.

"Thanks." Whitney wiped her lips. She didn't want Autumn's bright-red lipstick to mess up her stage makeup. She was Maggie, the female lead. She had on a pale yellow dress with a white sash, and her hair was ironed straight with a flip at the end. Alicia, who had flown in to see the dress rehearsal, grumbled about the irony of Whitney being African American and playing a Southern belle.

"You're amazing," Autumn said. "We're all freaking out about how good you are. Kyra and Laurel are jealous that they didn't get their acts together to audition."

Just then Kyra and Laurel wove their way through the art room, which was doubling as a dressing room with full-length mirrors and costume racks dividing the girls' and boys' sides.

"Hey, famous lady," Kyra said, sticking her butt out as she gave Whitney an air kiss.

Laurel grinned sloppily at Whitney. Their eyes were all squinty and bloodshot. They must have smoked up before the play. Weed was something that Autumn, Kyra, and Laurel majorly bonded over. Guys thought it was cool that they were stoner chicks, but Whitney thought it was lame. She hated the smell of weed and would never put it in her lungs, especially after she'd almost died of pneumonia last year.

"So," Laurel said as she hopped onto a metal table and swung her feet back and forth. "Are you too famous to come with us to Key West over spring break?"

"You guys are going to Key West?" Whitney asked. This was the first she'd heard about it.

Laurel glanced at Autumn, who looked at Kyra.

"My uncle," Kyra said. "You know, Lucas's dad? He said we could stay in his condo." Kyra smirked. She wasn't wearing her turquoise contacts, and her eyes were flat brown. "Too bad you think Lucas is a dick."

Whitney clenched her hands. *Focus, focus.* It was opening night. Her dad was filming her performance to submit to the summer acting program that she was applying to at NYU. She needed to kick ass, and Kyra couldn't throw her off course.

"Not like Lucas will be in Key West," Laurel said. "All we have to do is buy the plane tickets."

"So what do you think?" Autumn asked. She took a squirt of Whitney's frizz control and scrunched it into her hair. "Want to join?"

Whitney dusted powder across her nose. *Join.* That meant the plan with her three closest friends had formed without her. It would happen whether she went or not.

"Sure," Whitney said. "It sounds cool. I just have to ask my mom."

"When your mom hears it's us," Laurel said, pushing off the table, "she'll totally say yes."

"Yeah." Kyra slung her arms around Laurel and Autumn. "We're angelic. For stoner chicks, I mean."

Whitney tried to smile. She used to be the one they revolved around, and now she was the fourth wheel.

"Whitney," Ms. Godfrey called over. "Time to clear the dressing room."

Kyra, Laurel, and Autumn kissed her good-bye. Whitney's cheeks felt tight. She wanted to get onstage again. Recently she was more comfortable acting than being part of real life.

As she watched her friends leave, she noticed an oil painting propped on an easel by the supply cabinets. It was a self-portrait of a guy with long blond hair and green eyes. Whitney could tell immediately that it was Jake Rodriguez. People weren't kidding when they said he was a good artist. But what really got Whitney were the words painted in black across his face.

You're braver than you believe.

Maybe Jake Rodriguez was, but Whitney couldn't say the same for herself.

MARCH

GREGOR

"GREGOR?" HIS MOM called upstairs. "Does she drive an SUV? Because she's pulling into the driveway."

Gregor was lying on his bed, his pillow over his face.

"Are you going to get the door or do you want me to?" his mom asked.

He was wearing jeans and the creased T-shirt he'd slept in last night. He glanced at the dusty leather journal on his nightstand. He never wrote in it. It wasn't that he was depressed anymore. He was actually much better, and he was even playing drums again. But ever since his dad had died, he couldn't open his journal.

The doorbell rang. Gregor's stomach lurched as he heard his mom say hi to Nadine. He could hear Nadine saying something back. He pulled his shirt over his head and briefly examined the path of reddish hair running from his navel down into his jeans. It was weird the way his body was changing when so many other things were frozen in time. He put on a clean gray T-shirt and sank back onto the bed.

• • •

"Gregor?" his mom called upstairs in her forced cheerful voice. "Nadine's here."

His therapist, Jude, had been the one who said *go for it* when Nadine asked him out. It wasn't like he had much of a choice. Nadine was in band with him and Dinky and all their friends. If he said no, he'd look like a wuss.

"Coming," Gregor called. He walked slowly out of his room. All he could think about was how his dad used to harass Erica's ex-boyfriend Russell whenever he picked up his sister. It had been a running joke in their family.

Nadine was standing in the doorway. Her jeans were tight, her hair shiny, her lips pinkish red. It broke Gregor's heart to see how hard she was trying.

"Hey," she said, "I like your house."

"Cool," Gregor said, his voice cracking. "Thanks."

Gregor's mom sighed. "So you'll be back by dinner?"

Nadine and Gregor both shrugged. They hadn't made any real plans. Maybe food, maybe bowling, maybe a movie.

"Yeah," she said. "I'm guessing around five."

"Well, have fun," Gregor's mom said. "I'm going to stop by Nana Margaret's to check in on her."

Maybe it was twisted, but Gregor wanted his mom to tell them not to drink and drive, or to ask Nadine how she did on her road test. Just like how his dad used to do. Yeah, that was probably twisted. It would probably just make him feel worse.

In the car, Nadine turned on a pop music station. It was a mild afternoon, and the trees were starting to bud. They passed some runners heading into Mount Olive Park. Gregor looked away. After their dad had died, Erica quit cross-country and started smoking. She wasn't even secretive about her cigarettes. At first their mom let it go, but then they started fighting about it, screaming and slamming doors.

"Do you like this song?" Nadine asked as a girl band from England came on.

"It's cool."

"I know it's cheesy, but it gets stuck in my head. I have lowbrow taste." Nadine glanced into the rearview mirror. "Weren't you in orchestra last year? You played cello, right?"

Gregor nodded.

"Why'd you stop?"

Gregor's hands felt clammy. Jude would say, *Be honest.* Yeah, right. Like he was supposed to tell Nadine how his dad used to sit front and center at his cello recitals. After he'd died, Gregor never wanted to look into the audience and see that chair where his dad would have been. He slumped against the car window and pressed his cheek onto the cool glass.

"Are you okay?" Nadine asked.

"Actually, I don't feel so good." Gregor never thought about it until now, but what would his dad have said if he'd known Gregor had quit cello? The answer was obvious. He would have been disappointed in him.

"Do you want water? Should I pull over?"

Gregor shook his head. "I'm sorry . . . I think I need to go home."

• • •

Erica was tying her sneakers in the kitchen.

"What are you doing here?" she asked, standing up quickly. She was wearing her running clothes. "Didn't you go out with Nadine Turner?"

Gregor poured a glass of water. He was already dreading school on Monday. Maybe he'd take a sick day. He didn't want everyone giving him a hard time about bailing on Nadine.

"I'm heading out." Erica reached onto the hook by the door for a set of house keys. "Tell Mom I'll be back later."

"Where are you going?"

"Does it matter?"

Gregor shrugged. He couldn't deal with his sister right now. Once she was gone, he walked over to the closet where they stored his cello when it got shipped back from Michigan. He wasn't even sure who'd gotten it from the practice room at music camp.

He slid out the huge brown box and carefully tipped it onto its side. He tore off the packing tape and shoveled through Styrofoam peanuts until he reached his cello case. All four strings were loose. He was just lifting his cello onto his lap to tune it when he saw a piece of stationery at the bottom of the case. It said *Gregor* in small neat handwriting. He unfolded the paper.

Gregor,

I'm so sorry about your dad. You're awesome at cello and an overall great guy. I'm so glad I met you. Stay in touch, okay? I bet your dad was proud of you.

Love,

Ava

It had been eight months, and he could still smell Ava and feel her skin. It was tough thinking about her, being transported to the *before*. Back then, he had no idea there even *was* a before until he crashed hard into the after.

Gregor tuned the strings, pulled out the endpin, and tightened it into place. He started with Mozart, his dad's favorite.

ZOE

"GREAT TO MEET you!" Zoe forced a smile as she looked at her reflection in her full-length mirror. She had a job interview in twenty minutes and was practicing her answers. As with swimsuits, she and mirrors were not the best of friends.

She was applying to be a part-time barista at Bean. The manager's name was Kenny. Zoe had talked to him on the phone yesterday.

Kenny is thirty, Zoe imagined as she slid on a silver headband. *He's a heavyset guy with a buzz cut and baggy jeans.*

Zoe pictured Kenny sitting at a table near the brick wall. *Tell me about yourself,* he'd say.

I grew up in Southern California, she'd respond.

Stop! Smile. Zoe tried to smile, but it looked like a constipated grimace.

I've lived in Hankinson since the beginning of high school. I love to cook. I have my license and a car. I'm really responsible—

Zoe imagined Kenny cutting her off.

Is it true that your mom is Sierra Laybourne? he'd say. *Are you the spoiled brat from that video? Why the heck are you asking me for a job?*

Zoe scowled at the mirror and then turned away. She should

forget this whole idea. It wasn't like she needed money. She wanted to work at Bean because her afternoons were bleak. Ever since choir had gotten switched to mornings, she'd walk to the student parking lot after school alone. Sometimes she'd see Whitney or even that redheaded guy from her freshman orientation group. They'd be laughing with friends and she'd think, *Wow, they're doing high school so much better than I am.*

Then Anna texted her on Monday. Her best friend had an afternoon job at a candle shop across from Bean and had noticed a Help Wanted sign in the window.

Zoe turned back to the mirror. She slid off her headband, unbuttoned her tailored blouse, and tugged on a simple T-shirt. No expensive clothes. Nothing from LA.

Thanks for coming, another version of Kenny would say to her. Maybe he was Asian with angular hair and skinny jeans.

Thanks for having me, Zoe would say. They'd be at a table by the door. That was where she and Anna used to sit when they went to Al-Anon freshman year and would go to Bean for a brownie after.

I googled you this morning, this Kenny would say. *Can you get me an autograph?*

Zoe shook her head. It wasn't her fault that her mom was Sierra Laybourne. But it *was* her fault the way she couldn't face it so much that she hid from the world.

"Lame," she sniped at her reflection. Then she grabbed her car keys and walked downstairs.

JAKE

Jake: Hey, ML! How's life in Atlanta? I'm in German, but it's quiet reading time. Want to hear an awesome German word? *Lebensabschnittspartner.*

Mona Lisa: Leben*what*?

Jake: It's the German word for the person you're hooking up with . . . today.

Mona Lisa: Are you suggesting that's what I call my next fuck buddy?

Jake: Uh-oh. Mr. Fritz is waving me up to his desk.

Mona Lisa: Busted for texting? Delete this conversation. I just said fuck buddy. Oops, I said it again.

Jake: I'm back. Oh shit.

Mona Lisa: What?

Jake: Oh. Shit.

Mona Lisa: WHAT???

Jake: I had a stomach bug during the SATs last week. I'm taking a makeup at a school thirty minutes away next Saturday.

Mona Lisa: And . . . ?

Jake: Mr. Fritz is the football coach.

Mona Lisa: I'm confused.

Jake: He is TED'S football coach. He told me that Ted has to take the SAT makeup too.

Mona Lisa: Oh shit.

Jake: He said Ted needs a ride. He asked if I'd drive him.

Mona Lisa: What did you say?

Jake: I'm trying to breathe.

Mona Lisa: TELL ME WHAT YOU SAID!

Jake: Yes.

Mona Lisa: Looks like somebody's about to get himself a *Lebensabschnittspartner.*

APRIL

MIA

MIA FLIPPED ON her headlights, turned on the windshield wipers to clean the dew, and backed out of her driveway. Her dad said she could borrow his car instead of taking the bus. At six forty-five in the morning, the world was quiet and gray, like driving through a fallen cloud.

Mia had a mission. She was going to school early to get out the envelope that her group hid during freshman orientation. She'd gotten her SAT scores the night before. They were high enough to have her pick of colleges. Mia had just read *Love Story*, which made her want to apply to Harvard. But for real, Swarthmore was her ultimate choice. As she was brushing her teeth last night, she decided she wanted to print the SAT scores and put them in that envelope. She'd stuck a few other things in there over the years, like that stolen photo of Brock Sawyer, a perfect report card, her completion certificate from IMLI. It was Mia's lucky charm, her version of a penny tossed into a fountain.

On the way into school Mia shivered in her lime-green hoodie. She waved at the librarian and then hurried through the door and down the stairwell. She opened up the fire extinguisher cabinet, pulled out the envelope, and slid onto the floor.

"Hey, what's up?" a guy's voice asked.

Mia sucked in her breath. There, standing above her, was Brock Sawyer.

"You're Maya, right?" he said, grinning. "What are you doing down here?"

"Mia," she managed. Her pulse was so jumpy, she could feel it in her throat. She tucked the orientation envelope into her backpack.

"Mia. Sorry, I knew that. Are you new here? You started last fall, right?"

Mia had lusted after Brock since middle school. For all of seventh grade she recorded what kind of sandwich he brought to lunch and what color shirt he was wearing. Her obsession had eased a bit in high school, but he *was* incredibly hot. His reddish-brown hair crested in front, like a cartoon superhero. His eyes were copper and he had a sexy dimple in his cheek. Mia would give anything to touch that dimple.

"No," Mia said. "I've been in Hankinson all along. We actually went to middle school together."

"You must think I'm an idiot. That's cool. I probably am." Brock slid next to Mia and cupped his hand over her knee. "Can we start over? What's up? I'm Brock."

"Mia," she said. Generally, Mia would be paralyzed by the fact that *Brock Sawyer* had his hand on her knee, but the whole thing was so bizarre that Mia was forgetting to die.

"Do you want to get out of here?" Brock asked. "I came in early for a varsity club meeting, and I'm just not feeling school. I was thinking about going for a hike. I know this great waterfall."

Mia pressed her lips together. They had fifteen minutes until the first bell rang. "Can we?"

"I have a car," Brock said, pushing himself up. "Come on, before the hall monitors mobilize their troops."

Mia didn't know what to say. Hours and weeks and months and years of Brock Sawyer fantasies, and now . . . this.

"You know you want to," Brock said, extending his hand. "I'll call the office and pretend I'm your dad. I'll say you're sick."

"What about you?"

"I'll figure something out. I'm an idiot only sometimes." Brock hoisted Mia to her feet. "You know you can't resist."

It was true. Mia couldn't.

Two hours later, deep in a ravine south of Hankinson, Mia and Brock were making out in front of a waterfall in the pouring rain. Talk about surreal. But what was even more surreal was that they actually got along.

On the drive down, Brock told her he used to hike here with his dad and brother, but now his brother was in college and his dad lived in Albany and he only saw him twice a month. That was the kind of stuff they talked about. Mia told him about growing apart from Sophie and how her parents were workaholics and how she was obsessed with college applications.

"I can't believe this," Mia said when they came up for air. She was pointing to the waterfall, but really she was talking about today. This kiss. The whole thing.

Mia touched her tingly lips. Brock's mouth was warm and soft and inviting.

"I know," Brock said.

He pressed his hand against her back and pulled her close to him.

"You seem different than the other girls at Hankinson," he said the next time they broke for air. "I can really talk to you. It's not all shallow stuff."

Mia's hair was soaking and her jeans were so waterlogged, she could barely bend her legs. The rain wasn't bothering her though. She couldn't believe it was fourth period at school right now.

"You're also hot, by the way. I've been seeing you around." Brock grinned at Mia. "Don't get me wrong. This isn't all about talking."

Mia stroked Brock's cheek, pausing at his dimple.

On the hike back, Brock dragged a stick in one hand. He seemed quieter now, deep in thought. "Do you think people can reinvent themselves?"

"What do you mean?" Mia asked.

"I've been the same person for so long. It's getting old."

"I think you can. I think anyone can decide who they want to be and then go for it."

Brock chucked his stick down the gorge. "Maybe you can change in college. But I don't think so. You are who you are."

"Did you know I had purple hair last year?" Mia asked. "Green, too."

"For real?" Brock squinted at her long blond hair. "I can't even picture that."

"I'm just saying, you can change anytime you want."

When they got back to the car, they turned on the heat. Mia peeled off her wet hoodie and curled into Brock's arms. Brock slipped his hand up her shirt and unhooked her bra. Mia let him touch her breasts and even pull up her shirt to get a look at them.

"Awesome," he said before going in for another feel.

But once they started driving, Brock checked his phone and then didn't say much. Mia didn't say much either. It was almost like they were preparing for reentry into Hankinson, where Brock Sawyer and Mia Flint didn't make out at a waterfall in the rain. But Mia was okay with that because today *did* happen and no one could take it away from her.

WHITNEY

——————

AT FIRST THEY thought Laurel had sun poisoning or had eaten bad sushi on Duval Street, but then she admitted that her period was really late. It was their third day in Key West, and Whitney was counting the hours until the end of the trip. It had been a mistake to come along. At least Kyra's uncle was at work most of the time. As soon as they'd arrived at his condo, Kyra told him that Whitney thought his son, Lucas, was a dick. Ever since then he'd been icy cold to her.

"Puking and a late period," Kyra said to Autumn. Laurel had just gone into the bathroom to throw up for the second time. Whitney was flipping through *Entertainment Weekly* on the couch. There was a picture of Zoe's mom doing publicity for her new movie, set in Paris. "She's totally pregnant."

Autumn nodded. "She was being such an idiot with Russell, like it couldn't happen to her. With Zach, I went on the pill right away."

Whitney still didn't like hearing about Autumn having sex with Zach. Not that she wanted him back, but it felt icky.

"But Laurel hasn't done it yet," Whitney said, closing the magazine. Laurel had been going out with this older guy, Russell, but she always said she was going to wait until college. Even a few months ago they'd joked about how they were the last women standing.

"Apparently, she has," Kyra said, laughing. "How else do you get pregnant, Whit?"

"La?" Autumn called out. "You okay?"

Laurel moaned. As Autumn and Kyra clambered into the bathroom, Whitney went into the guest bedroom and lay on the rumpled comforter.

"Whit?" Autumn called in a few minutes later. "We're going to buy a pregnancy test! You coming?"

Whitney bit her lip. "I'm going to hang out here."

"Come on," Kyra said. "How many times in your life do you get to buy a pregnancy test?"

"That's okay," Whitney said.

"Whatever," Kyra said.

Seconds later the door to the condo slammed shut.

JAKE

ON THE LAST day of spring break Jake was doing sit-ups when he got a text from Ted.

Wanna chill?

Sure, Jake wrote back. *Where?*

My house. No one's home.

Jake flew into the shower. He shaved and put on new boxers and faded shorts that looked good but not like he was trying too hard. Ever since they'd driven to the SATs, he and Ted had been texting and talking at school. But so far they hadn't hung out.

Jake hopped on his mountain bike and started toward Ted's. It was a Sunday at two in the afternoon. He was sixteen and ten months. The sky was blue and the daffodils were butter yellow and he felt so much incredible promise awaiting him at that exact moment.

"What's up?" Ted asked as he opened the front door. "You can just leave your bike in the garage. It's open."

"Cool," Jake said, grinning. Ted smiled too. His hair was wet and his cheeks were chafed. He must have just shaved too.

"Want to go downstairs?" Ted asked after Jake rolled his bike into the garage.

Jake followed Ted through the kitchen to the basement stairs. The stairs seemed smaller than the last time he'd been there, over three years ago. He had to duck his head to clear the ceiling.

"It's exactly the same," Jake said as he eyed the brown shag carpet and the denim beanbag and the TV with the old Wii hooked up.

Ted reached into the mini-fridge and handed him a beer. It was a Heineken, just like back in middle school.

"I know," Ted said, popping a beer for himself. "Time warp."

"How's your tolerance now?"

"Not bad. You?"

"Not bad either. Better than eighth grade."

They tapped their bottles together. Ted seemed nervous the way he was perched on the edge of the couch. Jake wiped some sweat off his forehead and leaned back in the beanbag. Did Ted used to bring Marin to the basement, or that boyfriend from last fall? He couldn't picture it. This felt like his place with Ted, like no one else had ever been here.

"Want to play Wii?" Ted asked.

Jake shook his head. "I'm okay just hanging out."

"That's cool."

They both sipped their beers. Maybe Jake should have said yes to Wii. Things were feeling a little too quiet.

"Okay, screw it," Ted said. He set his can on the coffee table and slid onto the beanbag.

Jake reached for Ted's hand. They weaved their fingers together and then pressed their mouths against each other. Jake had kissed a few other guys, but he knew instantly that this was different. This was intense.

"Wow," Ted said.

"I know," Jake said.

Their cheeks were close and they were still holding hands, neither of them wanting to let go. Jake could smell Ted's breath, tangy from the beer. All he could think about was kissing him again.

"I don't know how to say this," Ted said, "but I'm sorry for being such a dick. You knew and I didn't. I didn't know for a while. That must have been shitty."

"That's okay," Jake said. "We're here now."

Ted pulled Jake's shirt off and then wriggled his own over his head. Jake touched Ted's chest, muscular with a coat of golden hair. Damn, he'd wanted to do that for so long.

"Can I admit something?" Ted asked.

"Sure," Jake said. He didn't know where this was headed.

"I knew you had to make up the SATs too," Ted said. "I overheard you telling someone in the cafeteria. That's why I told Mr. Fritz I needed to ride with you."

"You really didn't need a ride?" Jake asked. He'd had no idea! On the way to the SATs, Ted even said how both his parents were using their cars.

"I guess I lied," Ted said. "Maybe I could have gotten a car. But that wouldn't have changed the fact that I *needed* a ride with *you*."

They leaned in for another kiss. As soon as their bodies touched, skin on skin, their hands were flying all over the place. They unzipped their jeans and reached into each other's boxers.

"It was a white lie," Ted whispered a few minutes later.

They were lying in a wilted heap on the beanbag, their arms around each other.

"Cool," Jake managed to say, and then he fell asleep.

MAY

ZOE

AFTER MONTHS OF lusting after Dinky, Zoe couldn't believe
it when he walked into Bean right before the end of her shift. It was
the Sunday of Memorial Day weekend, and the place was empty.
Her boss, Keni—not Kenny, it turned out—was in the back. Zoe
was arranging blueberry scones on a platter. She happened to be
wearing a low-cut tank top and a push-up bra. Sometimes life was
awesome that way.

Keni was a lesbian anarchist with a deep voice and a mega Afro.
The best thing was that, at the interview, she told Zoe, "I don't give
a fuck about the Sierra Laybourne thing. I don't even watch main-
stream movies." Zoe had been working at Bean for three months
now.

"What's up?" Dinky said, approaching the counter. "You're Zoe
from American studies."

"I am." Zoe smiled. There was something so sexy about Dinky's
slow speech, his broad shoulders. "Can I get something for you?"

"That's cool," Dinky said. "Whatever."

"You mean you don't want anything?"

Dinky shook his head. Zoe glanced at the back of the café. Keni was still in the supply closet. Sometimes she went in there to sneak cigarettes and text with her girlfriend.

"I wanted to see if you can hang out," Dinky said. He drummed his fingers on the countertop, lifting up the tip jar and putting it down again.

"How did you know I work here?"

"Anna said I should ask you out. I was like, 'Her mom is a movie star, dude. She's probably stuck-up and there's no way she'll say yes,' but Anna said if I asked that you'd say yes."

Zoe's cheeks flushed. She busied herself placing a glass top on the platter of scones and then opening a box of muffins.

"I walked over here." Dinky grabbed a straw and twisted the wrapper at one end. "But you have that sweet Beemer parked out front. If you want, I can try driving your car."

Zoe stared at Dinky. "You want to drive my car?"

"No," Dinky said, shrugging. "I'm just nervous. I'm messing this up." He blew into the straw, shooting the wrapper onto the countertop. "I should probably depart."

"Yes."

"Yes, depart?" Dinky brushed his brownish hair out of his eyes.

Zoe had an urge to trim his bangs. "Yes, I'll hang out," she said quickly. "Yes, you can drive my car. I don't care. I finish in ten minutes."

Dinky grinned. His front teeth overlapped slightly. "Dude, you're not a bitch. Awesome."

Zoe smiled back. She liked the way Dinky said whatever he wanted. It was the opposite of her, and in a good way.

JUNE

GREGOR

"COME IN," GREGOR said when he heard a knock on his door. He'd already shaved, and was just slipping an EpiPen in his backpack. Even though the ceremony was inside, he always carried an injection just in case.

Erica pushed the door open. She was wearing her cap and gown, her red hair hanging down her back. It was weird seeing Erica dressed for graduation. It made it so much more real that she was leaving for the University of Maryland in a few months. Ever since she'd quit smoking and started running again, she seemed much better. She and their mom were still arguing, but it wasn't as bad. Back over the winter Gregor was surprised neighbors weren't calling 911 on them.

"Mom just left to get Nana Margaret," she said. "She'll be back for us in a few minutes. I haven't been in your room in forever. You still have that thing from Dad on your mirror?"

Gregor glanced at the Post-it that his dad had stuck on his mirror last summer, right before he'd died. It said, *Stay true to yourself.* A few weeks ago the sticky finally gave out and the note had fluttered to the floor. Gregor pressed it back into place with a curl of Scotch tape.

"Yeah," Gregor said quietly. He was thinking about how his dad would never get to see Erica in her cap and gown. Gregor had stopped meeting with Jude a few weeks ago. They'd both decided he was done with therapy. Even so, it didn't mean the sadness wouldn't hit now and then.

"So this is random." Erica plopped on Gregor's bed and pressed her thumbnail into a mosquito bite on her knee.

"What's random?" Gregor checked out the tattoo of a sneaker with wings that she'd gotten on her ankle on her eighteenth birthday. She'd done it to honor their dad, but their mom still flipped out, and they'd had a big argument over that one.

"Were you just looking at my tattoo?" Erica asked.

"Not really."

"Whatever. I guess I don't care."

"I actually like it," Gregor said. "I don't agree with Mom on everything."

"Anyway," Erica said, shaking her head, "this is random, but I wanted to tell you something. You know that time Russell dumped me? Like, two years ago?"

"You were outside the band room," Gregor said, remembering back to the last day of ninth grade.

"I never told you this," Erica said, "but I actually came to the band room to look for you."

"You *did*?"

"I needed to talk to someone I could trust. I just wanted you to know that."

Gregor sat on the bed next to his sister. He was debating whether to hug her. He wanted to, but Erica wasn't the touchy-feely type.

"Now you know," Erica said, standing up. "But don't get all emotional on me. No hugging."

Gregor had to laugh.

Erica was walking to the door when she turned around. "Did you hear he got someone pregnant?"

"Russell?"

"It's a girl in your grade. Laurel. I guess she's due in October. He's such an asshole."

Laurel was blond, jocky, and popular. She was part of Whitney's crowd.

"At least it wasn't you," Gregor said.

Erica shrugged. "I guess there's always a silver lining."

SUMMER AFTER
JUNIOR YEAR

JULY

JAKE

"WHAT TIME DID you say Mona Lisa's getting here?" Brock asked, shading his eyes. The sun was still high even though it was five fifteen.

Jake reached for his phone, which was sitting on the railing of the deck. "Probably around six."

"Da Vinci!" Ted and Brock shouted as they high-fived.

Jake rolled his eyes and looked out at Cayuga Lake. Ted had been to his cabin once before, but it was Brock's first time. Brock was Ted's best friend. They'd driven up together for Jake's seventeenth birthday. Mona Lisa was supposed to join them as soon as her flight landed and her grandparents drove her here.

Jake and Ted had been boyfriends for two months, and they were going strong. They were all drinking Coke and eating cherries, spitting the pits over the cliff. The sun was casting a glittering path of gold on the water. Ted and Brock were wearing swimsuits, their chests bare and tan. They were talking about football. Every now and then, Ted touched Jake's leg, sending warmth through his entire body. Even Brock didn't seem so bad right now. Jake had never been crazy about Brock. He was one of those loud popular guys. But he was Ted's friend, so Jake was putting up with him.

Plus, the setup would be awesome if it worked.

Mona Lisa was going to text when she got to her grandparents' cabin down the road. Jake and Ted wanted Mona Lisa and Brock to hit it off. For one, they were both straight. For two, it would solve the friend-boyfriend problem. Ever since Jake had texted Mona Lisa about being together with Ted, she'd barely written him back anymore. Jake figured she was jealous, and Brock would be the perfect solution. Girls loved Brock. Also, if Mona Lisa and Brock became a couple, then maybe Jake's parents would let them all go camping in the woods and it wouldn't be so obvious that he and Ted wanted to spend the night together. Which they *really* wanted to do.

Did you land yet? Jake finally wrote to Mona Lisa. *I thought I'd hear from you by now.*

Yep, she wrote.

Yep what? Where are you?

We're driving to the lake now.

"She's on her way," he told Ted and Brock.

"Da Vinci!" Ted said, and Brock laughed.

Jake scratched at some paint stuck to his arm. "Remember not to call her that. She was named after the Mona Lisa, but she doesn't need to be reminded of it all the time."

"She's definitely cute?" Brock asked.

"Yeah, she's cute," Jake said. Mona Lisa had long curly hair and big boobs. Guys were always checking her out.

"But more important," Ted said, "can she keep up with my man? The Brockman has some moves, you know."

Brock nodded and swigged his Coke.

Jake shook his head. Sometimes he couldn't stand being around Ted when he was with his friends. It's like he was one person when they were alone. He was sweet, sensitive, and funny. And then with his buddies he turned into an alpha dude.

Ted and Brock are here, Jake wrote to Mona Lisa. *Come on over for hot dogs and b-day cake.*

Mona Lisa didn't text back. Finally, after five minutes, his phone pinged.

Just so you know, she wrote. *I didn't say yes to this setup when you asked me before. I said I'd think about it. I'm actually not sure I want to.*

But they're here, Jake wrote. *Brock is right HERE.*

Jake squinted at his phone. This was definitely not like Mona Lisa. She was always hooking up with random guys.

So you're not coming over? Jake texted.

Remember what I said last summer? I said I can't deal with you having a boyfriend. I know I sound heartless, but I'm going to bail tonight.

"I've got to take a piss." Brock stood up and crossed the porch.

As soon as he was inside, Ted leaned over for a kiss, but Jake pulled away.

"What's wrong?" Ted asked, shading his eyes with his palm.

"Mona Lisa was texting. She doesn't want to meet Brock."

Ted clapped his hands and started laughing.

"What?" Jake asked, confused. Just minutes ago everything was falling into place. Now it was falling apart. Not to mention that after years of listening to Mona Lisa blabber about her boyfriends, Jake couldn't believe she wouldn't even come over to meet his. It felt as if he was losing his oldest friend right before his eyes, like she was making him pick friendship or relationship.

"Sorry," Ted said. "It's just awesome that a girl is saying no to Brock. His ego needs some bruising."

Ted popped a cherry in his mouth. He spit the pit toward the railing, but it toppled onto his foot.

"See how far you can get a pit," Ted said, gesturing to the bowl. "It's going to be easy to beat me."

This was what Jake loved about Ted. He yanked him back from the abyss. Jake set down his phone and picked two cherries. He chewed around the pits and then blasted them out of his mouth while Ted cheered him on.

WHITNEY

———

THE CHEERLEADING EXTRAS were onscreen for about two minutes throughout the entire movie. But whenever they came on, everyone in the audience screamed. Whitney and a bunch of other people were at a private screening of *This Is My Life*. It was over at Downing College, where Whitney's dad was a professor. People were saying the movie was never going to make it to theaters. This was their chance to see it before it died forever.

"You look hot up there," Lucas whispered in her ear. He flicked his tongue around a bit. "I'd do you."

Whitney wriggled away from Lucas and wiped the spit off her earlobe. She was honestly surprised by how pretty she looked shaking those pom-poms. That was only a year ago, and yet it felt like she was watching someone *else* with mocha skin and a wide smile, someone who had all the answers. And there was Autumn cheering alongside her. That was back when Autumn's hair was long. Back when they were still best friends.

"Anytime you want to," Lucas said, running his hand across Whitney's leg, "you know where to find me."

Whitney pushed his hand off her leg. *God!* Why did Kyra's

cousin have to come over and sit with her? She couldn't believe she was ever with him.

When the lights came on, Lucas slugged her arm. "I've got to split. Work."

As soon as he was gone, she saw Autumn and Zach making their way to the exit. Laurel was lumbering behind them. Six months pregnant, she was wearing a loose sundress and her blond hair was pulled into pigtails. Whitney had a quick image of summer soccer with Laurel before ninth grade, racing around the field in their brand-new cleats.

"Hey, Whit," Autumn said, waving. "You didn't tell me you were coming."

"You didn't ask," Whitney said. She didn't mean to sound frosty, but that was how it came out.

Autumn raised her eyebrows at Zach.

"What's up?" Zach asked.

Whitney shrugged. "What'd you guys think of the movie?"

"It was sort of dumb," Autumn said. "But it was cool to see us all up there. You looked great. It's annoying how great you always look."

Whitney wasn't sure how to take that. "You looked good too," she said.

Autumn rolled her eyes. "Yeah, if you ignore my huge honker."

Laurel sighed heavily and shifted from one leg to the other.

"How're you feeling?" Whitney asked.

Laurel stretched her hands over her swollen belly. "Huge."

"I heard it's a boy."

"Yep."

The screening room was stuffy and hot. Whitney fanned her cheeks.

"What are you up to now?" Autumn asked.

"I have to pack," Whitney said. "I'm leaving for NYU tomorrow. Summer theater program."

"Oh yeah," Autumn said. "I forgot. Have fun. Don't forget to text."

They all walked toward the exit together.

"We're voting on baby names," Laurel said as they reached the parking lot behind the film center. "Hunter or Aidan?"

"What has more votes so far?" Whitney asked.

"Hunter. Definitely."

Whitney clicked the key to unlock her dad's car. "I'll go with Aidan."

GREGOR

EXACTLY A YEAR after his dad died, Gregor's grandmother was going into a nursing home. Ever since Nana Margaret had broken her other hip last fall, things had gone downhill. She was forgetting to drink water and getting dehydrated, and she barely knew who they were most days. Even though Nana Margaret was his dad's mother, his dad had been an only child. That was why Gregor's mom was handling the details. What Gregor kept hearing her tell people was, "We're waiting for a bed to open up for Margaret."

A bed. That killed Gregor. All he could think was how you spend your life filling the rooms of your house, opening and closing your pool, expanding your world. And then, in the end, you're reduced to a bed.

In early August a bed opened in room twenty-seven of the Cedar Hill Center. A few years ago, back when Gregor's family could laugh about sad things, they'd driven by Cedar Hill and joked about how depressing places always have a tree (pine, cedar, oak) and a natural location (hill, grove, valley) in their name.

They'd gotten the call from the nursing home director on a Monday. On a sunny Thursday morning Gregor's mom, Erica, and

Gregor drove Nana Margaret to Cedar Hill. In the trunk they had two suitcases, sheets, a humidifier, and a copy of *The Joy of Cooking*, which was tragic because Nana Margaret insisted on taking it yet she wasn't ever going to have a kitchen again. In Gregor's lap he was holding a box with framed pictures of Gregor's dad when he was little, and of Gregor and his parents and sister. Whenever Gregor looked at the photo of the four of them on their deck the summer before he started high school, his throat squeezed tight.

Nana Margaret was in the backseat next to Erica. She was humming "Hey Jude" by the Beatles. Gregor thought about the therapist he'd seen for most of junior year. He tried to figure out what Jude would say about today. She'd probably say, *It's terrible, but there's no way around it. The only way out is through.*

They pulled into the parking lot of Cedar Hill. Gregor, his mom, and Erica climbed out. Nana Margaret was still in the car. It almost looked like she was smiling.

"This is too much," Erica said to their mom. Her face was pinched like she was going to cry.

"Want to wait in the car?" Gregor's mom asked. "It'll be a while."

"I'm just going to run home," Erica said. "I have my phone."

Erica stretched her hamstrings and then took off onto the road. Sometimes Gregor hated the way Erica did whatever she felt like without caring how it affected other people. It wasn't like he *wanted* to be here, but he wasn't going to leave his mom alone.

"I'll take Nana Margaret to registration," Gregor's mom said, helping his grandmother into a wheelchair. "Can you go ahead of us and make her bed? I think that'll help her feel more settled when she sees her room."

Gregor lifted up the plastic crate with the sheets. That was when he almost lost it. Inside the container he could see her faded floral comforter. He thought about all those times that he, Erica, and Nana Margaret had snuggled in her bed under *this* blanket, watching movies and eating popcorn. Like it would go on forever. Like it would never end.

Forty-five minutes later they kissed Nana Margaret good-bye.

"Give my love to Charlie," she said, smiling at them with her milky brown eyes.

Charlie was his *dad*. Gregor looked questioningly at his mom, but she took his elbow and squeezed it.

"It's harder for us than for her," she said as they buckled their seat belts and pulled away from Cedar Hill.

Gregor wiped back a few tears. "How do we know?"

"I guess we don't for sure. I just think so."

Neither of them said anything. His mom was dabbing her eyes as she drove.

"We need corn," she said, pulling into a farm stand on the outskirts of Hankinson.

Gregor nodded. The farm stand was in a valley full of maple trees. Nearby there was probably a hill with cedars.

"Why don't we ever call things what they are?" he asked as his mom shifted into park.

"What do you mean?"

"There weren't any cedar trees at Cedar Hill. Or hills. It should just be called The End."

They shucked six ears of corn, and then they grabbed cucumbers and fuzzy warm peaches, a muddy bunch of carrots, even cilantro. They loaded two baskets so full, they had to balance the blueberries on their arms.

"It's not the end," Gregor's mom said as they set their fresh produce across the backseat where Nana Margaret had been an hour ago. "It's life. Life goes on."

Gregor didn't say anything. There was nothing left to say.

AUGUST

ZOE

ZOE PUSHED BACK her sheets. Even though it was midnight, she was craving sour cherries. She and Aunt Jane bought two pounds of them at the farmer's market in Santa Monica, and they were going to bake a pie tomorrow. Aunt Jane was out here for the opening of her mom's movie, an independent film with a summer release. It was the one she'd shot in France. *Sierra* had actually invited Aunt Jane out. Hopefully, that meant they were finally getting along.

As she started down the stairs, Zoe heard them talking in the kitchen.

"Tell her *what*, Janie?" Sierra asked. Her voice was high and fast. "You haven't said anything, have you?"

Zoe sat down on a step and hugged her knees.

"Has she been asking?" Aunt Jane said.

When her mom didn't respond, Aunt Jane said, "Has she?"

Zoe bit down on her bare knee. So much for the sour cherries. She should turn around and get back into bed, maybe wake up Dinky with a middle-of-the-night text. She wished Aunt Jane would stop pushing her mom. Her mom was stressed enough already with her movie coming out. She'd been to five AA meetings in the past three days. Every time Zoe walked by her mom's bedroom, she was worried she'd find her crying in there.

"This is about you and me still, isn't it?" her mom finally asked.

"No, it's about Zoe. That's what this has always been about."

Then again, if they were in any way discussing her father, she deserved to know. She hurried down the stairs and walked into the kitchen. They'd been sitting at the counter, drinking tea. As soon as they saw Zoe, their faces paled and Aunt Jane jumped to her feet.

"Are you talking about my biological father?" Zoe asked.

Aunt Jane looked at Sierra. Her mom reached for her tea but accidentally knocked the mug onto the granite floor. It broke instantly, shards of ceramic spraying everywhere.

As Sierra knelt down and began sweeping together the fragments, Aunt Jane stared hard at Zoe. She knew something. Zoe swore she did. But instead of anyone explaining anything, the two sisters began cleaning the mess while Zoe turned around and went back to bed.

MIA

MIA SPOTTED WHITNEY Montaine in the pharmacy line at PriceRite. First she saw her braids, and then her model-gorgeous profile. Mia was picking up a prescription for her mom, plus mascara for herself. Also she'd tossed some Manic Panic in her basket. Maybe she'd put a few pink streaks back in. Nothing major. She didn't want to look too out there for college interviews.

Whitney was ahead of Mia in line. A year ago Mia would have split, come back later. But with senior year starting tomorrow, Mia didn't want to be terrified of popular people anymore. She wanted that to be over.

Whitney glanced backward. "Hey, Mia!" she said, waving with her fingers. "What's up?"

Mia tried to remember to breathe. "I'm picking something up for my mom."

"Me too." Whitney hesitated. "So, how was your summer?"

"Okay . . . what about you?"

"Pretty cool. I just got back from New York City. I did a summer theater program at NYU."

"Is that where you want to go?" Mia asked. She was dying to

know who was applying where, how many essays, *U.S. News and World Report* ranking. Sophie called it Mia's college porn. Maybe it was a joke for Sophie, but for Mia this was her chance to escape. Three years ago, at freshman orientation, Whitney had written in her letter that she wanted to escape too. Mia wondered if that was still true.

"If I get into NYU," Whitney said, laughing. "It's crazy competitive. What about you?"

"Swarthmore. I'm going to apply early decision."

"Wow," Whitney said. "I've heard Swarthmore's as hard to get into as—"

"Harvard," Mia said, finishing her sentence.

"Whitney Montaine?" the pharmacist called out. "Your medication is ready."

Whitney pressed her lips together. As she approached the counter, the pharmacist handed Whitney a white paper bag and asked if she had any questions. Mia pretended to be engrossed in her phone, but she was straining to listen. Whitney had said she was picking up something for her *mom*, but it seemed like this medicine was for her. It was strange to think how even people like Whitney had things to hide.

"See you around, Mia!" Whitney waved as she walked by. She smiled broadly, her usual perky self. "Good luck with applications."

"You too," Mia said. She'd give anything to read what Whitney was going to write in her college essays.

SENIOR YEAR

SEPTEMBER

JAKE

Ted: So . . . we need to chill.

Jake: Chill where?

Ted: No, us. Chill. I want to experience senior year as a single guy.

Jake: Hang on. Are you breaking up with me over TEXT?

Ted: I'm sorry. I would start cyring in person.

Jake: Cyring?

Ted: You're my editor now?

Jake: I can't believe it. We're happy, right?

Ted: You're happy.

Jake: You're not?

Ted: I need to chill on the boyfriend thing fro now.

WHITNEY

"DON'T YOU FIND it strange that you've only been with white guys?" Alicia asked.

They were sitting on the striped Ikea rug in Alicia's dorm room, waiting for their toenails to dry. Whitney pressed a ripple of maroon polish with her thumb. She never should have come to Oberlin to visit Alicia. When her mom proposed the idea of flying to Ohio by herself for Columbus Day weekend, it sounded cool. But she forgot that she and her sister couldn't stand each other. It was only the first night, and she already wanted to scream.

Whitney thought of Gus and Zach and Lucas and a few others. All white, but it wasn't like she was keeping track. "I've been with whoever I want," she said sharply.

"But you've never been with a black guy. Admit it."

Whitney chucked a cotton ball at Alicia. Just because her sister was suddenly hardcore about being black, why did she have to drag Whitney into it? When Whitney had driven to Oberlin last spring with her dad, she'd met a bunch of her sister's college friends. They were African American, biracial, white, Indian, Asian. But from the second she arrived today, it was a different story. All Alicia's friends were black. She was only listening to music by African Americans. She had pictures on her wall of Kanye and Nelson Mandela and posters of Basquiat graffiti.

"Your silence is saying it all," Alicia said.

"All I'm thinking is that I don't have to tell you who I've been with."

"You've said enough." Alicia reached into the mini-fridge for a bottle of water.

"Screw you," Whitney said, rolling her eyes. She could hear music thumping in the room next door, and people shouting outside the window. It made her wonder about college and where she'd be next year.

"Also, you could have been nicer to my friends," Alicia said. "You didn't even try to talk to them at dinner. What was up with that?"

The dining hall had been loud and hot, and Whitney had only focused on making it through the pasta bar without losing sight of her sister. Not to mention that Alicia and her friends sat on one side of the dining hall, and the white kids sat in a different area. College was supposed to be liberal, not back to the days of segregation.

"I was fine," Whitney said. She unzipped her duffel to find a cute shirt. Alicia was taking her to a party tonight and maybe even a bar.

Alicia drained the water bottle and tossed it into the recycling bin. "Your problem is that you don't know how to hang around black people. Your little group of friends, Kyra and those girls, they're all white. That's your world."

"What's that supposed to mean? Anyway, Mom is white and

Dad is black, so it's not like we're one or the other. It's not like we have to pick."

"Is that really what you think?" Alicia asked. She was digging through her jewelry box for a nose ring. "Are you really that dumb?"

Whitney pushed up off the rug. She honestly wanted to smack Alicia. "What's your problem?"

"I'm trying to help. You obviously have some identity issues."

Whitney yanked her phone charger out of an outlet. "You know what? I'm out of here."

She packed her SAT math prep book and slid her feet into her Chucks. It was going to ruin her toenail polish, but screw it.

"Where are you going, Whit?" Alicia slammed her jewelry box shut. "Don't be stupid."

"Will you stop calling me stupid?" Whitney asked, choking up. "Will you stop calling me dumb?"

"Will you stop acting like it?"

Whitney didn't even answer. She slung her bag over her shoulder and walked out the door. Tears were streaming down her face.

"You okay?" asked a guy with a long black ponytail. He was sitting cross-legged in the hall, using a spoon to eat hummus out of a container.

"Where's the common room?" Whitney asked him.

He pointed down the hall and then went back to his hummus.

Whitney flopped onto a stained couch and looked up Greyhound times from Cleveland to Hankinson on her phone. She wiped her eyes and blew her nose into a napkin. She felt strangely calm as she called for a car service to the bus station. The website said it was a forty-minute drive, which would be crazy expensive, but her mom had given her emergency money. Maybe it was insane to take a twelve-hour bus ride in the middle of the night when she had a plane ticket for Monday morning. But she was sick of Alicia treating her like there was something wrong with her. Not that she even hung around Kyra and Laurel and Autumn anymore. Not that Alicia had cared to ask.

"You're too pretty to be on a Greyhound bus," the guy next to Whitney said. It was past eleven, and they were zooming through eastern Ohio.

He didn't say it in a creepy way. Whitney had been watching him, too. He was maybe eighty, a grandfather type. He'd spent the first twenty minutes of the bus ride carefully peeling the tin foil off a picnic his wife must have packed for him, sampling each item before wrapping everything up again. Then he dug out an ancient flip phone and called to tell someone he was going to sleep.

"I just need to get home," she said.

The man was white with thick gray hair and a small dollop of a nose. Whitney imagined him coming from a large Irish family. He'd married young and worked hard, like, as a carpenter, and he and his wife had raised four boys. They'd gone to church on Sundays and bowling on Mondays, and now they had ten grandchildren. Whitney guessed he was on his way to visit his first great-grandchild, who was born two months ago.

"Who made you that picnic?" she asked the guy after a few minutes.

He looked startled. He must have been dozing off. "What picnic?"

"The food you were eating before."

"Oh," he said. "I made it myself."

"Your wife didn't?"

"I was never married."

Whitney felt a stab of sadness for those four strapping sons and the ten grandchildren who never existed. "Then who did you call before?"

The man cleared his throat. "A social worker who checks in on me. I'm visiting my brother. He had a stroke. They're not sure he'll make it through the weekend." Then he switched off his overhead light and closed his eyes.

OCTOBER

ZOE

"CAN YOU LOVEBIRDS go get a hot glue gun from the art room?" Nadine asked.

"Ugh," Zoe grumbled.

"Which part do you have a problem with?" Dinky stretched his arm around Zoe and tickled her waist. "The *love* part or the *bird* part?"

"Or the hot glue gun part?" Anna said, giggling.

Zoe scowled at Anna. "Don't make this worse."

When Dinky had asked Zoe to work on the senior class homecoming float, she'd said no. She wasn't into the high school spirit thing. But then Anna signed up, so Zoe was tagging along. The theme was "Outta Here in Outta Space," and it was a low-key group. Dinky's friend Gregor was there, and this girl Nadine who had a crush on Gregor. Everyone knew it except Gregor, which was kind of funny.

"I like hot," Dinky said, squeezing Zoe's butt.

Zoe yelped and jumped out of the way.

"Glue gun," Nadine said, rolling her eyes. "*Hot glue gun.* We need one. Jake . . . You know, Jake Rodriguez? He painted us a bunch of meteors that we have to glue on tonight."

"He's the senior class president," Anna whispered to Zoe.

Zoe nodded. She had no idea who he was. It was lame how she still didn't have anyone in Hankinson figured out.

"Okay, boss," Dinky said. "We're on it." He grabbed Zoe's hand and tugged her down the dark hall.

As soon as they were out of sight, Dinky pressed Zoe against some lockers. Zoe ran her fingers through Dinky's hair, and they started making out. After a while he guided her hand down to his shorts, but she pulled away. There were still janitors mopping the halls. She didn't feel like getting busted.

In so many ways Dinky was the perfect boyfriend. He was funny and cute, and he didn't push Zoe to be a twenty-four-seven girlfriend. Zoe never wanted to be the kind of girl who texted with her boyfriend every time she left the house, every time she poured herself a glass of juice. Actually, that would be impossible with Dinky. He had a bit of ADHD, and he was always losing his phone or forgetting to charge it. Often he wouldn't even get her texts until the next day.

All that said, Zoe was having a tough time being with Dinky right now. She was moody this fall. She was snapping at the important people in her life. Aunt Jane and Anna, but Dinky was getting the worst of it.

Dinky squeezed Zoe's hand and then leaned in to her. She could feel him, hard against her thigh. "We could get out of here," he whispered into her ear. "I don't think my parents are home tonight."

"No, we should get the glue gun," Zoe said, wriggling away.

He moved in for another kiss. "Just another minute . . ."

"Down, boy." Zoe wiped off her mouth. "Take a cold shower."

Dinky shrugged and started down the hall, shaking his head. She'd hurt him. *Fuck.* This was how it had been since she'd gotten back from California, a sour mood that she couldn't seem to shake.

MIA

Mia,

Do you remember me from IMLI two summers ago? I was the guy from Kansas. Just wanted to say hey and see where you're applying.

Jeremiah

Jeremiah,

Hey there! I can't believe you remember me. I've changed a lot since California. Or maybe I was possessed that summer and now I'm back to my regular self. Okay, shut up, Mia. MIA is in JereMIAh. See, I remember you! You had blue hair and vintage shirts. I'm applying to Swarthmore early decision. The fall option. What about you?

Mia

Mia,

Swarthmore, early decision. Fall option.

Jeremiah

PS My hair is now regular brown.

Jeremiah,

No way!!!

(About Swarthmore, not your newly brown hair.)

Mia

PS My hair is now partially pink.

Mia,

I can't picture you with pink hair! I toured Swarthmore last month and loved it. I'm writing my essay about growing up a dorky punk-music-loving guy on a farm in Kansas. Either that, or about the (formerly blond) girl I met one summer in California and how I was too chicken to tell her my feelings.

Jeremiah

GREGOR

—————

TWENTY MINUTES INTO senior lit, a bunch of girls started whispering and checking their phones. Gregor looked around, trying to figure out what was going on. Ms. Hewitt had stepped out for a few minutes, and they were supposed to be reading a chapter from *The Namesake*.

"Did you hear?" asked the girl behind him. Her name was Kyra. Her dad was the principal, and she was always at the center of the girl dramas.

"Hear what?" Gregor asked.

"Laurel went into labor!" She shoved her tablet in her purse. "That's my best friend. I'm out of here!"

As soon as Kyra left, two other girls dashed after her. Laurel was the one who Russell had gotten pregnant. Good old Russell. Back in September, Gregor had seen Laurel wobbling down the hall in her stretchy maternity top, and he thought about what he'd said to his sister. *At least it wasn't you.*

"Do you know what she's naming the baby?" a voice whispered behind him.

Gregor whipped his head around. Whitney had moved into

Kyra's desk. She usually sat over by the window.

"No . . . what?" Gregor asked.

"Hunter."

"No way."

"I know," Whitney said. "I don't want to be negative . . ."

Gregor grinned. "But who names a kid Hunter?"

"Exactly." Whitney nodded. "Like, is he going to hunt?"

"It's like naming him Gatherer."

Whitney giggled. "Or Fisherman."

"Exactly."

Gregor and Whitney smiled at each other, and there it was, this sudden flash of understanding. They *got* each other. Gregor felt something in his stomach, something low and deep and surprisingly happy. All those years when he was lusting after Whitney, he never realized that he might simply *like* her as well.

NOVEMBER

ZOE

"FUCK," ZOE SAID, dropping her phone on the kitchen counter.

"Zoe! I really don't think that's—" Aunt Jane froze when she saw Zoe's face. "What? What happened?"

"My mom's doing it again," Zoe said, her voice flat. "You know, drinking. Like she was a few years ago."

It was the Monday before Thanksgiving, and the house was sweet with stewing pumpkins. Aunt Jane had a smudge of flour on her cheek.

"Are you sure?" she asked.

Zoe nodded. She didn't feel like crying. She barely felt much. Two days ago she'd broken up with Dinky. She said they should stay friends, but now he wasn't talking to her. Anna was pissed at her for hurting Dinky, especially since Zoe couldn't even explain why she dumped him. How could she say that she was upset about what she'd overheard between Aunt Jane and her mom that night in California? She didn't even know what they'd been talking about or why it was making her so monumentally upset. Whatever it was, though, it made her not want anything happy or good in her life right now.

"Should I call Max?" Aunt Jane asked.

"He already knows. He was in the background, trying to get my mom off the phone."

Aunt Jane sank into a chair and massaged her temples with her thumbs. She was going gray around her part. "What about Al-Anon? I know you stopped going, but I'm sure we can find you a meeting tonight. Maybe Anna will go with you?"

Zoe shook her head. She hadn't been to Al-Anon in two years. She'd thought that was over. "I'm going up to my room."

"Can you at least call Anna?"

Zoe pointed to the stove. "Your pumpkins need more water. They've stopped steaming."

As Aunt Jane hurried to the sink, Zoe walked slowly up the stairs.

DECEMBER

WHITNEY

WHITNEY COULDN'T BELIEVE the stuff that was coming up in therapy. After she and Alicia had that fight and then she'd run away from Oberlin, her mom had suggested she talk to someone. Her mom found Jude, and so far she was exactly what Whitney needed.

Every Monday afternoon, now that soccer was over, she hopped in the spare car and drove to Darien Coffee Company. She'd buy tea and then go to Jude's office, which was in a tall brick building along the canal.

It was freezing cold today, a few weeks before Christmas. Whitney got a cup of chai with steamed milk. As she walked toward Jude's, she ran her free hand up and down her thighs. She was wearing thick corduroys and tall boots, but her legs still felt like blocks of ice.

"You said you wanted to talk about death?" Jude asked. It was the beginning of the session. At the end of last Monday's appointment, Whitney had dropped *that* bomb just as she was walking out the door.

Whitney liked how Jude always remembered her stories. Jude

was probably fifty, and she was also biracial, black and white. Whitney liked that, too. There was so much she didn't have to explain about having a black parent and a white parent, about being neither and both. In one of their first sessions, she told her how her sister said Whitney didn't know how to be black. Jude said that there wasn't necessarily *one* way to be black. Also, she reassured Whitney that no one expected her to be fully cooked about racial identity at seventeen, especially since she'd grown up in a mostly white community. As Jude talked, Whitney found herself nodding constantly.

"It's just—" Whitney paused. Her mouth felt dry, so she reached for her chai. "I never really talk about this, but when I was in ninth grade, there was a car accident at the end of my driveway. It was on New Year's Eve, and I was in my dad's car with Kyra and Laurel. We didn't know Autumn yet."

"Was that when your dad lived in the house?"

Whitney nodded. "It was right after my parents split up. It was a head-on collision. Sometimes I still think about how Kyra and Laurel and I were all holding hands and crying. I thought we'd be close forever."

Jude nodded. She knew Whitney didn't hang out with them anymore. They talked about that a lot.

"The guy died," Whitney said, swallowing back tears. "The driver of one of the cars. His name was James. He was a junior."

Jude gestured toward the tissues. "Did you know him?"

"Alicia did, a little. She went to the memorial. Everyone did. It was the thing to do."

Jude sipped her water. She always had a glass on the table next to her. "Did you go?"

"No, that's what I'm saying." Whitney crossed her legs and uncrossed them again. "Anything having to do with death terrifies me. There's this guy at school, Gregor. His dad died a few summers ago, and here's how lame I am. I couldn't even tell him I was sorry."

Jude took another sip of water. "You said his name was Gregor?"

"Yeah. Gregor." Whitney wiped her nose with her hand. "It's horrible, right? I feel so horrible about myself."

"Well, that's why you're here. It's normal to be scared of death. Let's talk more about why you feel so bad about yourself."

Whitney exhaled slowly. She'd never had someone ask her so many questions, or listen to what she had to say. She'd never talked about herself for so long. She'd never had so much hope that things could be better.

JAKE

_____

JAKE CLUTCHED HIS plastic cup of Sprite and looked around the crowded gallery. He was combusting in his button-down shirt. Why hadn't he just worn a T-shirt? *Smile.* Why did he have to smile? His face was exhausted.

Allegra skipped over and put her arm around him. "Hey, sweaty boy," she said. "Your painting is amazing. You deserved the prize."

"Thanks." Jake tried not to jerk away. He and Allegra were in art together again, but he was careful to keep his distance. He was keeping his distance with everyone. Mona Lisa had recently texted him for the first time in months, and he hadn't even written back. "Yours was great too."

"Yeah, well." Allegra adjusted her bra and then dug around in her purse. "It's not like I was quoting *Peter Pan*. The literary thing scored you points."

"Not *Peter Pan*," Jake said. "*Winnie-the-Pooh*."

"That's what I meant." Allegra slid on red lipstick and then bounced over to the refreshment table.

Jake studied his canvas. He'd painted it last winter in art class. It was supposed to be a self-portrait, but one afternoon he was in the library when he saw a Winnie-the-Pooh poster that said, "You're braver than you believe, and stronger than you seem, and smarter than you think." The next day in art he'd scrawled *You're braver than you believe* in black letters across his portrait.

Last spring Ted had come by the art room and seen the painting. He thought it was crazy good and told Jake to send in a photo to the Anacorte Emerging Artists contest. The winners would receive a cash prize. Also, the winning paintings would be part of a month-long show at the Anacorte Gallery in Darien Shoppes.

That had been back in June. In September the Anacorte Gallery contacted Jake to arrange a viewing of the actual painting. Ted had just broken up with him. Jake barely even remembered putting them in touch with his art teacher. And then Jake had gotten the news two weeks ago that he was the grand-prize winner. His painting would be featured at the show. A couple was even interested in buying it.

The only thing Jake wanted to do was call Ted. But he couldn't. Ted had said they should stay friends. Screw that. Jake didn't want to be *buddies* with the guy he loved. He wanted to be *with* him, holding him, kissing him, being held by him.

"Your painting is extraordinary," a middle-aged woman said to Jake. She had short auburn hair and rimless glasses. "It makes the viewer want to be brave."

"Thanks," Jake said. The muscles in his cheeks were aching.

"I'm Lydia Montaine." She reached out to shake Jake's hand. "You might know my daughter Whitney. She goes to Hankinson too."

"Yeah, I know Whitney. She's great." Whitney was on student

council with Jake. She was the one who'd helped him get elected a few years ago, which Jake was eternally grateful for. He hadn't realized her mom was white. They didn't look anything alike.

"I agree," Whitney's mom said, "but I happen to be biased."

Jake glanced over her shoulder. Where was *his* mom? His face was flushed and his underarms were leaking.

"How's your college search going?" Whitney's mom asked. "Do you know where you're applying?"

Jake nodded. That was all anyone asked about these days. "A bunch of SUNYs with strong fine arts programs."

"Is there just one application for all of them?"

"Yeah."

"Thank goodness," she said. "I know it can be overwhelming."

After Whitney's mom wandered off, Jake wiped his face with a napkin. He spotted his mom and waved desperately to her.

"Ready?" she asked, walking over and tucking his damp hair behind his ears.

"Yes . . . please."

It was freezing out. On the walk to the car, Jake started shivering.

"Your dad and I hate book parties," his mom said. "For us it's about the writing and the art. But talking about it? It's the opposite of what we do. We'd much rather be loners."

Jake burrowed his chin into his scarf. Snow was swirling around the parking lot, and his sweat was turning to ice. Honestly, he didn't want to be a loner. He actually liked people. He'd been elected senior class president, and there had even been buzz that he and Ted would be voted homecoming kings for the first time in Hankinson history.

That was before Ted dumped him.

"Want to drive?" Jake's mom held out her keys.

"No, thanks," Jake said.

"It'll get better. You'll slowly start feeling better about what happened with Ted. I promise you will."

"It doesn't feel like it," Jake said as he climbed into the passenger seat.

Jake's mom turned the heat to high. "It never does."

Jake leaned back in his seat. When he and Ted had gotten together, he dove headfirst into the relationship. He let himself free-fall because he thought it would never end. Well, he messed up big time, and now he was paying for it.

MIA

ON DECEMBER 15 at 2:59, Mia blasted the Clash and logged on to Swarthmore's admissions site. She kept hitting refresh until it showed up.

She'd gotten in.

Mia clutched her chest.

She was going to Swarthmore!

Last year it was ranked number one in *U.S. News and World Report.* At least five Swarthmore alumni were Nobel laureates, one in math. It was outside of Philadelphia, about three hundred miles from Hankinson. But in Mia's mind she was rocketing to another planet.

She reached for her phone but then set it down again. Her parents would lecture her about the expense of a private college. They'd say how they went to state schools and that worked out fine for them.

Mia texted Jeremiah from IMLI instead.

So . . . I got in. You? PS Listening to "Welcome to Paradise."

They'd been texting every few weeks, and they promised to check in with each other today. As Mia waited to hear from him, she thought about calling Brock. She and Brock didn't hang out in person, but they had this phone thing going on. Sometimes Mia would get a text from Brock in the middle of the night saying *Are you awake?* She'd text him back, and they'd stay up talking for hours.

Mia's phone pinged. Jeremiah had written, *Greetings from Kansas. I'm listening to the Suicidal Tendencies.*

Oh no, Mia wrote.

I got the big W. Waitlist. You rock. I'll roll with it.

Mia was about to write back to Jeremiah when her phone rang. It wasn't a number she recognized.

"Hello?"

"Oh . . . hey," a girl's voice said. "Mia, right? It's Whitney . . . you know . . . from school."

As if she had to clarify.

"What's up?" Mia asked. She tried to sound like it was normal for Whitney Montaine to be calling her.

"I was talking to Brock, and he gave me your number."

Mia's breath caught in her throat. She didn't even know where to begin. Whitney and Brock were talking about her? Never in a million years would she have imagined that.

"Maybe this sounds weird," Whitney said, "but remember that time you told me you were applying early decision to Swarthmore?"

"Yeah," Mia said. It had been in the pharmacy line at PriceRite, the day before senior year started.

"It made me want to apply early to NYU."

Mia smiled. Now *this* was a subject she could talk about. "So did you hear?"

"Did you?"

Mia's face erupted into a smile. "Yeah. I just got into Swarth-more!"

"And I got into NYU!"

Before Mia could stop herself, she shrieked into the phone. Whitney shrieked too, which made Mia shriek even louder. If all that prep work was college porn, then this was definitely a huge college orgasm.

GREGOR

GREGOR PUT OFF college applications until winter break. Now, no joke, it was down to the wire. His guidance counselor was leaving for Belize tomorrow. She told Gregor that she needed to know first thing in the morning where to send his transcripts and recommendation letters. The other seniors' deadline was two weeks ago, but she'd given him an extension.

Gregor leaned against a pillow and turned to a new page in his journal.

December 23

I can't decide where to apply. How can I make this choice about the rest of my life? City or small town? Liberal arts or big university? Music conservatory? Every decision I make sets my life on a different course. Here's something else. Whitney and I are starting to talk in school. STOP. Goal: get through one journal entry without mentioning Whitney. (I will try.)

Okay. College.

- *Reed. My dad went there. I still have a Reed sweatshirt.*
- *Ithaca College. They keep sending me catalogs.*
- *Berklee College of Music. Top music conservatory. Ava is a sophomore there. Yes, that Ava. We've texted a few times, no big deal.*
- *Juilliard. I'd never get in.*
- *University of MD. My sister goes there.*
- *Manhattan School of Music. I have a good chance of getting in with cello. Whitney just got accepted to NYU. We'd live in the same city.*

(So much for not mentioning Whitney.)

JANUARY

ZOE

ON NEW YEAR'S Day, Zoe was playing piano in the living room when the doorbell rang. She slipped a sweatshirt over her tank top. Rich Morrison, Aunt Jane's ex-husband, was shivering on the doorstep. As Zoe opened the door, an icy wind blasted into the foyer.

"Hey, Zoe," Rich said, shutting the door behind him. He set a tote bag on the ground and kicked off his boots. "Happy New Year."

"Yeah, Happy New Year."

Zoe crossed her arms over her chest. She'd never talked much to Rich at family gatherings, but he seemed friendly enough. He was her cousin David's father, and he and his wife, Glenda, had that little girl, Mariah. At David's college graduation last year, Zoe had seen him blowing raspberries on Mariah's stomach and that seemed cute.

"Is Jane here?" Rich asked. "I'm dropping off containers from Thanksgiving. I told her I'd swing by."

Zoe shook her head. "She's at a brunch with people from Downing. She'll be home around three."

Aunt Jane had invited Zoe to the brunch, but she needed to work on her song. Anna was coming over later with a draft of the lyrics, and Zoe was supposed to have the melody figured out. Anna signed them up to perform an original song for the Class Acts talent show in April. She said it would help get Zoe out of her funk.

"I'll leave the containers on the counter," Rich said, draping his coat over the couch. "I need to grab a bill for David too."

Rich headed into the kitchen, and Zoe sat at the piano again. She'd come up with a sequence of notes, but when she tried it now, the song only lasted seven seconds. *Damn.* Everything felt so crappy right now. Zoe's mom was drinking again and refusing to go to rehab. She'd told Max who told Jane who told Zoe that she felt a "moderation approach" to alcohol would be more effective. On top of that, all everyone at school talked about was college and where they were applying. Zoe had no clue what she wanted to do next year. She'd applied to Downing because that was where Aunt Jane worked, but she wasn't even sure she wanted to go to college. Maybe she'd take some cooking classes or work full-time at Bean.

"Are you composing?" Rich was standing under the archway in the living room.

Zoe flinched. She hadn't realized Rich was listening. "My friend and I are trying to write a song."

"Did Jane tell you I play piano?"

Zoe shook her head.

"In a band on weekends. We write our own stuff."

Rich slid onto the piano bench next to her. He rubbed his hands together to warm them up and then played a ragtime tune. He was good, like, *really* good.

"That's amazing," Zoe said.

"I wrote it last fall. Want to learn it?"

"Sure."

Piano was the one thing that got her out of herself. She'd recently restarted lessons with a teacher whose house was two streets away from Bean.

Rich played with his right hand, showing Zoe the notes. Zoe picked out a few notes herself.

"You're fast," he said. "How long have you been taking lessons?"

"On and off. I just started again."

Pretty soon they were both playing, Zoe's fingers alongside Rich's on the keyboard. They sounded solid together. Zoe was getting into it.

She gave Rich a grateful smile. This was what it meant to push beyond the gloom. These were the moments when Zoe realized that, somehow, she was going to muddle through.

WHITNEY

——————

WHITNEY CLIMBED ONTO the school bus. It felt silly to be taking a field trip like they were back in fifth grade. Pretty much everyone had their driver's licenses by now! But her senior lit teacher wanted them to go to the Downing Library to learn about academic research, to get ready for college next year.

"Hey there," Whitney said as she sat next to Gregor and unbuttoned her navy pea coat. It was hot on the bus and smelled like sweaty socks. "The school bus makes me feel like one of those clowns in a car that's too small."

"Or those big guys who ride tiny dirt bikes," Gregor said, smiling. His voice was deep, and he'd gotten tall this year, like almost six feet. For the past few months Whitney and Gregor had been joking around in their classes. She'd even gone to his jazz band's holiday concert back in December. Whitney had watched Gregor onstage wearing a black shirt and black jeans, his hair spiked. The audience went crazy whenever he had a solo. It was obvious he was a rock star on the drums. But then, back at school on Monday, his hair was messy and he was his usual semi-geeky self. It was kind of adorable.

"When's the last time you rode the bus?" she asked Gregor.

"Never, really," Gregor said. "I walked in middle school, and then my dad used to drive me before I got my license. I guess I've just taken the bus on field trips."

Gregor's dad. Whitney's tongue felt heavy, and saliva was pooling in her mouth. They'd never talked about his dad before.

"I'm sorry," she said. "About your dad. That must have been terrible."

"Yeah . . . well," Gregor said quietly.

The bus pulled onto the main road. Whitney watched a police car zip around them, the siren on but the lights off.

"I think my mom knew him," she said after a moment. She was remembering what she heard last year, how her mom had had a secret crush on his dad.

"Really? Is your mom a lawyer too?"

Whitney shook her head. "They went to high school together. My mom mentioned it once. Isn't that crazy?"

Gregor stared at her. "Your mom grew up here?"

Whitney told him the year that her mom had graduated from high school.

"I think that's the same year as my dad." Gregor paused. "I wonder if they were friends."

The light changed to green, and the bus rolled forward.

"I hope so," Whitney said. She wasn't going to tell him the parts about the car running over his dad's foot or her mom's crush.

"I should check his journal from high school," Gregor said. "What's your mom's name?"

"You have his *journal*?" Whitney couldn't imagine what it would be like to read her own dad's journal! She had no idea what occurred in his brain, maybe chemistry formulas and tropical fish and the occasional realization that he had daughters to deal with.

"I haven't read it," Gregor said. "Maybe someday. I have a journal like it. He gave it to me freshman year."

Kyra and Brock and Ted were in the back bellowing to each other like they owned the bus. Whitney wished they would shut up, even though two years ago she would have been right there with them.

"What do you write about?" she asked. Maybe she was getting too personal, but she'd never met a guy who kept a journal. It seemed so soulful, like Jack Kerouac or Kurt Cobain.

Gregor's cheeks were flushed, and he was looking into his lap. "I write about anything, I guess. Whatever comes up. It's weird to talk about this. I don't usually—"

"Me neither," Whitney said. "I've always wanted to have a journal. I've never told anyone that."

As Gregor drummed his thumbs against his thighs, she had this crazy idea to reach over and hold his hand.

"If you want to hear something else about me that no one knows," she said, "I sleep with a teddy bear. Dorky, right?"

Gregor grinned. "Really?"

"It's cute. It's small and red and says *coup de couer.*"

"*Coup de couer?*" Gregor asked.

"It means—"

"'Falling in love,'" he said. "I took French for seven years."

"But it's more than that. It's supposed to be like a shock of love. At least that's what I heard. The bear saved my life."

Gregor was staring hard at her. He had nice teeth, white and straight.

"I know . . . it sounds silly," Whitney said. "I was in the hospital with pneumonia sophomore year. Someone gave me the bear and then I got better. I guess it's my lucky charm."

Gregor shook his head but didn't say anything. Whitney wondered what it would be like to kiss him, but she quickly pushed that thought away.

"That's cool," he finally said, his voice cracking. "I mean . . . about your bear."

"Lydia, by the way."

"What's that?"

"Lydia Gibson. That was my mom's name in high school if you ever look it up in your dad's journal."

FEBRUARY

JAKE

"DID KENI TELL you that's okay?" Jake asked. His friend Zoe was walking around Bean, taping up hearts that she'd cut from construction paper. It was six thirty on Valentine's Day, and they were expecting a rush of customers. "She's a lesbian anarchist after all. She may be offended by little pink hearts."

"I doubt they're going to offend anyone," Zoe said. "It's Valentine's Day!"

"It offends *me*," Jake said.

Zoe handed him a pile of hearts. "As assistant manager," she said, "I command you to hang these hearts on the brick wall."

"Fucking power trip," Jake muttered, reaching for the tape.

"Fuck your broken heart," Zoe said, laughing.

Jake had started working at Bean in December. His parents had suggested it because he needed something to get him out of the house and help him get over Ted. Also, he wanted to make spending money for college. Keni was the general manager, and she was the one who hired him, but most of his shifts were with Zoe.

Zoe had actually been in his freshman orientation group. Not that she remembered, but Jake forgave her for that. It must have been insane to have a famous mom having a public breakdown and then to randomly show up at Hankinson High School.

But the crazy thing was, he and Zoe instantly hit it off. It was nothing like his friendship with Mona Lisa, where she ordered him around and always had to be the star of the show. Zoe and Jake even had the same swearing habit. Jake also loved Zoe's other best friend, Anna. She worked across the street and came in on breaks. The three of them called themselves JAZ for Jake-Anna-Zoe. It was a joke on how people named their cliques back in middle school.

"Did you brew the Brazilian blend?" Zoe asked after Jake had finished taping up the hearts.

"Yep."

"And you inventoried the cakes? You checked red velvet? That's a big one on Valentine's Day."

"Done. Or should I say, *Yes, Your Royal Highness*?"

Zoe rolled her eyes. "I'm going to get some tea from the supply closet. Need anything?"

"To have today over with," Jake said.

Once she disappeared, he snatched up a pen and some blank receipt tape. Even art wasn't cutting it these days.

For Ted

I could spend a July afternoon
sitting next to you
spitting cherry pits
rapid fire
sun dipping

I pucker my lips and inflate my cheeks
bing
smile when you tell me I look like a camel

"A *camel*?" Zoe leaned over Jake, her palms pressing hard on his shoulders. "Are you writing bad poetry again?"

"Fuck you!" Jake flipped over the paper. "Who said you could read it? And it's not bad. See how I said *cherry* and then *bing*? Get it?"

Zoe groaned. "You should have called it *Fro Ted*."

Jake had to laugh. He'd recently admitted to Zoe that Ted's breakup text had been full of typos.

"Honey," Zoe said. She took the pen and put the cap back on. "You're obsessing about someone who broke up with you *six months ago*. Do I need to call an emergency JAZ summit? When things ended with Dinky, I felt fine within days."

"That's because *you* dumped *him*," Jake said. "Also, you guys are hooking up again. Duh."

"Oh, right." Zoe fanned her face with her hand. "Silly me."

"Ted and I had history," Jake said. "We were in love. This hurts all the time. I never stop thinking about how much this hurts."

Zoe stretched out her arms and pretended to play a goddamn violin.

Screw her.

An older couple walked through the front door. The woman was carrying a bouquet of roses, and the guy had a cleft in his chin.

"I hate them," Jake muttered to Zoe. "I bet he's going to top off the evening with a box of Russell Stover assorted chocolates."

"Turn that hate to love." Zoe swiped her card in the register and patted Jake on the back. "Because it's time to deliver some Valentine's cheer."

MIA

MIA SET THE bowl of popcorn on the coffee table. "What do you want to watch?" she asked, holding up the remote.

Sophie was scrolling through pictures on her phone and didn't look up. "I don't know . . . whatever."

"Something Valentines-y?"

"I'm not in the mood for romance."

"*Doctor Who*?" Mia asked. "I'm obsessed with it right now."

Sophie rolled her eyes. "That's boring, all sci-fi and stuff."

Don't mess with the doctor! Mia wanted to say.

She tossed Sophie the remote and said, "You pick. I'm fine with whatever."

Mia and Sophie hadn't had a Saturday movie night since last fall and hadn't even hung out since New Year's. Mia rationalized it as both of them being busy with senior year, but on some deep level she knew they were growing apart, that their friendship had run its course.

When Sophie texted her yesterday to say she'd gotten accepted to a Catholic college in Buffalo, Mia called her right away and invited her over for a celebratory movie tonight. But now that Sophie was here, she couldn't figure out what on earth they used to talk about.

As Sophie scrolled around Netflix, Mia pulled a pillow against her stomach, hugging it with both hands.

"You have a text, Mia," Sophie said. "Can't you hear it?"

Mia grabbed a handful of popcorn and reached for her phone.

Hey, babe, Brock had written. *Can you talk?*

Hang on, Mia wrote back. *Give me a minute.*

"I'll just be a little bit," Mia said to Sophie as she pushed off the couch. "I have to call a friend."

"What's up?" Mia asked, settling on the floor in the kitchen. That was where she often sat during her and Brock's marathon phone calls, with easy access to the fridge for water or the cupboards for fruit leather and wasabi seaweed.

"Nothing," Brock said. "I'm lying low. I hate Valentine's Day."

"I can't picture you caring about Valentine's Day."

Brock laughed. "Me? Why wouldn't I care?"

Mia picked at some polish on her toenail. She and Brock talked on the phone so much that, at this point, they could say anything they wanted. "You've had girlfriends since, like, second grade. Everyone loves you. You're immune to all the romance bullshit."

"Ha. Not true. In fact, will you be my girlfriend?"

Mia shook her head. "You know we'd be terrible together. You're all popular and I'm—"

"Beautiful and smart and mysteriously cool."

Mia flushed. "Maybe when we're thirty."

"When we're thirty *what*?"

"If neither of us has found the one by the time we're thirty, then we'll get married."

"Ah, so I'm your backup plan," Brock said.

"Something like that."

From there, Brock played a song for Mia, and Mia told him the plot of a *Doctor Who* episode that he'd missed and she busted into a bag of SunChips and they were deep into a conversation about which one of them had a sexier voice when Sophie stomped into the kitchen.

"I'm going to go," she announced.

"Who's that?" Brock asked.

"Just my friend," Mia said. "No big deal."

"That's what I thought," Sophie said, sliding her feet into her boots.

"Hang on," Mia said into the phone. Then to Sophie she said, "I'll be off in a second. You don't have to go."

"So you're ditching me for your friend," Brock said, laughing.

"No," Mia said into the phone. "I mean, yes."

But before she could hang up, Sophie said, "See you around," and then walked out.

"Did she storm out?" Brock asked.

"Sort of."

Mia felt a cold wind as the door closed behind her. So it was true. Their friendship really was over. In a way Mia had been waiting for this moment. She actually felt relieved.

"Good," said Brock. "Now I get you all to myself."

MARCH

WHITNEY

EARLY IN THE morning Whitney rolled over in bed, scratched at the tag in her T-shirt, and looked out at the graying snowdrifts. She was somewhere between asleep and awake when she realized, *I like Gregor Lombard.*

He wasn't her typical type, but that was good. Another good thing—she'd discussed this with Jude—was that it was time for her to pick the guy she liked. In the past she'd always let them come after her.

Whitney walked into the bathroom, turned on the shower, and stripped. Her stomach was flipping like crazy. She couldn't wait any longer. She was going to tell Gregor today.

GREGOR

THE SKY WAS damp and gray when Gregor woke up. He'd stayed awake past midnight reading his dad's high school journal. It was Whitney who'd gotten him curious. At first he was just going to skim for her mom's name, but once he started reading, he couldn't put it down.

Mostly Gregor's dad had written about school pranks he'd done with his friends and trails he'd run for cross-country. He also wrote about girls, though not anyone named Lydia Gibson. His dad had had crushes in high school, but he'd never asked a girl out. Instead he put them on pedestals and suffered as they got together with other guys.

Gregor turned over in bed, his cheek against the pillow. It was six forty. He didn't have to get in the shower for a few more minutes.

Holy crap.

What his dad did was pretty much what he'd done with Whitney. For all of high school, he'd obsessed about Whitney when, in reality, he'd been too nervous to talk to her. But now they were getting to know each other. And the crazy thing was, Gregor could honestly say he cherished her friendship. Even if they never got together, which was probably the case, he was still happy to know her.

Gregor sat up in bed and reached for his phone. It was time to move on. It was time to make things happen with Nadine. They'd kissed last fall when the marching band was at an away game. It was a little sloppy, but nothing terrible.

Want to go to the senior prom together? he texted her.

Nadine wrote back almost immediately. *Yes!*

Dinky once told Gregor that if you ask a girl to the prom in March, you're destined to become a couple by May. Gregor set his phone on his bedside table. He was on his way to having a girlfriend.

APRIL

ZOE

ZOE HELD A brown bag over her mouth. Someone backstage said it would help, but as she inhaled the papery air, she thought she might suffocate. She crumpled up the bag. Anna was puking in the bathroom. Screw the Class Acts talent show.

"You must chill." Jake kneeled in front of her and steadied her shoulders with his hands. "I command you to chill."

Zoe nodded weakly. Anna returned from the bathroom and sank into the folding chair next to Zoe. Her eyes were red-rimmed, and her face was pale.

"And, you," Jake said to her, "no more throwing up."

"I was dry-heaving," Anna whimpered.

"Your song is good," Jake said. "Don't mess it up with all this stage-fright bullshit."

Zoe nodded again. Their song was called "You, Me, Together." The lyrics were sweet and soulful. Aunt Jane's ex-husband, Rich, had helped them compose the melody. It was so catchy that even Jake had been singing it, and he hated love songs.

"Zoe and Anna?" A skinny sophomore girl with an earpiece and a clipboard walked over to them. "You're next up. About two minutes. Oh my god! You're Zoe Laybourne!"

As soon as the girl walked away, Zoe moaned, "Fuuuuuck."

Anna buried her face in her hands. How did she and Anna agree to sing an original song and play piano in front of the entire school? What if their song actually sucked and no one was telling them the truth? What if someone filmed it and posted the clip and everyone commented that Zoe Laybourne was ugly and looked nothing like her mom?

"I told you that you should have done a shot," Jake said.

"Yeah, right." Zoe rolled her eyes. "Like being drunk would help."

Jake grinned. "A shot isn't going to get you *drunk*. Duh."

For months now Jake had been trying to convince Zoe and Anna to try alcohol. He knew they both had issues because of their parents, but he said they needed to let go of that and live like graduating seniors.

Anna hugged the neck of her guitar.

"We never should have signed up for Class Acts," Zoe said.

"What's so bad?" Jake said. "You guys will be together onstage. I'll be in the front row, right near your aunt. Everyone you love is here."

Zoe bit her lip. She hadn't told her mom about the show tonight.

Jake squeezed Zoe's leg. "I mean, there are a lot of people who love you here."

Zoe nodded. Jake was right. Even Dinky had come. They weren't officially together again, but they'd decided to go to the prom, and they were fooling around whenever they felt like it. Rich had come too, since he'd helped write the song. He'd taken Zoe and

Anna out for blueberry pancakes this morning to wish them luck.

The girl with the clipboard nodded to Zoe. "Sorry about before . . . I was just starstruck . . . uhhh . . . Are you ready to go on?"

"Don't worry about it," Zoe said. "You won't be starstruck when I blow it out there."

Jake reached for Zoe's hands and pulled her from the chair. Then he yanked Anna up next.

"I'm going to get you both drunk before graduation," Jake said as he looped Anna's rainbow guitar strap over her neck.

"We'll see about that," Zoe said.

Jake smiled. "Do you always have to have the fucking—"

"Last word?" Zoe asked, grinning. "Fuck, yeah."

Then she and Anna pushed through the curtain and stepped onto the stage.

MIA

Dear Jeremiah,

We just kissed good-bye. You're also in the Philadelphia airport. I'm waving to you over in Terminal F. Do you see me in Terminal B? I'm the dork wearing the Swarthmore sweatshirt, carrying the Swarthmore tote bag. Oh yeah, so are you. (Yay, Admitted Students Weekend!)

We only spent two days together, and yet it feels strange to be apart. I'm counting the months until we can move into the dorms. I can't believe we both love DuPont Science Hall even though everyone else thinks it's ugly. And last night. I can't believe last night.

Oops! My plane in boarding. Back in a few minutes.

Here I am. I just got your text that your plane is taking off. I'm looking out my oval window, waving as you zoom down the runway. I still can't believe we were both at IMLI two summers ago and never hung out. That's my fault. I will make it up to you.

I'm in my seat now, by the way.

Last night when we talked on the lawn outside Parrish Hall, I felt like I could be myself for the first time in my life. And then we lay on the grass and watched the sky change from blue to black and you tucked my bare feet under your legs to keep them warm and we kissed. I'm sorry if this is cheesy, but I have to say it was amazing. And then you took that fortune cookie paper of your wallet and read it to me with the light from your phone. "There is no fear in love for love cast away all fear." And you know what I thought when you read that? I realized that for my whole life, I've lived with so much fear. But I'm not scared anymore.

See you in four months.

Love,
Mia

MAY

GREGOR

A FEW DAYS before the prom Nadine called Gregor. He was sitting on the back deck, running the circulation system on the pool and waiting for the pool woman to come check the pH and chlorine levels. His mom had asked him to handle opening the pool this summer.

"I don't think it's working," Nadine said. "I mean . . . us."

Gregor held his phone against his ear and kicked at a dead spider, sending it into the grass. He'd been feeling the same way, but he was waiting until after the prom to end things.

Nadine sighed. "We should break up before the prom so we can both have fun."

Maybe he was a wimp, but Gregor was relieved that Nadine was doing it instead of him. "Probably a good idea."

He and Nadine had been attempting the boyfriend-girlfriend thing for two months, but it felt like they were buddies who happened to be fooling around. Not to mention that Nadine drank way too much. She always got plastered when they went out at night, which was getting old.

"What do you want to do about the prom?" Nadine asked. "I'm

thinking it'd be easier if we still go together."

"Yeah. We don't want to have to figure out dates and limo stuff."

"Exactly," Nadine said.

"Good," Gregor said.

"So you'll get me the lily corsage from Vine?"

"Yeah . . . of course."

They chatted for a few more minutes and then, when the pool woman pulled into the driveway, Gregor got off the phone.

Three days later they were in a limo heading toward the Hilton. It was him, Nadine, Dinky, Zoe Laybourne, Jake Rodriguez, and Anna Kimball. Gregor was trying to get into the prom thing, but he was feeling melancholy. He kept thinking about his mom and how she'd taken pictures of them on the front lawn before they left. It was moments like those when he felt like his dad should have been there taking pictures too, that it wasn't right *not* to have his dad there.

Nadine and Dinky were swigging from a bottle of spiked Dr Pepper, and occasionally they'd pass it over to Jake, the senior class president. Jake was going to the prom with Anna. Anna and Jake were best friends with Zoe, Sierra Laybourne's daughter, who was together with Dinky. When Dinky had first started going out with Zoe, everyone acted awkward around her because of her famous mom, but after a while they'd gotten used to it.

"Holy fuck!" Jake said, pulling Gregor out of his thoughts.

"What?" Zoe asked. She was wearing a low-cut violet dress and a diamond necklace.

Jake gestured at Gregor and Zoe. "I just realized that all three of us were in the same freshman orientation group."

Gregor nodded. That was so long ago he could barely even remember it.

"Wow," Zoe said. "We just need Whitney . . . and who else?"

"Whitney Montaine?" Nadine asked. "She's fucking gorgeous."

"Mia Flint," Gregor said to get off the subject of Whitney. Over the winter it had felt like he and Whitney were becoming friends, but as soon as Gregor had gotten together with Nadine, she'd turned chilly. She barely even talked to him anymore.

"Remember the letters?" Zoe asked.

"Oh yeah," Gregor said. He vaguely recalled writing about Whitney. Of course he had.

"What letters?" Nadine asked, grabbing for the Dr Pepper drink.

Jake raised his eyebrows at Zoe and then nodded at Gregor. It seemed like he was trying to signal them to keep it quiet.

"Nothing," Gregor said quickly.

"No letters," Jake added.

The prom theme was "My Heart Will Go On." That was a song from a movie called *Titanic*. The ballroom was decked out with porthole windows and ocean-liner images and choppy waves cut out of paper.

Gregor was sitting at his table by the lifeboats, picking at a dinner roll and thinking about how the shipwreck theme was demented. More than fifteen hundred people died when the *Titanic* sunk. It was like having a 9/11 prom.

"Why aren't you dancing?"

Whitney was standing above him in a knockout silver dress,

her skin smooth, her hair twisted back. She'd already kicked off her shoes and was pushing up onto her toes like a ballerina.

"I *was* dancing," Gregor said.

"For, like, one song. I saw you."

Whitney slid into the empty chair next to Gregor and fiddled with a prom program on the table. Gregor sipped his water. He considered asking who her date was, but he couldn't handle it if she said she had a boyfriend.

"Can you believe the theme is *Titanic*?" Whitney said. "Isn't that depressing?"

"I was just thinking the same thing!"

They both laughed. Maybe it was true, that tragedy plus time equaled comedy. Or maybe tragedy plus Whitney made everything okay. Man, he still loved her. No denying it.

Whitney folded the prom program into a fortune-teller like people used to make back in third grade.

"I filled out my roommate forms for NYU," she said.

"What did you say?"

Whitney reached into her small purse and took out a pen. "I wrote that I'm into the drama thing and I'm neat but not OCD. What about you? Did you decide where you're going?"

Gregor downed the rest of his water. "Manhattan School of Music."

Whitney's eyes widened. She began writing on the fortune-teller. Celine Dion was singing a slow song. Gregor could see Nadine wrapped around a junior guy, her hands massaging his butt.

"Do you realize we'll be in the same city this fall?" Whitney asked.

"Yes."

Whitney looked at Gregor, her hazel eyes staring into his, and he felt it like he'd never felt anything that clearly in his life. *Whitney liked him back.*

"Pick a color," Whitney said, scooping the fortune-teller onto her fingers. "Green, red, blue, or yellow."

"Green."

Whitney spelled out *g-r-e-e-n* and moved the points of the paper with each letter.

"Now pick a number," she said, "one through eight."

"Six."

She opened and closed the paper points six times.

"Now ask a question," she said. "It has to be a yes-or-no question, and after you ask it, you pick another number. You can pick one, three, five, or seven."

Gregor's hands were trembling. There was only one question he wanted to ask.

"You're not together with Nadine anymore, are you?" Whitney said suddenly.

Gregor shook his head.

"Ask a question," Whitney said quietly. "And pick a number. One, three, five, or seven."

"Can I kiss you?" Gregor asked. "Three."

Whitney counted to three and then carefully pried open a fold of paper.

She smiled at Gregor. "All signs point to yes."

JUNE

JAKE

—————

Ted: What's up?

Jake: Not much. Countdown to graduation. Doing some
art.

Ted: I don't know how else to say this. I basically suck.

Ted: And I'm sorry.

Ted: And I still love you.

Ted: You can say you hate me. I'd deserve it.

Ted: Jake, are you there?

Jake: Yeah. I'm just trying not to die.

Ted: Don't die. I'll be over to resuscitate. Are you home?

Jake: Huh?

Ted: I'm walking to my car.

Jake: Are you going to destroy my heart again? If so, you shouldn't come.

Ted: I'm driving over.

WHITNEY

WHITNEY HAD NEVER thought about happily-ever-after before, but that was what this felt like. Ever since she and Gregor had gotten together, every cliché in the world was her life. *Meant to be. Match made in heaven.* They joked that they should write cheesy greeting cards together.

She'd be wriggling on a dress or driving to school or shaving her legs, and she couldn't stop smiling. For one, it was amazing to fool around with Gregor. They went to her mom's house after school and kissed and moved against each other until they came. They texted nonstop, and he played cello for her on the phone every night to help her fall asleep. Her mom thought Gregor was adorable, especially when he taught them how to open the pool at their new house. Her dad said he seemed intelligent. Even Alicia said Gregor was her *best yet*, which was major coming from her sister. Alicia hadn't brought up the fact that Gregor was white, and honestly, being with Gregor affirmed what Whitney felt about race. She didn't want race to define her. She didn't want to be with a black guy just because he was black, just like she didn't want to be with Gregor because he was white. She wanted to love someone for who they were.

It was love. Yep. They'd said it.

After they'd been together three weeks, Gregor admitted to Whitney that he'd loved her since freshman orientation, that he was the one who brought her the teddy bear in the hospital, that she was his dream girl.

"You should have told me," Whitney said. They were sitting on her deck eating strawberries and pretending to study for finals. "High school would have been so much better if we'd been together."

"I don't think we were ready," Gregor said. "For sure I wasn't."

Whitney tried to remember what she'd thought of him at the beginning of ninth grade, but it was hazy. Honestly, she wasn't even sure if they'd talked.

"Anyway, we have next year," Gregor said. "We'll both be in New York City."

"The future is ours," Whitney said.

Gregor laughed. "Another one for the cheesy card business."

"Oh my god!" Kyra set down her phone and clapped her hand over her mouth. She'd painted her fingernails black in honor of the senior prank. *"Oh my fucking god."*

Whitney glanced at Gregor. He was slicing open a sandbag and spilling it onto the floor outside the principal's office. He was the one who'd come up with the idea of making a beach scene for the senior prank. It was ten at night, five days before graduation. Kyra had snuck the key from her dad and let them all into the school.

"What is it?" Autumn asked, tossing a rainbow beach ball to Whitney.

"My dad thinks I'm at your house. Anyway, he just texted me. I have to say it again," Kyra said. *"Oh my fucking god!"*

Whitney clenched her jaw. This time Gregor caught her eye. *It's okay,* she could feel him saying. *Don't let Kyra get to you.*

"Kyra," Zach said, swigging a beer. "Either tell us what Daddy the Principal said or shut up already."

Kyra rolled her eyes. "Fine. I shouldn't be telling you guys, but you know how Zoe's mom is Sierra Laybourne? Well . . . guess who's coming to graduation? Her manager got in touch with my dad to talk about security issues. She's staying at the Hilton, where the prom was."

"Oh my god!" Autumn squealed.

Whitney blew up another beach ball. She had to admit, it was cool that they were having a movie star at graduation. The final student council meeting was tomorrow, and graduation was on the agenda. Maybe Whitney should ask Jake to ask Zoe if Sierra could make a speech.

"Isn't Sierra Laybourne in rehab?" Zach asked. He set down his beer and burped loudly. "I thought she was a crazy alcoholic."

"Shut up," Whitney said, plugging a beach ball and rolling it onto the sand. At least Zoe wasn't here, but it was still uncool to talk about someone's mom like that.

Kyra giggled. "Maybe they're letting her out for the day?"

"If she shows up wasted," Zach said, "I'm taking pictures and selling them for a ton of money."

Whitney squeezed her fingers into fists. Enough was enough. "You guys are—"

"Whit." Gregor took her hand and pulled her down the hall.

"But they're being assholes," Whitney said. She was shaking all over. She tried to remember what Jude had told her to do when Kyra and the others were getting to her. *Breathe. Step away. Count slowly backward.* It was just so hard. She still hadn't told Gregor that she saw a therapist. She was planning to tell him soon. She knew she could trust him with that kind of stuff.

Gregor wrapped his arms around her, holding her tight. "They *are* assholes. But you're so much better than them."

"You're saying don't go there?"

"I'm saying they don't matter."

"But—"

Gregor's lips were on hers. She breathed him in. She didn't care what Gregor said. High school would have been ten thousand times better if they'd been together.

JAKE

————

"I WAS THINKING we should all meet up," Jake said to Whitney as they stepped through the heavy doors of school and into the harsh noonday sunlight. He'd just run into her in the hall. Jake had come to turn in his keys to the student council office and to empty his locker. Whitney must have done the same, because they were both carrying Hefty bags in their arms.

"All who?" Whitney asked, squinting up at Jake. Something about her seemed different. She usually wore a lot of makeup and dressy clothes, but now she was in shorts and a T-shirt, her long hair pulled into a ponytail. Jake thought she looked better, more relaxed.

"Our freshman orientation group," Jake said, remembering back to that day in the gym almost four years ago. "You, me, Gregor—"

"And Mia Flint and Zoe!" Whitney squealed. "Those letters! We made that promise to meet at graduation and read them."

"I think Zoe will do it. She hates being a joiner, and she'll probably bitch and moan, but I'll convince her. I've never told anyone about those letters. I like it being a secret."

Whitney shook her head. "That's so weird. I still remember when I wrote my letter."

"Me too." Jake paused. He'd been wanting to tell Whitney something for a while and now, two days before graduation, seemed like a good time. "You sort of saved me, by the way. I've always meant to thank you for that."

Whitney shifted her plastic bag into her other arm. "Saved you? How?"

"Remember when you helped me run for junior class treasurer? You got me all those signatures and convinced people to vote for me? I really wanted to be on student council but couldn't have done it myself."

Whitney shook her head. "I feel like I used you to beat Zach. Was I bitchy back then? I hope I wasn't too much of a bitch."

"No, never." Jake pushed his hair out of his eyes. He'd been thinking about cutting it short before college, but Ted had begged him not to. He said he loved Jake's hair. But Ted also said he'd love Jake even if he was a baldie.

They crossed the small street to the student parking lot. The ice cream man was parked at the curb, selling Popsicles to the younger kids who'd just handed in their last final.

"So, you want to plan to meet after graduation?" Jake asked. "You can ask Gregor, right?"

Whitney slipped her phone out of her purse. "I'm texting him now. I also have Mia Flint's number."

Jake remembered that time Mia knocked on his front door. He still had her number from then. "Okay . . . or I can ask Mia."

"Either way." Whitney shrugged. "By the way, I heard that you and Ted got back together. You two are so adorable."

"Yeah," Jake said. Even hearing Ted's name made his stomach

flip. People say there isn't a one and only, but Jake wasn't so sure. "I'm being more careful this time."

"Really?"

"Honestly . . . no. I don't want to be more careful."

"I know exactly what you mean." Whitney laughed. "I can't imagine being careful about Gregor. Hey, I wish we hung out more in high school. Why didn't we?"

"I was hiding," Jake said thoughtfully.

"Me too."

"You?"

"In my own way."

Hearing that made Jake wonder if they'd all been in hiding, if he hadn't been the only one who'd felt alone for so much of high school.

ZOE

—————

ZOE PULLED INTO the parking lot of the Hilton and shifted into park. She breathed in through her nose and out slowly through her mouth. Her mom had taken a private jet from Los Angeles and landed this afternoon. All Zoe had to do was get through dinner with Sierra, and then she was going to meet up with Anna and Jake.

Her windows were rolled down, and the music was pumping. The air smelled so sweet and grassy that Zoe couldn't help but feel happy. She loved the air in Hankinson, a summer night, a smoky fall, a wet and earthy spring. After four years this finally felt like home.

She checked her makeup in the mirror and then reached onto the passenger seat for the cooler. She and her mom were going to eat dinner in the hotel suite, just some salads that Zoe had made. Even though Max didn't come on this trip, he'd orchestrated everything. He suggested the idea of eating in the room rather than dealing with the publicity of going to a restaurant. Max had *said* it was about publicity, but Zoe figured it was because of her mom's drinking. He didn't want any viral videos.

As Zoe walked across the parking lot, the Hilton was a giant rectangular shadow in front of her. Last month she and Dinky went to the prom here and killed it on the dance floor. *Dinky.* They had tickets to a few concerts this summer, and Dinky was taking her camping before he left for college and she started her cooking classes. That was Zoe's plan for fall, to take a Mediterranean cooking class and a class in pastry arts. She'd also do her music and live with Aunt Jane while she formulated a real plan. Whatever that meant.

Zoe's mom met her at the door of the suite.

"Honey," she said, touching Zoe's cheeks with both her hands. There was a small bluish stain on the front of her white shirt, which was strange. Her mom hated stains. "It's good to see you again. It's been so long. Can you believe you're graduating tomorrow?"

Zoe smiled stiffly as she unzipped the cooler and began setting the table with salad containers and paper plates and a thermos of unsweetened iced tea. She'd just seen her mom two weeks ago when she'd flown to LA for Memorial Day weekend.

"Fancy food," her mom murmured. "You're going to be the star of your cooking classes."

It was obvious her mom had been drinking and it wasn't in moderation, but Zoe was going to force herself to get through dinner. In two hours Jake and Anna were coming over to her place, and JAZ was going to have a three-person party. It was the first time Zoe was trying alcohol. The irony wasn't lost on Zoe or Anna, but Jake promised he wouldn't let them become alcoholics. Zoe actually thought it made sense to try alcohol, to prove that her mom's demons didn't have to be her own.

Jake had gotten vodka from someone Ted knew, and he was bringing snacks and he'd even made a playlist. Around eight he was picking up Anna, and they'd drive over to Zoe's. At midnight Ted—who promised he'd be sober—would show up and chauffeur Jake and Anna home. When Jake and Ted had started dating again, Zoe was wary. But as soon as she saw them together, it all made sense. It was obvious they were in love.

"It's strange being in central New York." Sierra sipped the iced tea that Zoe had poured into two hotel glasses. "I said I'd never return . . . even on location. Tomorrow morning, right after graduation, I'm taking a plane back."

"When's the last time you were here?" Zoe asked. Her mom had never come to visit her. For the past four years Zoe had done all the traveling. And now that her mom had finally made it to Hankinson, she was leaving within twenty-four hours. In a way that was okay. Zoe wasn't exactly looking forward to the crowds that would swarm her mom tomorrow morning.

Her mom's cheeks were flushed in two perfect circles, like a Raggedy Ann doll. "*One Precious* was filmed a few hours north. That's the last time."

"Seriously? Why didn't you come back after that?" Zoe crossed one leg over the other and tugged at a thread on her skirt. She wondered if it had to do with her grandparents who'd died. Maybe being in this area, so close to where she'd grown up, reminded Sierra too much of that tragedy.

When her mom didn't respond, Zoe said, "Aunt Jane is driving you to graduation. She'll pick you up here in the morning."

"Is Rich going to be there?" her mom asked.

Zoe nodded. They'd gotten a graduation ticket for Aunt Jane's ex-husband. He said he wanted to be there. Zoe wanted him there.

After he'd helped her write the music for "You, Me, Together," they'd been jamming on the piano every week or so.

"Now *that's* funny," her mom said. She downed her iced tea and wiped her lips with the back of her hand.

Zoe's stomach clenched, but she was determined to act like things were normal. She was not going to let her mom get to her. "My cousin David and his girlfriend, Tamara, are driving up from Brooklyn," she said. "That's where they live now."

"Your *cousin*." Sierra cocked her head at Zoe. "I never really thought about that."

"I don't think I understand," Zoe said.

"Oh, you know the story, Z. How I came down to Hankinson on a break from filming *One Precious*? I was going through a hard time then. . . . I'm sure Jane told you about our fight."

Zoe's hands began to tremble. After all these years she suddenly wasn't so sure she wanted to hear it.

"I'm surprised Jane hasn't told you," Sierra continued. She reached for a tissue and tore it into shreds. "David might not *just* be your cousin. He might be your half-brother."

Zoe suddenly felt like she was going to throw up. She had to get out of here. She looked at her sandals by the door. They were impossibly far away.

"Jane and Rich were already split up when he and I spent time together. Let's just say, we made some mistakes." Her mom pressed her pale fingers over her mouth. "It's funny to come back for your graduation, and Rich is here too. I know you want a simple answer about your father, but I can't give you that. Sometimes life is complicated."

Sierra let out a sob and disappeared into the bathroom. Zoe doubled over her knees, breathing fast. Was her mom saying that she and Rich had had an affair? That Rich could be her *father*? Zoe thought about their hands together on the piano, the same freckles, the same musical instincts.

"Did you lie to me?" Zoe shouted, standing up. "Why did you always say it didn't matter? Of course it matters!"

The sink was running, and it sounded like her mom was on the phone. Zoe wanted to bang on the door and demand the exact truth. Or maybe not. Maybe she didn't want it to be true. For the past four years she'd felt safe here in Hankinson, but everyone had been lying to her all along.

Zoe loaded the containers back into the cooler. She forgot to put the lids on. The beans spilled out, swirling around in the bottom of the cooler with the roasted zucchini and oil and chunks of mozzarella. She put on her sandals and walked out of the suite. She stabbed at the button for the elevator until it arrived at her floor. Her phone started to ring. *Jane.* She dropped her phone into her bag again.

MIA

"DOES EVERYONE TELL you that you have sexy toes?" Brock asked. They were dipping their feet into the pool in Whitney Montaine's backyard.

"Does everyone tell you that you are the king of clichéd come-ons?" Mia asked.

Brock kicked some water at her. "First of all, it's not a come-on. And how are *sexy toes* cliché? I just like the way your second toe is longer than your first. Supposedly, it's a sign of fertility."

"So, now you want me to have your babies?" Mia asked. "Remember, we have to be thirty and only if we're both single."

"I'm not saying anything about babies, woman. I'm just saying, you have sexy toes."

"Fertile toes," Mia said, kicking water back at him.

Ever since she'd gotten together with Jeremiah at Admitted Students Weekend, she and Brock had become actual in-person friends. She no longer cared that he was popular or that he'd gone up her shirt at the waterfall that time. They liked each other, and the friendship worked for them.

Mia swirled her sexy fertile toes around in the water. High

school was over, and honestly, so were the stupid labels. Whitney was together with Gregor Lombard from band. Brock had brought Mia to Whitney's pool party. And Laurel, one of the bitchiest popular girls, was here with her baby boy. Mia had cooed at Hunter in the kitchen, and Laurel had said she should come to the playground with them over the summer.

Not to mention that tomorrow was graduation and Mia was valedictorian of the senior class. She was even okay with the fact that she'd be standing at the podium tomorrow, giving a speech. A few days ago—the afternoon that Jake texted her about the orientation group meeting up—she'd slipped down to the basement of the school and put the envelope with the letters back in the hole inside the fire extinguisher cabinet. She'd taken out that photo of Brock that she'd stolen from Kyra's locker freshman year and also her SAT scores and report cards. Only their original five letters were in there, and Mia hadn't let herself reread them. She was saving that for tomorrow.

"Want to swim?" Brock asked Mia.

A bunch of people were splashing around in the water, dunking each other and having chicken fights.

Mia shrugged. "My suit is in the car."

"So that means I get to toss you in with your clothes on!" Brock grinned mischievously. The sun was casting a golden glow on his face, his auburn hair. "Awesome. The wet T-shirt contest begins!"

Mia leaned into Brock, and he put his arm around her. They joked around like this, but Brock knew he wasn't getting anywhere. Mia and Jeremiah were together. They texted all the time, and he even sent her a necklace that she wore constantly. He'd had *I wanna be your boyfriend* engraved on a dog tag. That was from their favorite Ramones song.

Just then Mia heard Whitney shriek from the porch. She and Brock jumped up.

"He's been stung!" Whitney was screaming. "Gregor's been stung! He's really allergic!"

Mia leaped off the pool deck and ran across the lawn. Whitney was sitting in a lawn chair, Gregor slumped between her legs. His eyes were closed, and he was clutching his throat and gagging.

"He needs an EpiPen!" Mia shouted. For the first time in her life she wished her mom was here. Her mom always carried samples in her trunk. "Where's his EpiPen?"

"It must have fallen out of his backpack somewhere," Whitney cried, her eyes filling with tears. "We can't find it. Oh my god, Mia. I don't know what to do."

"Has anyone called 911?" Brock asked.

Mia ran to get her phone. She'd left it up at the pool. She could barely feel her legs moving as she climbed the stairs. But just as she began dialing 911, she saw Brock helping Whitney and Gregor into the back of an SUV. She watched him fly into the front and peel down the driveway.

JAKE

JAKE'S DAD COOKED up a serious night-before-graduation dinner. Quesadillas, guacamole, grilled steak, salad, corn on the cob, homemade blueberry pie. Jake ate until he was stuffed, then he brushed his teeth, kissed his parents, and got into the car. He'd loaded the party supplies into the trunk earlier so he wouldn't get busted carrying a bottle of vodka down the driveway.

Before he put the car in reverse, he texted Ted to firm up plans for later. Ted was at a pool party with Brock and a bunch of other people. They'd invited Jake along, but he wanted to have dinner with his family and then hang out with JAZ. Ted was his boyfriend, but Zoe and Anna were his tribe. He couldn't wait to see them get buzzed tonight. Now *that* was going to be hilarious.

Jake texted Anna that he was on his way to pick her up, and then he plugged his phone in and headed toward Breakneck Hill. He was halfway up the hill when he slowed at a red light and adjusted the volume on the music. He looked up just in time to see a white SUV hurtling past him, Brock at the wheel. He glanced in the rearview. Brock wasn't even stopping at the lights.

GREGOR

ON THE DRIVE to the hospital, Gregor's body was on fire and he couldn't stop throwing up. His thighs were slimy with puke, but he was too out of it to care. He flopped his head loosely from side to side. Whitney was next to him, her phone at her ear. Her voice was high and tight. Gregor couldn't even understand what she was saying.

Was this what it felt like for his dad when he collapsed in Mount Olive Park? To be sort of here, but not really. Mostly, to be slipping away.

Gregor could feel his dad with him, holding his hand. He could see his dad's warm brown eyes and hear his voice telling him it would be okay.

"It'll be okay," Whitney was saying. "Gregor, don't fall asleep. . . . Seriously . . . keep your eyes open. Brock, can you drive faster?"

Oh . . . it was Whitney holding his hand. It was Whitney looking at him with her beautiful hazel eyes. His beautiful girlfriend. But why had he heard his dad's voice? Gregor was having a hard time keeping things straight. He tried to breathe, but it was impossible to get air. He vomited again. He wanted to wipe his mouth, but he couldn't lift his hand.

"Brock," Whitney was saying, "can't you drive faster . . . I don't think . . . The emergency room says . . ."

As Gregor drifted off, he thought about a quote his dad once told him. It was when his dad had been recounting the story of how he'd met his mom. He said to Gregor, *Someday, someone will walk into your life and you'll realize why it never worked out with anyone else.*

That was how it felt with Whitney. Maybe his dad had been passing on that wisdom so Gregor could tuck it away until he and Whitney got together.

That was what made Gregor realize he would live.

He would live and, in the fall, he and Whitney would move to New York City. They would be on their own campuses, Whitney downtown at NYU and Gregor at Manhattan School of Music up in Morningside Heights. They would talk every day, and on weekends they'd see live music in underground clubs and they'd eat cheap Indian food in the East Village and they'd walk across the Brooklyn Bridge and hook a padlock with their initials onto the metal lattice of the bridge.

After college, maybe when they were twenty-five, they'd be back in Hankinson visiting their families and they'd take a walk in Mount Olive Park. Gregor would get down on one knee and propose to Whitney and she'd say yes. They'd name their first son Charlie after Gregor's dad.

Give or take a few details, Gregor saw his entire future on the drive to the emergency room. That was what kept him alive.

ZOE

IT WAS GOOD her gas tank was full because Zoe drove for hours. She took small roads and big roads and, for a while, the New York State Thruway. She didn't even care where she went. All she wanted was to get away from this life that she thought was real but was actually a lie.

Her phone kept ringing and texts were coming in. Zoe read them whenever she stopped at lights, but she wasn't writing back to anyone.

Jake and Anna both wrote, *Where the hell are you?*

Dinky wrote, *What's up, babe? Are you okay?*

Aunt Jane wrote, *Call me. I need to explain.*

Rich wrote, *I'm so sorry you had to find out this way.*

Her mom wrote, *I'm having a hard time right now. Please try to understand.*

And then Max wrote, *Don't do this, Zoe. You don't run off like this. Not when you're in the public eye.*

Zoe slowed at a red light and texted, *Fuck off, Max.*

Then she turned off her phone.

• • •

As the sun was setting and the sky was streaked with pink and violet, Zoe pulled onto the shoulder and turned on her phone.

"Zoe!" Jake shouted. "What the hell? Where are you? Are you alive?"

As soon as she heard his voice, her chest squeezed up tight. She wanted to be at Bean, serving lattes with Jake, or drinking vodka with JAZ tonight. She didn't want to be alone on some roadside. But like everything in her life, Zoe didn't ask for it. It just happened.

"Is anyone with you?" Zoe whispered. She didn't want to talk to Anna, who would be so upset she'd start crying, which would make Zoe cry. And if Zoe began crying, then she'd never stop.

"I'm at Anna's," Jake said, "but she's in the bathroom. When you didn't come to your place tonight, we—"

"Listen," Zoe said. "I'm going to talk quickly and I want you to hang up as soon as Anna comes in."

"Why?"

"I found out tonight who my real dad is and basically that my life is a lie."

"I have no idea what you're talking about," Jake said. "Like, where are you? Everyone is freaking out. Your aunt wants to call the police."

"Tell her not to call the police," Zoe said. "Tell her I'll be okay."

"You're not going to do anything stupid, are you?"

"Duh . . . no," Zoe said.

"What about graduation?"

"I'm not going to graduation," Zoe said. "It doesn't matter."

When Zoe heard Anna's voice in the background, she hung up and turned off her phone again.

WHITNEY

—————

"YOUR PHONE'S RINGING, Whit!" Alicia called into the shower. "Want me to answer it?"

It was an hour before graduation. Whitney had slept over at Gregor's last night, just to be near him. For part of the night she was in a sleeping bag on his floor, but then she'd crawled into his bed and wrapped her arms around him, grateful he was alive. She'd gotten home a little while ago, downed a bowl of cereal, and jumped in the shower. She'd already shaved her legs, and now she was letting the hot water spray her stiff neck. Last night had been intense. Hopefully, she wouldn't get a migraine today. She'd started medication last summer to prevent them, but she still got headaches when she was stressed.

"Who is it?" Whitney called to her sister as she shut off the water.

In their mom's new house Alicia's and Whitney's rooms were connected by a shared bathroom. In a way it was nice to have neutral territory where they could meet. Two nights ago they sat on the edge of the tub and had a leg-shaving party.

"Jake Rodriguez," Alicia said. "Who's he?"

Why was Jake calling her? Maybe he was checking on Gregor. Jake's boyfriend, Ted, was at her pool party yesterday. All last night people kept texting to ask how Gregor was doing.

"Yeah, you can answer," Whitney said. "Thanks."

"Who is Jake, anyway?" Alicia called from Whitney's room. Whitney could hear her phone ringing. "Was he in that freshman orientation group? Group eighteen, right? His name sounds—"

"Just answer!" Whitney shouted, reaching for a towel.

"Touchy, touchy." Alicia cracked open the bathroom door. "Here's my sister," she said into the phone, and then handed it to Whitney.

Whitney lifted the phone to her ear. "Hey, Jake . . . what's up?"

"Hey," Jake said. "How's Gregor? Ted said he got stung by a bee and he's allergic."

"He's okay . . . thanks." Whitney sat on the toilet lid and squirted moisturizer in her palm. "The problem was that we couldn't find his EpiPen. That'll never happen again."

"But he's okay?"

"He's tired," Whitney said, "but he'll be fine. The doctor said he can come to graduation."

Jake sighed. "Speaking of graduation, you know how we were going to meet later? I'm not sure it's going to happen."

"Why? What's going on?"

"The thing is . . . Zoe is missing."

Whitney gasped. "Missing?"

"She had a fight with her mom last night, and no one knows where she is. I shouldn't even be telling you this, but—"

"No, it's okay." Whitney was trying to be a different person, more caring, less self-absorbed. In the past she would have been excited about this nugget of news because of the Sierra Laybourne connection, but now she was genuinely concerned about Zoe.

"I'm sure she's okay," Whitney said. "Has Dinky talked to her? Or Anna? Or anyone?"

"I did briefly, but she didn't say where she is."

"I'm sure she'll show up at graduation. But if she doesn't, will you let me know what I can do or how I can help or whatever."

"Thanks," Jake said quietly.

"Anytime."

JAKE

JAKE FOLDED HIS cap and gown into his backpack and biked to the high school. Ted said he could easily pick him up on the way to graduation, but Jake was hoping the ride would clear his head. Even though his mom and dad and Ted and Anna and even Whitney said that Zoe would turn up at graduation, he was the only one who'd talked to her, who'd heard how distant she sounded.

He had to get his shit together before he made his speech as senior class president. He was introducing the keynoter, a New York State assemblywoman. Right now his brain felt murky. For the past twelve hours he'd been talking nonstop with Anna and Dinky and Zoe's aunt Jane. Everyone was a wreck. Once, when he'd been on the phone with Jane, she'd broken down and started crying. She told Jake that she'd talked to Sierra, who told her what she'd said to Zoe about Rich.

"I never told Zoe because nothing was certain," Jane had said to him. "At least I didn't think it was. And Sierra had always threatened that if I said anything about it, she'd fly Zoe home. That was what she said."

Jake was stunned. *Rich?* The guy who helped Zoe write her

song? He shouldn't even be hearing this. He was in way, way over his head.

"Where do you think she is?" Jane asked Jake.

"No idea," Jake said. "All she said was that she was going to be okay and not to call the police. I'm sorry. It's sort of a blur."

"But what do you *think*?" Jane asked.

"I don't know. . . . I'm sorry."

It was almost like people were mad at him for not knowing more. It wasn't as if Zoe had given him a choice. She'd hung up before he could get any real information. On top of being worried about her, he was also pissed.

As Jake locked his bike to the rack outside school, his stomach was churning. He slipped into a side door, washed his face, and pulled on his gown and cap. Then he rushed to the VIP room to meet Mr. Bauersmith and the assemblywoman. In one hand he had his note cards for the speech. In the other hand he was holding his phone, waiting to hear from Zoe.

MIA

MIA HAD IT all planned out. She'd been thinking about it ever since Whitney texted her two days ago. After graduation the five of them would find each other. Mia, Jake, Zoe, Whitney, and Gregor. Four years ago, at freshman orientation, they said they would meet under the basketball hoop right after the ceremony and walk to the basement together to get the letters.

The way she figured it, when graduation was over, they would go to their families and take pictures and get their flowers. But then, after a few minutes, they'd see each other and drift together. Mia would say, "Do you think the letters are still there?"

Of course she knew they were there, but it wasn't like she'd admit that.

Then they'd go to the basement and read their letters to their future selves. When Whitney realized that she and Mia had written almost the same thing, they'd hug and say how amazing it was.

Talk about amazing.

It was amazing to think how much Mia had changed since the beginning of freshman year. Four years ago she would have *died* before talking in front of even her orientation group. Now she was going to make a speech as valedictorian to more than a thousand people!

Mia drove her dad's car to graduation because her parents were playing tennis, and she had to get there early to check in for her speech. She took the long way, meandering through downtown Hankinson, listening to music, thinking about Jeremiah. He'd already graduated from his high school in Kansas last week and made his speech as salutatorian. Mia had been teasing him because he was only number two in his graduating class and she was number one. He retaliated with his slightly higher SAT scores. Geek love all the way.

Mia went to the VIP room where the speakers were hanging out. She could hear people talking about how Gregor had been stung at Whitney's party last night. Mia knew from Brock that they'd gotten to the ER in time. She was just reviewing her notecards when she heard Kyra Bauersmith say, "Did you hear that Zoe Laybourne is missing?"

Mia glared at Kyra. She still couldn't stand her. That was one thing that hadn't changed in four years.

"Missing?" asked a junior girl. She was one of the marshals who'd be leading in the graduating class while the marching band played "Pomp and Circumstance."

"Yep," Kyra said. "My dad says she took off last night, and no one knows where she is." Kyra pursed her lips for emphasis. She was loving this. "Completely vanished. Which means, of course, that Sierra Laybourne isn't coming to graduation. Bummer."

Mia felt a rush of adrenaline. As she was driving around Hankinson this morning, she'd seen Zoe's car! It was that fancy white

BMW. But where? Crap. If she told Jake and the others that she'd seen Zoe's car but didn't know where, no one would believe her. Anyway, maybe Kyra was full of it about Zoe. She was definitely not someone to trust.

A half hour later, when Mia was onstage making her speech, she scanned the graduates for Zoe. The L section was a swirl of people in caps fanning themselves with programs. It was hard to tell anyone apart.

But then, when Mr. Bauersmith was presenting diplomas, he called, "Zoe Laybourne."

Zoe didn't come onstage.

The gym was silent.

At that moment Mia remembered where she'd seen Zoe's car.

"I have to talk to you," Mia whispered to Jake after the ceremony. She didn't even go find her parents. "It's about Zoe."

Jake had been standing with Ted and Ted's family. He took Mia's elbow and steered her a few steps away.

"The thing is," Mia said, sucking on her bottom lip, "I saw Zoe's car in the lot behind that café, Bean, this morning. I drove past there maybe two hours ago."

"Bean?" Jake asked. "We checked there last night."

Just then Whitney and Gregor came over. Gregor didn't look too bad, maybe a little puffy. Whitney was holding his hand tight, her forehead knotted in concern.

"Any news?" Whitney asked Jake. "Hey, Mia. Great speech."

"Mia saw Zoe's car behind Bean," Jake said. "I have my bike. I'll go over there. I know we were going to get the letters and you guys can do that, but—"

Mia reached into her bag for her dad's car keys. "I'm parked out front. Let's all go."

ZOE

MAYBE IT WAS a lame hiding spot, but Keni had let her spend the night in the supply closet on a threadbare recliner that smelled like stale smoke and Earl Grey tea. Zoe had called Keni after midnight because she didn't know where else to go and she was too tired to keep driving. Keni had just said, "Use the key. Feast on day-old scones." Keni was awesome that way. She never asked too many questions.

Early that morning Zoe had splashed her face and rinsed out her mouth and helped Keni brew the coffees and set out the baked goods. Once customers started trickling in, she retreated back into the supply closet. There was no window in here and no fresh air. Her neck was tight and she probably smelled ripe. Also, her phone was dead, and Bean didn't have a compatible charger. But in a way that was okay. She didn't want to watch the time and think about how graduation was happening—or maybe it was already over? She didn't want to see Aunt Jane's texts. Those were breaking her heart more than anyone else's. She loved Aunt Jane, but she couldn't deal with her now.

Maybe she'd move to Los Angeles. It wasn't like she'd live with her mom, but at least it was a place you could get lost. Then again, Sierra Laybourne's daughter could never truly disappear. They always found you.

But what about when you're also Rich Morrison's daughter? What does that mean?

"You're looking for Zoe?" Zoe heard Keni's deep voice saying from out in the café. "You see—"

"Keni," Jake was saying. "We know she's been here."

So . . . Jake had figured it out. It wasn't like she'd hidden her car very well. She'd just parked it in the back lot, by the Dumpsters. Zoe pushed her hair behind her ears and opened the supply closet door. Only it wasn't just Jake out there. It was Dinky's friend Gregor and Whitney and that tall blond girl, Mia. Oh my god! It was her freshman orientation group. The first people she'd met when she got to Hankinson. They were all wearing their blue caps and gowns. They must have come right from graduation.

Zoe tried to clear her throat, but no sound was coming out. Jake's arms were crossed over his chest. She'd hurt him. She could see it all over his face.

"Zoe," Mia asked, "are you okay?"

Zoe shook her head slowly, and just like that, she started to cry. She bit down on the inside of her cheeks, but the tears kept coming. Jake walked over and wrapped her in a hug.

"Come home," he said. "Come with us."

"But . . ." Zoe whimpered, wiping at her face. What about the lies? What would she say to Aunt Jane? Or Rich? It was all such a mess.

"We'll figure it out," Jake said. "You're not alone."

Zoe was too teary to talk. But in that moment she knew she would stay in Hankinson and make sense of things. Maybe it was the worst decision of her life. But it was probably the best.

IN THE END they decided not to read the letters. They agreed to leave them in the hole inside the fire extinguisher cabinet until their ten-year reunion or a wrecking ball toppled the school and built a modern solar-paneled structure in its place—whichever came first.

Instead they sat on the curb behind Bean, drinking complimentary iced coffees that Keni gave them in exchange for taking the drama outside. They all pulled out their phones, except for Zoe, whose battery was dead, and responded to texts about why they'd disappeared from graduation. Whitney and Gregor made a plan to meet up with their families for lunch, where they had a reservation at a nearby restaurant. Mia was going to Lake Ontario with Brock for a "purely platonic picnic"—her words. Jake told his dad and Ted and Anna that he'd found Zoe, and then he loaned her his phone so she could text Aunt Jane and make a plan to talk it out.

"So . . . ten years?" Whitney asked as she and Gregor tossed their cups into the Dumpster.

"Ten years," Mia said, smiling.

They all hugged and said congratulations and told Zoe that they hoped she was okay, and then they hugged again. It was hard to let go. Because right then, that moment, felt extraordinary. When they had written those letters at the beginning of high school, it hadn't seemed like much. But now that they were at the end, they were feeling how extraordinary it was. Not necessarily the beginning and not really the end, either. It was the infinite in between, all those miniscule and major moments when they'd dipped in and out of each other's lives. That had been their journey and somehow, even though they hadn't realized it, they'd been on it together.

ACKNOWLEDGMENTS

Three years ago, I went out for coffee with a friend from my son's school. Over steaming soy Americanos, I said, "I have an idea for a new novel. It's all formed in my head and I think I can write it in five weeks. Definitely before the school year ends." I think she just stared at me. She may have said good luck.

Good luck is right. Here it is, almost two hundred weeks later, and I've finally finished *Infinite in Between*. It was worth the trip. They say it takes a village to raise a child. Well, this novel took a metropolis. With infinite thanks to:

Jodi Reamer, who read a very early draft (maybe ten weeks in) and said, "This is exactly the novel I wanted you to write." The rest of the crew at Writers House, including Alec Shane and Cecilia de la Campa, who have made it this writer's *home* since the day I arrived.

Tara Weikum, for staying in this fictional universe with me through the entire journey. Also at Harper, Chris Hernandez, Alexandra Alexo, Alison Donalty, Michelle Taormina, Christina Colangelo, Patty Rosati, and Gina Rizzo for everything you do/are doing to make this book completely rock.

The whole team at Booje Media—Clio de la Llave, Tiffany de la

Llave, Leila Nadery, and Kristina Hermida—for understanding my love of coffee and making me feel much cooler than I actually am.

My writer-friends: Megan McCafferty (who read a draft, about sixty weeks in), Judy Blume, Wendy Mass, Gabrielle Zevin, David Levithan, James Howe, E.R. Frank, Jay Asher, and Mariah Fredericks. All of you help keep me sane (on the writing front).

My mom-friends, Jhoanna Robledo, Sarah Klock, Jen Bailey, Maxine Roël, Ismée Williams, Jenny Greenberg, Juliet Eastland, Martha Wilkie, and Raasa Leela de Montebello. All of you help keep me sane (on the parenting front).

Meredith Smart, Charlotte Exton, Sarah Ferguson, and Michael Lapinsky, for taking excellent care of my boys while I was writing.

The women from my Pilates group who jumped in when I was having title trouble and who keep me laughing (and core-strengthening) every Wednesday morning: Nitza Wilon, Valerie Vann-Oettl, Elizabeth Kaiden, Lauren Gale-Napach, Kyle Stokes, Bonnie Bertram, Martha Banta, and Ayala Fader.

My one set of parents, Ian Mackler and Debra Wolf, for offering to write a prologue for me when I was stuck. It's amazing what parents will do.

My other set of parents, Anne Dalton (who read another draft, about thirty weeks in) and Jeff Layton, for taking me in and feeding me vegetarian food that chilly winter week so I could write from sunup to sundown.

My aunt, Alice Dalton Brown, who read yet another draft (about one hundred and ten weeks in) and gave me valuable feedback.

Dr. Denise Chou, for saving my life.

Miles and Leif Rideout, for being awesome (and understanding) kids all those weekend mornings when I ran up to the library to write and came home, blurry-eyed, seven hours later.

And, as always, my husband, Jonas Rideout, who read every draft and was here, loving me, for all of those weeks.

JOIN THE

Epic Reads
COMMUNITY

THE ULTIMATE YA DESTINATION

◀ DISCOVER ▶
your next favorite read

◀ MEET ▶
new authors to love

◀ WIN ▶
free books

◀ SHARE ▶
infographics, playlists, quizzes, and more

◀ WATCH ▶
the latest videos

◀ TUNE IN ▶
to Tea Time with Team Epic Reads